The crack of  lled
up and down an   rget
in his sights dis   felt,
rather than saw, t   rist sniper was hit.

"This is Tango One. I think I got him," Peach said.

"We'll check it out, Peach," Getts said, already circling from the south to approach the sniper's position
from a flank. He spied the prone form of the sniper, his
weapon still pointing down the riverbed. The sniper's
camouflage ghillie suit was well made, as Getts suspected it would be, but he was no longer wearing his
hat. It had been blown off.

Getts took the sniper's rifle from his dead hands
and looked at the telescopic sight. A hole had been
bored through the lens, from front to back. Getts shook
his head and chuckled gruffly. He opened his lip mike.

"Tango One, I think it's safe to say you got
him. . . ."

Dead-Eye

NAVY SEALS

GREEN SOLITAIRE

Mike Murray

A SIGNET BOOK

SIGNET
Published by New American Library, a division of
Penguin Putnam Inc., 375 Hudson Street,
New York, New York 10014, U.S.A.
Penguin Books Ltd, 27 Wrights Lane,
London W8 5TZ, England
Penguin Books Australia Ltd, Ringwood,
Victoria, Australia
Penguin Books Canada Ltd, 10 Alcorn Avenue,
Toronto, Ontario, Canada M4V 3B2
Penguin Books (N.Z.) Ltd, 182–190 Wairau Road,
Auckland 10, New Zealand

Penguin Books Ltd, Registered Offices:
Harmondsworth, Middlesex, England

First published by Signet, an imprint of New American Library,
a division of Penguin Putnam Inc.

First Printing, July 2000
10 9 8 7 6 5 4 3 2 1

To Dean Minor, Roy Gaskin, and Gary Feramisco,
all now handicapped, and three of the toughest
fighters I have ever seen in action.

Chapter One

In a ten-day whirlwind tour of South Africa's superb nature parks and game preserves, including a memorable three days at the internationally famous Kruger National Park on the northeastern border of South Africa near Mozambique, Dorothy Mauser was nowhere near her fill of sights of animals in the wild. Her day bag contained dozens of rolls of unspent film and her heart was filled with anticipation over the baboons they expected to see at the Cape of Good Hope nature reserve where the Atlantic Ocean meets the Indian. It was her dedication to long daily walks that kept her forty-seven-year-old body looking much like it did when she led cheers for her high school football team in London, Ontario, and she was not in the least intimidated by the prospect of all that South Africa's park system could throw at her. Though her brown hair was now streaked with gray, and lines etched by sun and the years appeared at the corners of her mouth, in the eyes of her husband, Ronald, she remained classically beautiful.

An enormous flash of lightning lit up the late afternoon skyline of Johannesburg, and Dorothy rushed to the window of their hotel room to get closer to the energy of the oncoming thunder-clap. In the moments she waited for the sonic meeting of superheated, then cooled, air to come together, her eyes took in the panoramic view of what seemed to her an otherworldly city of gold. In the glow of summer evening, shafts of late daylight pierced thinning rain clouds to illuminate man-made mountains of mine tailings that dotted the city landscape in all directions. The small mountains, colored bright amber from arsenic used in processing gold, emerged from the ground like the lopped-off tops of Cairo pyramids, residing in locations where buildings, parks, and streets would have been built in any other city center. This was the epicenter of South Africa's "Golden Reef," a crescent of mineral deposits so vast and so rich as to tax the imagination.

When the peal of thunder arrived it rocked Dorothy back away from the window. Her excitement increased, anticipating the next lightning strike. There followed not one but three bolts of chain lightning, stretching across the southeastern quadrant of the city, the thunder rumbling, roaring, gathering its deafening momentum as giant cumulus clouds reached as far away as Dorothy could see from the twenty-second floor of their room in the Carlton Hotel. The rain now began to pour, the violence of nature exerting its forces in a show that thrilled her to the very tips of her toes.

She heard Ron's key in the lock and she turned toward the door as it opened to reveal her drenched, steamy, sorry-looking husband of twenty-six years, his flannel hat drooping over his ears like a helmet as he plodded into the room. He stopped short just inside the doorway while he removed his thoroughly soaked shoes and his sopping overcoat before moving toward the king-size bed to remove his sodden socks. "Hi, darling," Dorothy said. "Did you get wet?"

"Jesus, did I ever."

"Did you get the tickets?" she wanted to know.

"Of course I got the tickets. I had to cross this whole,

rotting city to find them," he said, continuing to peel layers of summer-weight clothing from his body.

"Why didn't they have them in the lobby?" she asked.

"I don't know, Dorothy."

"Didn't you ask?"

She was still wearing her pajama top and panties, her preferred bed attire for her afternoon "power naps" as she called them, and Ronald thought she still looked pretty damn sexy. If it were not for his chilled physical state and residing anger for the way Johannesburg had changed from the last time he was here in 1980, he would have drawn her to the bed and ravished her. Instead of moving toward his wife, however, he advanced to the bathroom and directly entered the shower. "I'm a college graduate, a trained researcher with thirty-five years of experience in the business of finding facts and separating them from fiction. Of course I asked! Do you think I'd walk, take trains and broken-down taxis through the streets of Johannesburg during a monsoon, if the goddamned tickets could be bought right in front of my nose?"

Shower water was beating him on top of the head as Dorothy responded—not that he cared what she said. He was not enjoying his vacation in post-apartheid South Africa. He felt that he was despised by the country's black majority population because he was white, and the reversal of roles consciously irritated him. He was sure he was not a racist while admitting to no one but himself that whites did things like running countries better than anyone else, the present American administration notwithstanding.

On the other hand, he recalled that on his last trip to Johannesburg, Durban, Port Elizabeth, and Cape Town, blacks were entirely separated from all things white, including public restrooms. It was true of his own country that such a system of caste segregation based on race prevailed well into the mid-1960s. Hard to believe. And he recalled that if he had been black and his wife had been denied the use of public amenities, he would have accepted a loaded rifle from any source and begun shooting whites. Any whites.

He toweled off with the bathroom door still open, aware that Dorothy liked to invent reasons to catch him in the nude. Though he spent most of his time behind a desk these days, he had not lost his devotion to daily aerobic workouts. "So what time does it leave?" he heard her ask.

"What?" he responded, though knowing to what she referred.

"The train, Ronald," she said, with no sign of impatience in her tone.

"Ten-ten," he said. "Wednesday."

"Isn't that tomorrow?" she asked, now poking her head around the corner of the bathroom and kissing him on the cheek.

"Yeah," he said, now very aware of the proximity of her beautiful legs.

"I wish I had been with you last time," she said.

"I was working," he pointed out. In fact he had enjoyed that visit more than his current, forced vacation, where he poked along behind his wife trying to be interested in fauna, flora, and white beaches about which he really couldn't have cared less. But it had been five years since he and Dorothy had been on a real vacation and he had promised that she could pick the time and place. He had silently, even sternly, promised himself that he would be a model traveling companion for his wife while realizing that his added baggage was a naturally grouchy personality. Still, Dorothy either loved him dearly or was the world's best actor. For his part, he found life without her of no interest whatever.

"I haven't finished my nap. You might as well take

one, too," she said, kissing him lightly once more. He grunted acceptance, happy that she had so easily offered a hoped-for invitation for afternoon sex.

At Vauxhall Cross, London, Melissa Witherspoon was early for work. She was the first, in fact, to arrive out of the entire Eastern European Franchise division. She was not attempting to polish up the brass, but had such a full and eventful evening with a helicopter pilot assigned to Whitehall that the hours had slipped away until it made more sense to come straight to work rather than waste time changing clothes at home. She would not have the chance to see Eugena before the child left for public school, but she was well looked after and Melissa would make it up to her this weekend. No family. Just the two of them off together to . . . well, they would think of something on the spur of the moment. She would let Eugena choose.

Melissa needed tea inside her throat to counterbalance the night's damage done by Scotch and secondhand smoke. Richard was a darling man but he lacked control over both his orgasms and his need to inhale two packs of cigarettes per day. It was a terrible habit—Richard admitted it readily—but habits, Melissa believed, were rooted in one's genes and she was not sure how much longer she could remain in his company before surrendering to a portable oxygen tank. By the time her tea water began to boil she had made a mental note to avoid Richard's calls, a state of mind that made her feel better about herself. Anyway, the flirtation was due to end by next Friday when Richard's beaming but banal wife, Pamela, was due back from the Caribbean.

Melissa found one of the many newspapers delivered to her department within her division of MI6 and tore it apart looking for the football scores. She knew that West

Brom played like they were in wheelchairs and more's
the pity that Tranmere was as dreadful as Port Vale, but
she was less drawn to their clumsy imperfections than the
points they had scored, which were tallied in the Lion's
Head Saturday pool in which she had invested ten
pounds.

Her pencil, with which she was handicapping next
week's Division 2 teams, was still clutched in her left
hand, her head resting at an uncomfortable angle in the
crook of her arm, when she was shaken gently awake by
Geoffrey Aills, a colleague.

"Ah, Melissa," he whispered nervously, glancing
about the cubicle in which employees served themselves
tea or withdrew memo pads, ink cartridge refills, and
other odd assortments of desk requirements.

"Oh, Geoffrey," she said, quickly approaching a state
of wakefulness. "You're early, too."

"No, not really. It's half-past ten," he said.

Her smile slowly faded. "Is that a joke? I just walked
in the door. It's . . ." She looked at her watch. "My God,
it's almost eleven! How the hell could that be?"

"You looked so . . . I mean, we thought you could use
the rest, Melissa. Sir Hogue Ortwith said . . ."

"Don't tell me the old dickhead saw me like this?" she
said.

"Yes, but no one appreciates your overgenerous con-
tributions to this organization more than Sir Hogue, and
he was showing it," Geoffrey said.

"That's utter bullshit," she said, reaching for a teapot
and pouring the now-tepid liquid into her bright yellow
Limoge cup and saucer. She drank daintily but with purpose until she had swallowed it all, then refilled the ves-
sel twice more and drained them, too. "Well, thank you
for your concern, Geoffrey, I think I can get on with my
work, now."

Geoffrey Aills, twenty-eight, watched with scarcely concealed yearning for the brain and body of a woman older than he, swaying beautifully past a phalanx of desks toward her own, located in the rear. In the two years and some months that Princess Melissa Radford-Gayles Witherspoon, Duchess of Kent, Countess of Beaumont, grandniece of Lord Earl Mountbatten, had taken "employment" in an obscure labyrinth of MI6, he, like all other men that knew her, fell helplessly in love. Those men who virtually worshiped the ground upon which she walked included their boss, Sir Hogue Anal-Ass, as they secretly called him behind his back. She was not quite beauty personified, but she was a searing sexual image to the beholder, Geoffrey thought before retrieving his locked folio and heading for the classified printing room.

Melissa wended her way to "Siberia," the nickname for the area where she occupied her own medium-size oak desk, chosen by her over the polite objections of her section chief, Rebecca Hazen. Now surrounded by fabric screens, filing cabinets, and a computer station, Melissa kicked off her high heels and slouched back into an overstuffed swivel chair and began to work.

Her assignment, considerably downgraded in importance since the reorganization of MI6 in 1993, was to maintain an electronic list of Russian technicians, scientists, and weapons experts—biological, atomic, as well as conventional. Their current whereabouts, as well as their movements within the Russian economic system and its orb of influence, might be of interest to UK threat planners and tendency analysts. The information was obtained by Melissa—and a dozen other such persons located within the walls of MI6—from a wide variety of sources, some of which included newspaper reports in their native country languages, television coverage, academic announcements, statistical reports, political party

communiqués, even the Internet. Melissa often down-
loaded printed material into the bowels of her computer
using a high-quality scanner. The computer program that
operated the data retrieval system, Ukr-3999-W/2, or
ATHENA, registered, sorted, evaluated, and, when certain criteria had been met, popped a given piece of
datum-arrhythmia out of the box for the operator like a
kitchen toaster. The operator, like Melissa, would take
cognizance of the change in data, and, if deemed necessary, forward the item to a tendency maven four floors
below ground level in the same building.

Upon her request for updated archival information
from *Pravda* in connection with chemists working at the
Zcaznoi fertilizer factory located in Saratov, on the Volga,
ATHENA had regurgitated the name Evileski, Dmitri M.
Evileski, the data read, was still employed after seven
years at the same location but recently promoted to assistant plant manager. As Melissa was typing an MI6 rune
into the database verifying the chemist's career move, her
pinkie finger struck two keys at once, causing her to replace Dmitri Evileski on her screen with Eveshenko,
Boris L. She swore under her breath and stabbed at her escape key but Eveshenko, Boris L., remained where it was.
She noticed, at first with little interest, that the item containing Eveshenko's name was the subject of a newspaper
report from Gaborone, Botswana. Melissa moved instinctively to return her screen to where it should have been but
hesitated long enough to read the very short news item. It
said that a drunken automobile driver had careered off the
street in downtown Gaborone and struck several people
waiting at a bus stop. Two were killed, a twenty-three-
year-old mother and her four-year-old son. Three others
were taken to a city hospital, the extent of their wounds
not yet known. Eveshenko, a foreigner, the article contin-

ued, was arrested at the scene but released from custody within three hours.

Melissa punched off the distracting screen so that she could finish her notation for Dmitri Evileski. In the back of her mind, however, she knew that vehicular manslaughter was a very serious crime in Botswana and wondered how Eveshenko, obviously Russian, had managed to get himself out of jail so quickly. She assumed that he was part of the Russian legation in that country. She considered dropping it there, but promised herself that if she had time before the end of day, she would confirm her supposition by verifying Eveshenko's name among the Russian consular staff.

Melissa made several telephone calls during her midday break, the most important of which was to her personal secretary who would, in turn, make dozens more calls on Melissa's behalf when not responding to a small mountain of correspondence she received weekly. Melissa's last call was to her best friend, Patricia Elmhurst. Lady Elmhurst asked for and received permission to use Melissa's beach home in Carstairs for the month. Divorced, as was Melissa, Patricia had sworn off men for at least the month of July, and Carstairs, she hoped, would serve as a perfect retreat for her and her two preteen children.

After hanging up her desk telephone and putting her head back against her chair, the name Eveshenko popped back into her brain like an unwanted, repeating jingle. She turned to her computer keyboard and began a search for the man, expecting to find him listed among either the SVR—formerly known as the KGB—or foreign service personnel. Neither form of inquiry revealed Eveshenko, Boris L. Now intrigued, Melissa was determined to locate the history of a Russian who could get himself sprung so quickly from a foreign country's jail cell.

* * *

Dorothy was perfectly comfortable in the sweltering heat of Johannesburg's great train depot. Despite the fact that July was a South African winter month, it could be colder where they were going in the south than in the northern part of the country. The local populace waited shoulder to shoulder on the platform, their baggage as colorful as their clothing, which featured gingham plaids, bright yellows, and aqua blues. She and Ronald waited in the main waiting room along with the great throng as they anticipated the arrival of the internationally famous Blue Train to arrive from Pretoria, only sixty miles away in the north. The twenty-four-hour sybaritic trip would take them from Jo'burg through the heart of the nation, crossing the Vaal, Kruger Park, south along the Free State via Bloemfontein, through Kimberly where the diamond mines were, and on to Cape Town by way of the beautiful wine country of Stellenbosch.

Ronald noted with undisguised admiration Dorothy's social ease, her ability to talk with anyone; not forced, just nice. She didn't talk politics, religion, or history. Instead she traded stories about dogs and cats, something that everyone was fond of, or art, which she loved and studied. She also liked to chat about theater and the ballet, which she admired for their intrinsic beauty. And old people and kids. She loved them, too. Apart from that she was a good listener. Actually she had a very short attention span but people took her blank stare for keen interest and just kept on talking.

Ronald was tempted to have a cold drink at the Blue Train lounge but knowing, or hoping, that the train would pull into the station at any minute caused him to wait. A drink in their stateroom might be more pleasant.

"Ron," Dorothy was saying while tightly holding the arm of a woman with blonde hair swept across her attractive face. "This is Danielle Hüüken. This is my husband, Danielle." Before Danielle and Ron could exchange formal greetings, Dorothy breathlessly continued, "She's from Holland. You'll never guess who she knows."

"Ludi Boekan," he said.

"Yes!" Dorothy almost shrieked.

"My goodness," Danielle said, eyes widening, "you're so clever."

"If I am anything on the face of this Earth, Ms. Hüüken, it is not clever. Ludi Boekan happens to be the only person we know in the Netherlands," he said, looking past her shoulder at the track where the Blue Train should appear at any moment.

"And this is my daughter," Danielle Hüüken said, in turn pulling the arm of a teenager who was taller than both her mother and Dorothy's five feet six inches by an inch.

"Isn't she darling?" Dorothy gushed, practically petting the hair of the girl whose name, Ronald learned by straining to hear over the babble of the crowd, was Reanna. To Ronald's surprise, Reanna was wearing a Girl Scout uniform. She was either self-conscious about wearing the uniform in public or she was shy, or both, Ronald thought, the girl's eyes avoiding his in favor of almost anything, anywhere else. Now that Ronald thought about it, Danielle also wore Girl Scout kneesocks and shoes.

"I am a troop leader," Danielle explained.

"Your troop is a long way from home," Ronald said, his mouth pulling into a disapproving frown.

"Yes, aren't we?" Danielle said.

"Who's taking care of you?" Ronald said with a note of concern in his tone.

"I am sorry? Oh, who is *helping*," Danielle smiled, glancing around at the crowd. "Alise Willicaze is my friend. She's helping. Really, I am helping her," Danielle giggled.

"Two women alone?" Ronald said, plainly rejecting the wisdom of their travel. "This is Africa, not Europe. Certainly not Holland," he said.

"Well, darling," Dorothy began, but her next words were drowned by the rapidly approaching Blue Train, its whistle blaring, the tracks creaking as the monster engine rumbled on rails that were only a few feet from where Ronald and his coterie of women stood. Dorothy was a feminist, Ronald mused, and no doubt she would argue that a Girl Scout leader should be able to travel anywhere in the world without the worry of harm coming to her. The world should change, not women's rights.

They were among the first to board the train when its doors opened to passengers. A uniformed porter showed them to their suite in one of the elegant first-class cars. Dorothy had been on trains before, but after riding from Toronto all the way to Los Angeles, she put trains low on her list of preferred transportation, just above camels and walking. But viewing the compartment that she and Ronald would share all the way to Cape Town almost took her breath away. There were five gracefully curtained windows looking out from their compartment at the countryside; a comfortable double bed with soft, overhead lighting; and a small, linen-covered dining table with a silver service that included a champagne bucket and flower vase. And there were two well-stuffed wingback chairs to maximize their comfort while eating or lounging.

"Oh, darling," she said, tossing her khaki safari jacket onto the bed where it would most likely lie until Ronald picked it up and put it away, "it's wonderful! What a great idea. Have you been on the Blue Train before?"

"You've asked me that three times. No," he said.

Dorothy fell into one of the wingback chairs, found that

it fitted her body comfortably, then flung herself from there onto the double bed. "Perfect. Just damn perfect."

"Time for your nap?" Ronald asked, sarcastically.

"Hmm."

He should have known better than to suggest it. It was still mid-morning but she was always ready to launch a power nap. He thought about closing the curtains for her but decided to let the sun do its work and maybe restore some solar energy to her system.

"Unpack," Dorothy mumbled, already an eyelash from sleep.

"Too soon," Ronald said, distracted, looking carefully out of a window. This side of the train overlooked the marshaling yards and switching tracks. Passengers still boarding for second- and third-class accommodations were not visible. Ronald made a mental note to walk his car's corridor the moment the train began to move. When he turned back toward Dorothy he was surprised to see her sitting up on the bed, wide-eyed. "Hey, sport," she said, "let's have a drink."

"Let's wait a bit," Ronald said, pulling down a stowage door that swung down from the ceiling of the car. He glanced inside, then snapped it closed.

"Wait for what, darling? I'll be too damned old to enjoy our next vacation. Say, why don't I ask Danielle to join us?" Dorothy said.

"She's too busy, I'm sure," Ronald said, settling into one of the wingbacks.

"She could bring her daughter. We have lots of room," she said.

"She has a whole scout troop to take care of, Dorothy," he replied.

"Okay, you're right," she said, seeming not to have noticed the irritation in his response. After all, she was well accustomed to his abrupt personality.

*   *   *

In the same car, in the last compartment, Bishop Kimo Jimini was removing his unseasonable serge suit jacket and was immediately relieved to wear only his clerical collar, a short-sleeve orchid-colored shirt, and trousers. He took in the ambience of his compartment, noting that he would not need the wine cooler nor the whole of the large double bed that occupied so much of the suite. He opened the door to the compact washroom and, while rinsing his hands, looked into the mirror before him. His eyes behind gold, wire-rimmed glasses were bloodshot but, despite his sixty-plus years, the skin beneath them was remarkably unlined. His hair was now heavily grayed, caused in part, he supposed, by a career of unceasing stress. He sat gingerly in one of the wingback chairs, unaccustomed to the luxury surrounding him now despite a lifetime of traveling by all means, trains included. He would not be here now, sipping from the chalice of extravagance, were it not for the insistence of his wife, Jasmine. There was money flowing in like a river from varied sources of headwaters, and they had earned it, she said.

Comfort was in the mind, he told her, and his mind would be much more at ease if he were riding several cars down the train with the third-class passengers. But since his elevation to bishop by the Anglican church and his international visibility as a leader against the apartheid government that preceded Mandela's victory over white oppression, Jasmine had found their new social and economic fortune to her liking. It was not written in stone, certainly not in blood, that a human being need wear rags while serving his or her constituency, a term she preferred to use when referring to the common blacks of South Africa. He was now much more than a minister of God who preached to a semiliterate flock, she told him. He was, in truth, an enduring, resolute figure of black humanity who not only refused to submit to the morally illegal laws of the white man in South Africa, but one who flourished while fighting against them peacefully. Rumors abounded that he was high on the list of candidates for the next Nobel Peace Prize. Not that he cared for official recognition, but Jasmine insisted that he be aware that both of them had worked tirelessly to pull themselves, as well as others, out of South Africa's red-clay, low-caste existence and into the modern world. She argued that he was special, and that he should admit it, if only to himself. But Kimo Jimini had never been able to follow his beloved wife's exhortations, even privately.

Yet, he liked the idea of a few hours of uninterrupted quiet, even if gained at the cost of a ticket he would not himself have bought. The train was moving, pulling away from Johannesburg station, as Bishop Jimini stepped across the compartment from his chair to his double bed. "Just for a few minutes," he said to himself. He had no idea how right he was going to be.

The Blue Train was never intended for high-speed travel but it would reach speeds in the middle 100kph range when special sights like Kruger Park did not warrant slowing it down. Still, it was accelerating through 62kph when the engineer, Heward Beoverwan, saw the damaged track ahead. He immediately pulled the red emergency stop handle inside the cab of his diesel/electric locomotive in an effort he knew was too late. The train's tool-steel wheels locked up, but it would have taken a minimum of three-quarters of a kilometer to stop the train and there was less than half that to go. Heward shouted at his fireman and his two assistants, the words hardly out of his mouth when the sabotaged track, the spikes removed from their ties, fell aside and the seventy-five ton locomotive dug straight into the exposed rail bed. The locomotive

slid for 280 feet, as though in slow motion, tipping over
on its side and crushing one assistant fireman to death.
Passenger cars followed, jackknifing from the tracks,
some rolling over onto the graded embankment while others remained in a more or less upright position.

The sounds of grinding metal upon metal, and metal
upon rock, seemed to go on for an eternity for the 312
souls on board. Thrown around inside shaking, rolling
metal cars, slammed into seats, ceilings, and glass windows, women, men, and children shrieked and howled in
pain and panic long after the tangled chain of crumpled
metal had come to a halt. The quiet that followed was
punctuated by the hiss of escaping air from rubber brake
lines, steam from the galley, and moans of the injured.

Most passengers, while bruised and battered, escaped
life-threatening wounds. Two of the first-class cars, while
pushed and pulled from the steel rails, nevertheless remained on the track bed and did not overturn. At the time
of the derailment, Dorothy had been in bed so that she
could watch passing scenery with her neck resting on a
pillow. When the train crashed Ronald had been sitting in
one of the wingback chairs that was touching the bulkhead of the connecting stateroom. He had been reading a
book, a pillow placed carefully at the small of his back to
support a chronic arthritis condition, more of a nuisance
than a handicap. Neither he nor Dorothy were injured.

"Oh, God," Dorothy said, picking herself up from the
carpeted floor of their stateroom, "I'm going to find
Danielle and those girls. They must need help."

"Stay where you are," Ronald ordered, a crackle in his
voice that demanded obedience.

"But all of those girls . . ." she began before he interrupted.

"It wasn't a violent crash," he said, only half truthfully, "and the last thing authorities need are more people running around the crash site."

Dorothy hesitated. She had been an RN in her earlier life, and while her skills could still prove useful, she believed her husband had probably assessed the situation correctly. She would wait calmly until the situation clarified. She looked again outside their windows, none of which had broken, and realized that the dust had literally not yet settled. The geography was flat, the weather was still warm, and they were located not more than about thirty-five miles from Johannesburg. That would put them, Ron pointed out now as he referred to one of their several tourists maps, about five miles between Meyerton and Vereeniging. Both towns, as well as Jo'burg, would have dispatched medical staff and ambulances to tend to the injured, he said. All they had to do was sit tight.

He was right, Dorothy thought, and she turned toward her day bag, where she kept a pair of walking shorts and shoes. Her safari blouse and jacket were just right for the occasion. She was just tightening the laces on her shoes when she heard strange sounds. Strange, at least, considering their circumstances. They sounded like gunshots. "Do you hear that?" she said to Ronald.

"Yes," he said, in an almost surreally calm voice.

"What is it? Gunfire?" She could hardly believe her own words.

"Yes," he said. "Stay calm, Dorothy."

She was calm. Ron's presence accounted for most of her lack of panic, she believed. After all, the man had spent his life in wars and international intrigue—he certainly had the capacity to evaluate their current emergency. "So, what the hell is going on?" she asked.

"I don't know," he said. "We're in a politically unstable country. Shit like this happens. You just have to use your head and go with the flow."

Dorothy heard shouting both outside and inside the train now. She heard men pounding against the doors and windows with what she assumed were rifle butts, then there was banging immediately outside their own compartment. "Out!" she heard in a voice directed at them as smashing, thudding sounds continued on the door. "Get out! Out of the car. Hurry, dogs, or you die!"

Ronald opened the door just as a rifle butt struck it and it smashed open hard against the bulkhead. A small black man wearing jungle camouflage and a black sweatband tied around his head pointed the barrel of his assault rifle at Ronald's face. At a glance Ronald recognized the distinctive features of a Vektor CR 21 5.56 compact assault rifle, made in South Africa by a company who had worked diligently to become a player on the world stage of military weapons. The man on the other end of the gun had a passive face, dead eyes, and was in a hurry. Ronald took Dorothy's hand and pulled her through the door as the man with the rifle commanded.

Standing just behind the wrecked engine and track was Walter Felinda, commander of the forty armed men who brought about the mayhem around him. While his men herded passengers together, Felinda made sure a satisfactory number of them were watching him as he flicked the fingers of his right hand in the direction of one of the third-class coaches. As though the scene had been rehearsed many times, which indeed it had, members of Felinda's uniformed gang began to systematically execute the passengers from an entire car, including women, children, and the elderly, black and white alike. The terrorists' assault weapons, on full automatic fire, raked lines of victims who were standing with their backs to the derailed cars. Two members of the killing team walked among the fallen and delivered coup de grace shots into the back—and front—of heads. The action was done swiftly, efficiently, without remorse. The desired effect on the survivors from the first-class carriages, for whom the atrocity was being staged, was achieved. Adults hugged children to their bodies, most young people and many adults cried. Felinda, satisfied with their work, turned his attention to the first-class passengers who had been assembled before him.

"You are hostages of the SADL, the South African Democratic League. If you do exactly as you are told, you will live. If you disobey any order by me or one of my men, you will die. There are two buses over there." He pointed to a service road only a few meters from the wreck. The hostages, surrounded by Felinda's men, could hear intermittent shots ringing out even as Felinda talked. "Leave your baggage and get into the buses. Now!"

Without a moment's hesitation the hostages, including Danielle Hüüken, her daughter, her twelve Girl Scouts, and her assistant, Alise Willicaze, moved toward the buses. In addition to those persons, although neither Ronald nor Dorothy knew them, were a group of seventeen American touring inner-city youths and their adult counselors from Cleveland, Ohio. Apart from them were eight American adults including Dorothy and Ronald Mauser. Bishop Kimo Jimini, along with two more South African citizens, were also among the fifty-one of Felinda's hostages. Ronald suspected that those selected for this destination with terror had been deliberately chosen. But why?

The bus ride, made under heavy armed guard, was short. It was less than four kilometers to the Salisbury mine. As bus doors were opened passengers were pushed to the ground, kicked, and shouted at by their captors. As the hostages arrived at the entrance of the mine, their screams and quavering moans became all the more hysterical. And indeed they should.

Chapter Two

The telephone awoke President Les Elling with a special chime. He groped for it in the dark hoping that he could reach it before it woke Rachael. But his wife was a light sleeper, often getting up in the middle of the night to read in their adjoining sitting room when worries jabbed at her psyche. "Yes?" he said into the instrument, making no attempt to turn on a light or even locate his eyeglasses in order to see his digital clock. Elling recognized the voice on the other end of the line immediately, one of the few persons in the government who had more than once intruded on his rest at this hour. "Who are they?" he asked, then continued to listen. "Jesus." He listened for another minute, then said, "Okay, come on up. Bring Dekins with you. And call Spencer. I don't think he'll contribute much but it'll save time. Ten minutes ought to do it." He hung up the telephone.

"What is it, Les?" his wife said.

"South Africa. Some nutcases, I don't know who yet, hijacked a train and took hostages. Americans among them." Elling turned on his bedside lamp, looked for and found a pair of pajama bottoms, which he stepped into.

"My God," Rachael said, sitting up in bed. "Was anybody hurt?"

"Apparently a number of South Africans were shot to show that the terrorists meant business," he said.

"How many?" she asked.

"I don't know, Rachael. Give me a chance to find out," he said irritably as he dropped his glasses into a satin robe pocket and walked into the bathroom.

"Is there anything I can do for you? I'll call down for coffee," she said, swinging her legs out of bed.

"Thanks, Minnie," he said, calling her by a pet name. "Have the cook include some coffee cake or something. Pete Dekins will be there. He might want to eat a side of beef."

The get-together took place in the president's den adjacent to the sitting room. It was a large, comfortable room with bookcases lining three walls, a modest showing of artwork including sculptures and portraits of renaissance men—among them Michel de Montaigne, one of the president's favorite classical thinkers. Overstuffed furniture guaranteed comfort for the president's visitors and there were tables, high and low, upon which papers could be spread.

National Security Advisor David Magazine and his aide, Army Brigadier General Peter Dekins, were the first to arrive. Dekins had been on the premises talking with the duty officer when the Code Five message arrived from South Africa. Dekins's first telephone call had been to his boss, Dr. Magazine. The president greeted both men as cheerfully as he could under the circumstances and asked them to sit. "Coffee and tea are on the way up. Pastries, too. I worry about you getting enough to eat, though, Pete. How about some scrambled eggs?"

"No, thank you, sir, I think coffee will do just fine," Dekins said. Dekins did not wear all of the medals and badges to which he was entitled because he had been on duty in "the cave" when the signal came from Pretoria. But like most field-grade officers on their way up, Dekins was parachute qualified, Ranger trained, and owned a battle star earned in 1991 in Iraq. Dekins had been picked in the first round of the major league baseball draft before graduating from West Point in 1983, the scouts figuring the guy would still be able to hit the long ball when he finished his five year military obligation. Problem was, for the Cincinnati Reds who drafted him, that he never came back. Dekins got a rush jumping out of airplanes, firing guns on the run, and leading fraternal men in combat, that no amount of home runs could equal. Dekins's friends calculated that he would be earning somewhere around five to seven million dollars per year if he hadn't been struck with an unaccountable desire to stay in. Now, at thirty-nine, Pete Dekins was considered to be a lock to make full general before he retired.

"Did Spence answer the phone when you called, Dave?" the president asked his security council advisor.

"Elaine did," Magazine said.

The president snorted. "Personally, I think she had the phone put on her side of the bed just so she could monitor Spencer's moves. Did you talk to her or him?" the president wanted to know, enjoying himself at the vice president's expense.

"To her. I just said that we had an urgent meeting taking place in your quarters," Magazine responded as he reached for a pastry that had just arrived on a linen-covered trolley.

The president leaned back and laughed. "That was it? You didn't tell her why? Great. It'll drive her right out of her mind. Pete, after Spencer comes in, put a napkin over the keyhole in case she's outside."

They were still laughing when the vice president arrived. General Dekins turned slightly red when the president said, "Come on in, Spence, we were just talking about you."

"Nothing good, I'll bet," Vice President McGraw said,

zeroing in on the Dutch pastries and helping himself to coffee before nodding in the direction of the others.

"If you can't say something bad about somebody, don't say anything at all," the president said. "My mother always said that."

"I think you have that backward, Les," McGraw said, cutting his pastry in half.

"You never met my mother. Okay," the president said, his face sobering. "Fun's over. Let's hear it, Dave."

"I've got it all down here in the signal," the president's advisor said, referring to a document in front of him, "but Pete talked to South Africa's top cop. I'll let him tell you."

"Good idea," the president said. "Shoot."

"We don't have all the intelligence we want, sir, but General Johannes Boord, state security police, said that four hours ago a train was intentionally derailed south of Johannesburg about forty-five kilometers out of the station. A group of well-armed and well-trained men took hostages from the wreckage—"

"How many armed men?" the president interrupted.

"General Boord couldn't say, sir," Dekins replied. "Witnesses at the crash site thought there were maybe a hundred. But witnesses, especially under these circumstances, are unreliable. Also, that's a high number for a terrorist operation. If that's what it is."

"Any question about what it is?" the president asked, pouring himself a cup of coffee.

General Dekins shrugged. "Seems like it, Mr. President. Worst thing is that they took the hostages to an abandoned gold mine. They're two thousand feet down."

"Holy mother of God," the vice president said.

The president, too, was startled. "Two thou . . . good Lord."

"The obvious fact is that we don't have a hell of a lot

of options, rescue-wise," David Magazine said. "Apparently, there is only one way in and one way out, and that's the main mine shaft."

"Two thousand feet down," the president repeated the number, shaking his head in astonishment. "Who are the hostages? How many Americans?"

"The hostage takers—they say they're the SADL, South African Democratic League—are holding Americans but won't say how many or who they are. General Boord says he'll try to get that for us," Pete Dekins said.

"They want to deal with a top official of the United States. They shot a whole carful of passengers from the train just to let us know they mean business," Magazine added.

"We haven't heard their demands, yet?" President Elling asked.

"Not yet, sir," Magazine said.

"Have you started on options, Dave?" the president wanted to know.

"Well, sir, on the way over Pete and I talked briefly about getting a negotiator over there, fast. Somebody from the Bureau. They've probably got the best. And . . ." Magazine hesitated.

"What else?" Elling urged.

"Well, we haven't had any time to discuss this, but if we send a military man for them to talk to, maybe it should be a dual-purpose guy. Somebody who has hostage rescue training, like a Delta man or a Navy SEAL."

"Makes sense," the president said. "Anybody come to mind?"

"I don't see why Pete couldn't handle it," Magazine said, nodding curtly toward General Dekins, "but to back him up I think I'd want to go with a SEAL Six man. I'm thinking about Bob Getts."

"How 'bout it, Pete?" the president said. "Want to take it on?"

"Yes, sir, I think I could handle it," Dekins affirmed.

"Could you work with Getts?" the president asked.

Dekins nodded his head emphatically. "Good choice, in my opinion. Smart, tough son of a bitch, and a real cool head."

"Okay, I'll think about everything you just said." The president looked at a desk clock. "It's almost three-thirty. Check with the Bureau and the navy and anybody else you can think of. Wake everybody up and let's get some more input. I'll make the decisions by seven o'clock in my office." The president looked at Vice President McGraw. "Anything you want to add, Spencer?"

"Yeah, I have a question. Who the hell is the SADL and what the fuck do they want?" McGraw said.

David Magazine answered, "General Boord never heard of them, Mr. Vice President, and so far we have no idea what they want."

Mr. Bucks, the H. P. Carlisle Foundation's head gardener, sat uncomfortably across the desk from his employer, Bradley Wallis. In contrast to Wallis's expensive Italian wool slacks, navy blue linen double-breasted blazer, club tie, and sparkling white shirt, Mr. Bucks was perfectly comfortable in his bib overalls and chambray shirt. And while Wallis's delicate hands were well manicured, Mr. Bucks's fingers were rougher, thicker, holding a delicate teacup and saucer in a way that appeared almost ludicrous. Still, Mr. Bucks had come to appreciate good English tea after dozens of impromptu meetings with the fastidious Wallis, where their conversations ranged widely. This morning it centered upon Mr. Bucks's plans for landscaping the grounds.

"I would strongly suggest that we remove the peony plants, Mr. Wallis," Mr. Bucks was saying.

"Trees," Bradley corrected the gardener.

"Technically, yes sir, but they're still shrubs. Call 'em what you like, but they've grown to become a hazard near the north gate," Mr. Bucks said.

"Not the Chinese peony. They are my favorites. I won't have them removed," Wallis said petulantly. He considered eating another scone but the thought of murdering a peony left him without appetite.

"Well then, Mr. Wallis, we're both in luck because I'm referring to the Moutan bush, not the Chinese," the gardener said, following Wallis's eyes to the scones. He helped himself to another.

"Hmmm." Wallis leaned forward to refill Mr. Bucks's delicate gold-trimmed China teacup with English Breakfast. "It isn't much of a concession. Can't you just cut off some of the plant? You need what, two feet for your cameras to see?"

"I thought you might say something like that, Mr. Wallis. That can be done, of course, but it isn't a permanent solution, is it? I have another plan that I think you will like very much," Mr. Bucks said, reaching into one of his several pockets and withdrawing a photograph. Wallis looked at the photo with interest.

"Beautiful, isn't it?" the gardener said. "Purple loosestrife. It comes from your home grounds, you know." Mr. Bucks was referring to Britain.

"Hmm," Wallis said again, turning the photo in his hand, hating to admit that he was quite pleased with the lush flowers shown in the glossy photo. "And you think this will solve your problem?"

"Well, yes, sir, at least to the north."

"Good heavens, man," Wallis said, sitting almost upright in his executive chair, "surely you don't mean to say that you're ripping out my gayfeathers next? I mean what else, in the name of God?"

"I didn't say that, Mr. Wallis. Not at all. The gayfeathers are doing everything that we could ask of them. And so are the others on our perimeter. But I am thinking of replacing our gold heart with morning glory around the main building."

"Why? Gold heart has done us very well over the years. Damn it, Bucks, sometimes I think you harbor personal grievances against some of our indigenous plants," Wallis said, turning sideways in his chair, his eyes averted from his gardener.

"You know that isn't true, Mr. Wallis. I've come to my conclusions without becoming emotional. Something you might consider yourself, if you don't mind my saying so. The morning glories are far more pleasing to the eye than the gold heart, and that isn't just me saying so. My staff will back me up on that."

Wallis stifled an unkind remark that a staff willing to lay down its life for Mr. Bucks would certainly not shrink from endorsing a subtropical plant on his behalf. Instead he said, "Well, we are not pressed are we? I mean, it isn't in the same category with the peony, is it?"

"No, indeed, Mr. Wallis," the gardener said to his superior. "Take all the time you need to consider."

Wallis exhaled with relief. Nothing caused him so much concern as tinkering with the grounds. Vegetables had spiritual life, he believed, and while there is an end for all things, he was reluctant to squander so much as a blade of grass prematurely.

The meeting obviously finished, Mr. Bucks replaced his cup on Wallis's desk and thanked him for the tea and the two scones that he had eaten. As he leaned forward to rise from the deep easy chair, the gardener felt an uncomfortable jab in his ribs through the pliable material of his bullet-proof vest. It was the MP-5, sans suppressor. It never seemed to hang quite right inside his overalls, but he knew that after a few minutes on his feet he would feel easy.

Having delayed his visit to the basement—a place he loathed—Wallis stepped into an elevator that allowed its rider entry only after an electronic retinal scan. As the machine descended deeper below the surface of the earth through a series of concrete walls hardened to withstand 20,000 psi of overhead pressure, the aging spy again considered retirement. As he stepped through the elevator doors into a maze of luminescent screens, controlled lighting, and purified atmosphere, he realized why he yearned to be somewhere else. He missed people. He regarded himself an insightful interrogator, a highly trained listener, and a skilled diviner of the human psyche. All of these skills were lost, however, in an environment that was absent of people. Oh, there were bodies around him, to be sure, but they operated machines, probed electronic cavities pulled in from space, or deciphered harmonious blurbs originating from one set of silicone users to another. Life and death was now measured in population-megatonage (Pop-Meg), lethal exploitation arrays, and force multipliers. It was a Dick Tracy, wrist-radio business of faceless men and straight-butt women who sold out their countries for no more reward than television consulting fees. Yet, since the death of his wife twelve years ago, Wallis had no place to retire to. In many ways he was glad Hildy was not here to see what had become of him. He was becoming little better than those he despised. He had even fallen into the habit of attending the wretched cocktail parties for which the city had become infamous.

"Is Captain Getts in yet?" he asked Major Bing.

"Good morning, Brad," Major Bing said, causing Wal-

lis to visibly stiffen at the sound of a subordinate calling
his superior by his first name. Not even his first name, but
a nickname. Wallis's hand went to his upper lip as he
stroked his mustache, a nervous reaction that he recognized as a personal failing. It affected his poker playing
so he gave up the game just as he was beginning to enjoy
it. Major Andrew Bing—soon to be lieutenant colonel at
age thirty-one—was a product of the top of his West
Point class, the youngest graduate of the U.S. Army
Combined Arms Center, and was a platoon commander,
First Bat., 5th Special Forces Group (Airborne). In contrast to his predecessor, Colonel Adrian Barnes, Major
Bing was anything but spit and polish. Conformity had
been Barnes's game. "Nope, Bobby has been in and gone
out again. Shooting guns, I should think. Should we ring
him up?"

Ring him up? I should think? Is this child mocking
me? Wallis asked himself. "Yes, we need to talk."

"Yes, sir. I suppose it's all about the hostages?" Bing
probed.

"As a matter of fact, it is," Wallis said. "How the devil
did you know that?" David Magazine had spoken to Wallis in the early hours of the morning. The entire affair was
highly classified until the president released the information himself.

"General Dekins called. He wanted to know if we had
anything on SADL," the army officer said. "Naturally he
had to fill me in. Up to a point."

"And what did you tell him?" Wallis asked.

"Nothing. We didn't have a thing. I searched our files
and even called some of our assets in South Africa. Nada.
Zip," Bing said.

"Well, we do know something," Wallis said, a surge of
exultation coursing through his breast.

"We do? About the South African Democratic League?" Bing asked.

Wallis resisted the temptation to smile at Bing's sudden anxiety at giving the National Security Council incorrect information. Their business rested upon complete confidence of its product analysts. "Well, in a fashion. This Walter Felinda character was a minor officer in Mobutu Sese Seko's so-called Congo army more than a dozen years ago. The man is a homicidal maniac."

"How do you know him, Brad?" Bing asked.

Maybe I should force myself to get used to it, Wallis said to himself. Perhaps if I drank an ale with him I would loosen up and . . . oh, hell. "One of my people had him in his crosshairs out in the bush. There was a ceasefire, about an hour old, and the man toyed with the idea of pulling the trigger anyway. Pity for the world that he didn't."

"I see. Well, NSC will want to hear from you ASAP, sir. They're meeting with the president right now," the army officer said, chagrined.

"Ah, well, I need to finish one or two things around here. Why don't you call them yourself? Tell them that you've come up with a bit more information—no need to tell them where—and alert them that we think SADL is only a front name invented ad hoc for the present hostage action," the master spy said.

Major Bing was very aware that Bradley Wallis was giving him a face-saving way out of the fundamental mistake of passing on information based upon incomplete sourcing. But he wasn't about to make the same mistake again. "Uh, do we know that, sir? That SADL is a phony name?"

"No, we don't know that. I know that. Put it to them any way you think it sounds best. But call Getts first," Wallis said as he turned away.

* * *

Getts stepped out of a shower at Building 3408, Bachelor Officers' Quarters at Little Creek, Virginia, and weighed himself. One hundred sixty-two pounds, twelve pounds lighter than he knew was optimal for his body frame. He was already eating five thousand calories a day but needed more. The reconstruction of bone in his face had healed long ago and the puffiness had been replaced with a gaunt appearance. Even so, his body was all muscle, and Getts felt that he was still in peak physical shape. He eyed a bowl of fruit on his kitchen counter that contained, among other things, fresh bananas. He made a mental note to eat one after he found a clean shirt. He sat on a canvas chair near the phone. He was running late and he intended to call Peach. The sun was taking its time to set but Getts had been out of the rack and on his feet at 0430 hours, doing underwater demolition with a unit from SEAL 4.

Last week they had cleared mines and mapped beaches while locking into and out of a submarine lying three miles off shore. The work had taken high concentration and physical stamina. To make life more difficult, Getts was working with ST4 four days per week, then commuting to the Carlisle Foundation to work from Thursday evenings through Saturday afternoons. On Sunday, though he knew he needed some form of recreation in his life, he simply crashed and slept the clock around. It was a schedule he felt he had to adhere to if he was to maintain his SEAL skills while carrying out his assignment to the Foundation. It was now Tuesday and he planned to meet Peach at the officers' club for a drink. Or two. Peach was assigned to SEAL 1 in San Diego, a fact he never let his old skipper forget. "It's the cream out here," he explained to Getts the last time they met in Oakland during the holiday season. "The guys the navy can't afford to leave the service they assign right here in California so that we can get our dicks sucked twenty-four hours a day."

Getts was looking forward to hearing about Peach's romantic life because his own had been so poor. Peach wasn't nearly as handsome as Getts, Getts thought, but he worked at it harder so naturally the girls paid attention. When he heard the telephone ring he thought it might be Peach asking about when he was going to get his ass over to the bar. "Captain Getts," he said into the telephone.

"General Dekins, Bobby," the other voice said. "I work at NSC for the president. Did I interrupt anything?"

"Actually, General, I've already jerked off in the shower so if you're calling to fix me up with your daughter, it's too late," Getts said.

"I'm going to tell my wife you said that, Getts," the general said.

"You wish you had a wife, General," Getts said.

"As a matter of fact, I do," Pete Dekins said.

"My apologies then, sir. With your permission I'd like to withdraw my insensitive remark," Getts said.

"Captain Getts, are you all right? I don't have time to call back . . ." the general said, his voice dwindling.

As Getts listened to the electronic hum on the line he suddenly felt cold as a chill came over him. "Ah, this isn't Peach? This really is General Dekins?" Getts said, suddenly sweating despite the cold that he felt.

"That's right. Who's Peach?" Dekins said.

"Oh, God, General Dekins, I apologize, sir. I have this friend, Peach, a nutcase, sir, and he can imitate anyone's voice. Not that I know yours, but I'm supposed to meet him in a few minutes and . . . and . . ." Getts fumbled, despising himself.

"He a SEAL, too? That explains everything. No reason you should recognize my voice, Getts. Relax," Dekins said.

"Damn, I feel like a jerk," Getts said.

"You might feel like a bigger jerk when I tell you what kind of mess I got you and me into." There was a hesitation on Dekins's end of the line so Getts waited for the general to continue. "I just came from the head shed. I'm not on a secure phone so you and I have to get face-to-face," Dekins said.

"Understand. Where are you now, sir?" Getts said.

"We're thirteen-thousand descending, fifteen out from Norfolk NAS, ETA twenty-one," the general said.

Getts understood that Dekins was in an aircraft fifteen nautical miles from Norfolk Naval Air Station, descending from thirteen thousand feet, expected arrival twenty-one minutes. "Roger, General. Suggest we meet here at NAVSPECWARGRU-TWO. I'll have ground transportation waiting, sir."

"Your place is good, negative transportation. We've got that waiting," came the reply.

On Getts's nightstand was a bottle containing 100mg tablets of Desyril, an anti-depression drug in the Trazodone family. He considered taking one now but immediately rejected the idea because of the drowsiness the drug caused. Better to be suicidal than accidental, he thought grimly. It was, in fact, less than twenty minutes when Getts, hair still damp, entered Building 3801, NAVSPECWARGRU-TWO (Navy Special Warfare Group Two). He hardly broke stride as he walked through the front door. A PO First Class, despite the late hour, rose to his feet as Getts appeared.

"Army General Pete Dekins is on his way in. My door's open when he arrives," Getts said.

"Aye, aye, sir," the yeoman said as Getts passed his desk.

"Larson," Getts called out from within his office.

"Sir," the yeoman said and stepped into the doorway.

"Call SEAL Team Three in San Diego. Run down First Class Petty Officer Heggstad, put him on priority transportation to this station. I want him here tonight. No excuses," Getts ordered.

"Yes, sir," the yeoman said. "Are we on alert, Captain?"

"They didn't send Dekins down here on a public relations tour. Whatever it is, I want to be ready," Getts said.

Getts kept travel bags packed at all times, one of which occupied a place in the corner of the room. He immediately began disposing of a stack of paperwork atop his desk by tossing some on to smaller piles or dropping others into an already overflowing trash can. He was in the process of tossing out the last of it when he heard sounds in the outer office. He rose to meet his visitor from Washington, D.C., as Dekins strode through the open door.

"Bob Getts, General," he said, saluting first, then shaking Dekins's proffered hand. The general was perhaps an inch taller than Getts's five-ten, but had big hands and long arms. Getts would have put the man at a flankerback if he had been running a football team. No way he could miss a pass with those flippers, he thought.

"Pete Dekins. Thanks for coming so soon, Bobby. Sit down."

"How about a drink, General?" Getts offered.

"Sure. Wild Turkey and water, if you have it," Dekins said.

"I can offer you Jack Daniels and Coke, General," Getts said.

"Sounds like shit but . . ." Dekins said, waving a hand.

"Larson," Getts called out, but before he could finish Yeoman Larson walked through the open door with a bottle of Jack Daniels, a bowl of ice, and a can of Coca Cola. He placed the tray on Getts's desk.

"Thanks, Larson," Getts said, pouring a stiff amount of booze into a glass from his desk. "Pour one for yourself and stand by."

"Aye, aye, sir," the yeoman said, as he accepted the glass of bourbon. He dropped two ice cubes into the glass and helped himself to the Coke. "Thank you, sir," he said and withdrew to his outer office.

Getts did the honors and handed Dekins his drink. "To the army," he toasted.

"I haven't had it like this since I was trying to get laid in high school," Dekins said. "How about you?"

Getts liked him immediately. "Sex never enters my mind, General. I've been saving myself for marriage."

"Not married?" Dekins asked.

"Never did, but I can hardly wait," he said, straight-faced.

Dekins laughed, then downed the rest of his drink. He waved away Getts's offer of another. "I spent the morning with President Elling and a few others. Your old boss was there. David Magazine," Dekins said.

"How is Dave?"

"Running his ass off right now. Said to say hello to you. They were looking for a shitty stick to attach a hand to. Mine was there. A group of very nasty people in South Africa wrecked a train out of Jo'burg and snatched the first-class passengers. Lots of Americans, though we don't know how many yet. We don't even know what they're after. They want to talk directly to a senior American military officer."

"You?" Getts asked.

"Yeah. Magazine thought I should take along somebody with hostage rescue experience. I was Delta at one time."

"Good thinking," Getts interjected.

"The FBI is supplying a mouthpiece. If there is any chance of getting those people out, I want heads-up troops for the job. I read the Tac-Ops file on your assault on that castle in Syria . . ."

"Fouquat," Getts reminded him.

"Right. Pretty slick. Whose idea was it to jump into the jet stream?" the admiral asked.

Getts smiled self-effacingly.

"How about cracking the walls. That your idea, too?" Dekins said.

"I had help on that one," Getts said.

"I liked the whole job. Naturally, I couldn't believe a sailor planned it because I didn't know you people ever had original ideas."

Getts loved the man immediately. "Are you trying to flatter me into volunteering to go to South Africa?" he asked.

"Yes. I'm going to be too busy doing liaison for these fucking maniacs to command an assault team. At least, that's what I'm telling myself because, frankly, I don't want to do it. I think the chances of getting those folks out alive is a red-cunt-hair less than zero and it isn't a function of bravery."

"That so?" Getts asked, leaning forward in his chair. He, like all SEAL Six personnel, had extensive training in hostage rescue in almost every conceivable venue, and Getts thought that he had just about heard them all.

"They're in the bottom of a gold mine shaft, two thousand feet down," General Dekins said.

Getts whistled. The various models for disaster immediately leaped to mind. He could see the terrorists clearing themselves out of the hole, depositing barrels of gasoline behind them, then dropping a match as they checked out. Or setting off explosives and sealing everyone inside. And defense? Perfect, if you're a bad guy. Nobody could get down the elevator shaft without staring a machine gun straight in the face. Naturally, an attacker could do the same as the bad guys, and pour gas down the pipe or drop bombs down the shaft, but the hostages would go up with them. Getts could see that an assault team was going to be about as useful as three dicks on a donkey.

"So? Do I see a shaky little hand in the air?" General Dekins was saying.

"You got it, Pete," Getts said. "Tremors and all."

Pete Dekins dropped a fistful of papers on the floor, completely missing the wastebasket and not caring. He put his hands briefly over his eyes, and shook his head slowly before regarding Getts. "Thanks, Bob. There wouldn't be a single officer in the entire navy or army who would blame you for turning down this piece of shit. I not only appreciate it, but I'll never forget it."

"Thank you, sir," Getts said.

"If you pull this off, I'll make sure that you get the credit I would have normally appropriated from my subordinates," Dekins said.

"Only if I fuck it up, you mean," Getts said.

"You'll go far in the navy, my friend. I'm leaving here by Special Air Mission at 1000 hours. My first order of business will be to clear your team for entry into South Africa with their authorities. Just in case that takes longer than we want, take our charter flight. I'll expect you and your people no later than eight hours behind me.

"Charter flight" referred to an L-1011 wide body painted to appear to be an American airliner, but which actually belonged to the SpecWarOps people and was, of course, flown by their own crew. The "passengers" would wear civilian clothes and pass themselves off as tourists or engineers or even a rugby team. "We'll be right behind you, General," Getts said.

"Who do you want?" Dekins asked.

"I don't see this as a big unit operation, as least not for the assault, if we execute one. Eight to ten, I think. More than that might get in the way. I've got Peach here on the base. He's a warrant officer so he'll be my exec. Heggstad is with SEAL Three in San Diego." *The rest are dead,* he thought to himself. *And now another assault. How many more dead?* "I'll get the rest of my people from SEAL Six," he added.

"Okay. You've got top priority. Don't bother with printed orders, use Green Solitaire for the code word. That's coming down from the top as we speak. All the aircraft you need are right down the street," the general said, referring to Norfolk Naval Air Station, a high volume flying operation which included dedicated NAVSPECWAROPS planes.

Getts had only to step into the next office where there was a secure telephone to set his team into motion. He first dialed the officers' club. He did not take the time to have Peach paged, but simply told the person answering the phone to find him and have him report to NAVSPECWARGRU-TWO immediately. His next telephone call was to the H. P. Carlisle Foundation. He identified himself to the duty officer by a seven digit number and was then put directly through to Bradley Wallis.

"Bob Getts here, Bradley. Can you talk?" he said into the phone.

"Yes, I can talk. How are you, my boy?" the older man asked.

"Just fine, Bradley. Is your end secure?" he asked.

"It is. I assume by your tone that something's come up. I think I can imagine what it is," Wallis said.

"You're probably right. I'm leaving for South Africa within six hours. Peach is here on the base. He'll go with me plus a SEAL Six squad. What do you know about the hostage takers?" Getts asked.

"Virtually nothing, at this point," Wallis said. "I think this SADL is a sham, of course, but Walter Felinda is very real, sorry to say. He was a junior officer in Mobutu's dustup in the Congo back in eighty-six, and then again in the massacres against the Tutsis in ninety-five. He has a passion for killing."

"Besides that, what do you know about him? Is he very smart?" Getts said.

"Socrates argued that no man who commits crimes against other men is very smart. Philosophy aside, I have no reason to regard Felinda as a candidate for distinguished scientific achievement. We're working hard right now to get solid information about him and his men. We're accessing DIA, CIA, and our friends overseas. I'll be very interested in what our colleagues on Boulevard Mortier can tell us," Wallis said.

Wallis was referring to the French intelligence agency located at 128 Boulevard Mortier, in Paris. They had moved to the fort at Noisy-Le-Sec but intended to retain their Caserne headquarters as well. "Yeah," Getts responded, "those folks should know if anybody does. Jean-Paul Bouvier is a good man at MI."

"I'll go directly to Claude," Wallis sniffed, meaning Claude Silberzahn, the French Director of Intelligence. "In any case, I'll send along intel as we get it," Wallis said.

"Good. I'll be moving fast but I'll have a day pad and so will Peach," Getts said, referring to the efficient but simple one-time day pads to use for coded communication. He was just hanging up the telephone when the looming figure of Peach entered the door.

"Hi, Peach. You're getting fat," Getts lied as he held out his hand.

Peach, almost six feet four inches tall, black hair worn insolently long and slicked back, had beautiful olive skin that most women would die for. His teeth were bright, shining pearls and his dark brown eyes revealed that there was always somebody home behind them. He had been Getts's friend since they were teens and Getts loved him second only to his mother.

"That's because the natives bring me rare fruits and forbidden foods to eat. I am worshiped at SEAL One. Men fight each other merely to stand in my shadow while their wives and sisters fight to fondle my incredibly large reproductive organ."

"I happen to know that you are the pathetic victim of drugs and alcohol and that you will perform indecent acts with pack animals for even one drink of whiskey," Getts said.

"Yes, but it has to be Canadian whiskey."

"We've got an op in South Africa, hostages two thousand feet down in a mine shaft," Getts said, interrupting.

Peach whistled, sitting upright in his chair. Getts continued, "General Dekins is liaison, FBI is doing the talking, and you and I will be working on an assault plan. I want to be off the ground in five hours. I know Heggstad is available. We need six, plus you and me. Pick 'em yourself and I'd recommend SEAL Six people. Agree?"

"Agreed," Peach said.

"We'll go over in our L-1011, civilian clothes and funny cards," Getts said, meaning forged identification documents. "We can have a company aircraft follow us over with equipment and special weapons when we figure out what we'll need."

"I recommend we stow our thundersticks and tac gear in the hold of the 1011. If their customs people want to make an issue about that, we'll deal, but we're saving time if they don't," Peach said.

"Good. I'm setting up the transport right now. You name the personnel and call them in to the skipper over at Six. Code word for this one is Green Solitaire. It opens all the doors," Getts said. "Meet me at the POD at"—Getts looked at his watch—"2300 hours."

"Roger, skipper. Pleasure to be back in business with you," Peach said. The two men shook hands briefly, then turned toward executing their urgent duties.

In Pretoria, South Africa, Captain Robert Getts, U.S.N., waited in the office of General Johannes Boord, commander of State Security. Getts did not have time to scan all of the available personnel profiles on South African military people, but the name Boord rang a bell. There was a Colonel Boord in a branch of the S.A. state police who was widely feared during the apartheid years. He was a torturer, it was alleged, and a cold killer. The man abhorred all blacks and had little more respect for other people of color. He was, if Getts recalled correctly, the very manifestation of all that was evil about the old political system. Getts assumed that when the ANC took over, Boord had been arrested and either imprisoned or executed. Boord was a common name, though, and the man Getts was waiting for could not be the same.

The office was comfortable, as one would expect the head of national security to inhabit, with the obligatory framed photographs of various police and army detachments adorning the walls, oil paintings of previous occupiers of the office—all white, like the present official. Although Getts had brought a uniform with him, today he wore civilian clothing.

The intelligence community was having problems drawing profiles on the hostage takers. They were desperately hoping that the intelligence people in-country had the answers they needed. Nor was Getts pleased that the South African security service had not provided them with the full military support they had requested.

"You got to believe they have 'em all, Skipper," Peach had said earlier in the day as they loaded arms and other equipment from their aircraft into four-wheel drive vehicles they had obtained from a safari supply house. "I mean, I'll bet their Committee knows the middle name and blood type of every fucking man or woman holding an assault rifle on the continent. Hey, it's how they stay alive in these parts," Peach said.

The door opened at that moment, causing Getts to look over his shoulder. A man in an immaculate khaki uniform of the South Africa's security police stepped into the room and closed the door behind him. He was black, of average height, and affected an air of efficiency set off by his highly shined brown boots and bemedaled jacket. He was not young, perhaps in his late forties. His head nodded slightly to the American. "Captain Getts, I am Major An Louden, deputy to General Johannes Boord. General Boord conveys to you his compliments and asks me to offer you a drink." The South African's heavy eyebrows raised in anticipation of the forthcoming drink order.

Getts blinked. "A drink? That's real nice of the general, Major, but I'm a little pressed for time."

"Entirely understandable," Louden said. "The general has a great deal on his plate at the moment, as you can imagine. He knows you are anxious to see him. Now, would you care for coffee? Tea? Anything at all?"

Getts simply turned his head away from Major Louden, pointedly ignoring him. He forced himself to think about the military situation they faced. The hostages were in a hole in the ground. To get them out, an assault team would have to somehow get into that hole with them.

He lapsed into a kind of free association of thoughts, sorting through the problems that stood in the way of seeing any hostage emerge from below ground alive.

At last the door opened again and a slender man of average height entered the room. The man who extended his limp, boney hand with indifference and said his name was Johannes Boord seemed extraordinarily young for the position he held. He had the cherubic face of a teenager and his brown hair hung carelessly across his forehead. His ears were slightly large, which only contributed to his adolescent appearance. His lips were of such a dark red hue that Getts wondered if the man suffered from poor blood circulation. His eyes danced from point to point, never looking directly into the eyes of another, and his delicate fingers flicked at imaginary particles on his uniform. He gestured that his visitor was to sit while he took a nearby chair. When he crossed his legs, Getts could see how scrawny the man's legs were, his kneecaps looking to pierce the khaki material of his uniform trousers.

"Sorry to keep you waiting," Boord said loftily. "Major Louden has offered you a drink?"

"Yes," Getts said, attempting to convey a sense of urgency to South Africa's security czar, "but we're pressed for time." Getts leaned forward in his seat as he waited for General Boord to speak.

"The hostage situation? Is that why you are here?" he asked, the fingers of his right hand fluttering like a bird. "Then tell me how I can help you."

"General Boord," Getts said, "General Dekins and I are the senior United States officers present in your country. General Dekins is the man the hostage takers want to talk to. I am his deputy. It's up to us to represent our country not only to the terrorists—if that's what they are—but to the independent nation of South Africa, as well. Our orders come directly from President Elling. We hope we can count on your support in dealing with the terrorists."

"Yes, yes, I appreciate that," Boord said.

"My understanding is that many, if not most, of the hostages are Americans," Getts said. "The threats being made against the hostages are aimed at the United States. What we need from you, sir, is cooperation. We need access to your intelligence on who these terrorists may be, Walter Felinda in particular, and who he's associated with. We need details about the mine the hostages are being held in, including maps, technical drawings and interviews with mining engineers. We need security support for me, and for our FBI liaison, and I need your permission to operate a U.S. Navy hostage rescue team in South Africa. Then there is communications and logistics to be sorted out and . . ."

"Please," General Boord said, shaking his head and holding a slender hand in the air, palm out. "You are asking for too much. We are not one of your states. This is not Virginia, Captain. Or California. You are welcome as guests, of course, but we do not permit foreign armed troops in our country. We have our own resources. And they are very good. The United States is new to the terrorist business but here, in Africa, we deal with it every day." The general shrugged as he uncrossed and crossed his legs. "These black people in the Salisbury mine are thugs. They are violent and they make demands, as all thugs do. If we jump when they say jump, they are in control. We think it is best to let them sit for a while. Let them become nervous worrying about what we will do. Then we will contact them." The general looked at the watch on his wrist. "If you will excuse me, I have other appointments. Will you be at your hotel if we should need to contact you?"

Getts rose to his feet, livid with fury. He leaned closer to South Africa's security chief as he spoke. "My mistake, Boord, was in dealing with a fourth-rate, pompous bureaucrat about an important issue. You're an insulting, egotistical son of a bitch, but I'm not going to think much about that. Instead, I will tell you that my Navy SEALs are in your country right now and if you get in our way of rescuing United States citizens, you'd better put every hospital in South Africa on emergency status because we'll damn sure fill 'em up for you. Then, after we finish off your local bullies, we'll deal with the terrorists."

Major Louden dropped his glass, shattering it.

As Captain Getts walked toward the door, General Boord spoke harshly to his back. "I don't respond to threats. This business will be handled our way, not yours." His words were meant to intimidate but they did not even register with Getts.

General Pete Dekins was present when Getts spoke on a secure telephone within the hour on a conference call with President Elling, David Magazine, and Bradley Wallis. He recounted as accurately as he could the conversation he had with General Boord. It was difficult, if not impossible, to remove the rage he felt from his narrative.

"Jesus Christ," Magazine muttered into the phone.

The president chuckled. "Did you really tell him that? About filling up his hospitals?"

"Yes, sir, I did."

"Did you mean it?" the president asked.

"Yes, sir, I'm embarrassed to admit it. It sure wasn't very diplomatic," Getts said.

"Don't apologize, Getts. Sometimes I'd like to say that to some of the ambassadors I have to deal with. Anyway,

I'll talk to President Kwisi as soon as we hang up the phone."

"Something is wrong, here," Wallis said.

"Damn right, something's wrong," Magazine said. "Bobby, could this be some kind of personality conflict between you and Boord? Don't misunderstand, I'm not looking for a place to put blame, but did this guy suddenly take a disliking to you or something?"

"I guess that's possible, Dr. Magazine. I don't want to think this brushup was my fault but I suppose I should give that some serious thought. If I'm the cause, then you better get somebody over here to replace me ASAP."

"Getts isn't here as a diplomat," interjected General Dekins. "He's a combat team leader. If anyone gets replaced, it should be me."

"Hold on, everybody, it isn't hari-kari time yet," Magazine said.

"That isn't what I meant," Wallis said.

"What are you thinking, Bradley?" President Elling asked.

"General Boord is a powerful man in the South African government. Any head of state security police would be. Goes with the position. Even so, it isn't likely that he would take the risk of alienating a nation like the United States unless he was very sure of his ground."

"You mean concurrence from above?" President Elling said.

"Yes," Wallis responded. "Something else is going on, I think."

"I see where you're going," Magazine said, "but we don't have time to sort out African politics. General Dekins has to get his people to work, fast."

There was a momentary silence connoting agreement on the line. Then the president said, "Is the FBI guy—what's his name?"

"Arlen Gibbs, sir."

"Yeah. Where is he, now?"

"He's at the mine, sir," General Dekins said.

Gibbs was a shade less than average height, in his early to middle forties, slender, and wore bifocals perched on a prominent nose. His dark hair was quite thin on top and he had a way of looking a person straight on as though he were very interested in everything you had to say. He was a man hard to disconcert. But inside he felt a nagging frustration in the physical setup under which he was forced to work.

The mine complex had been abandoned for more than thirty years. It now served as an infrequent tourist attraction, so that the buildings, the derrick, the hoisting equipment, and the elevator cage, while weather-beaten, were maintained in good condition. The platform itself was about four feet high and about eighty feet on each of its four sides. On the west side of the platform was an unpaved road that serviced the rig and equipment shed, while on the east side of the derrick tower was a power station that included an electricity-producing diesel engine. On the north side was another large, two-story building, once used for first-stage processing of ore as it was brought up from the tunnels below. There were, to Gibbs's liking, far too many civilian and uniformed personnel—military and police—standing around him, interfering with his attempted communication with the hostage takers. It took almost a full day to obtain and deploy a simple telephone line that would reach from his place ten feet from the adit to the depths of the main shaft, 2,000 feet below. This, despite the fact that almost all of the existing phone line was still in place from the 1950s.

Someone, not surprisingly, had tipped off the media.

Television trucks and crews, turned away from the paved parking area, parked at the perimeter, marked by cyclone wire fence. Their towers were raised and transmitters hummed from generators within the trucks. Reflectors and lights were erected near the scene and directed toward the platform.

When at last he established contact with the SADL below, he was constantly given instructions over his shoulder from various officials of the South African government, almost all of which he ignored. Pete Dekins was on hand, virtually at his side, but waged what seemed to be a losing war among representatives of the bureaucracies that came upon them in waves. Most distracting of all was a lack of intelligence about the SADL and the individuals who kept the prisoners below, which was so vital to Arlen Gibbs's bag of negotiating tricks. Finally, it seemed that state security police, grim-faced, armed, uniformed personnel numbering in the hundreds, controlled access to and from the site of the captives. The only positive note in which Gibbs could take solace was a fully capable communications system from the hostage site to Washington, D.C., and other vital bureaus such as the NRO, DIA, and the Carlisle Foundation. By 1430 local time of the first day of hostage captivity, Navy Captain Getts had appeared at the site, bivouacked in what was once the mine's main parking lot. He had with him a group of Navy SEALs.

Now, with the telephone in place and working, Gibbs attempted to locate the leader of the so-called SADL. "Say your name, please," he said into the telephone. The response was faint and incomprehensible. "I cannot hear you," he said slowly, distinctly. "Give me your name, please. I need to have your name." Again, he waited.

Abruptly, in a clear and strong tone, a different voice

boomed over the line into Gibbs's ear. "I am General Felinda. Who are you?"

"Ah," Gibbs said into the mouthpiece, "my name is Arlen Gibbs. I am here as a representative of the American government. I also have the authority to negotiate . . ."

"There will be no negotiations, white massah. I will give orders, you will carry them out," Felinda said with no discernable passion.

"General, there must be understanding on both sides if we are to move this problem, your problem, forward. What I suggest . . . Hello? Are you there? Hello?"

As Gibbs slowly replaced the telephone in its cradle, Pete Dekins, seated in a canvas chair, raised his eyebrows in question. "He hung up," Gibbs explained.

"Who is *he*?" Dekins said.

"Walter Felinda. Calls himself a general, now."

The weather, in contrast to events on the ground, was too warm to be pleasant, the temperature hovering in the mid-90s, unseasonably warm for the Free State province. Tall pine trees cast narrow shadows from a blazing sun only 12 degrees off vertical azimuth.

Mopping his brow, Dekins, like Gibbs, did not like the abrupt disruption in telephone contact with Walter Felinda. "What do you make of it?"

Gibbs shrugged. "Maybe he wants to be dramatic. Maybe he wants to make us sweat."

"You have made a mistake," Major Louden said from the comfort of his own chair placed ten feet from the lattice-iron fencing that surrounded the elevator. Next to him was a folding table on which he maintained ades, ice tea, and a generous supply of American cigarettes. "You have caused Felinda to become angry."

"You know the man?" Gibbs asked.

"Only by reputation," the state security officer said. It

was clear, at least to Gibbs and Dekins, that Boord's minion had attached himself to their enterprise until it was concluded. Maybe not a bad thing, Dekins thought. They could at least appeal directly to the state for help, even though it might never arrive.

"Then let us know what you know," Gibbs said.

"What I know is that he hates white people. He helped drive them from his land in Zaire. When you do not show him proper respect, he will be quick to anger. That is what I know," Major Louden said, lighting yet another cigarette and inhaling the smoke deeply into his lungs.

Gibbs swiped absently at his temples with a damp cloth, then punched three digits on his telephone that would cause the phone to ring two thousand feet below. He held the telephone painfully close to his ear but there was no answer. He exchanged eye contact with Dekins who shifted from one foot to another, then paced the wooden planks of the tower platform.

Dekins jumped inwardly, as did the other men at the platform, when the hoisting machinery sprang into life, actuated by electric switches located below as well as above. As heavy-lift cams and gears were turned by the power of a large electric motor, doubled steel cable began moving up from the depths, pulling a cage forty-nine square feet in size. The cage's running time, Gibbs and Dekins knew, would be slightly over three minutes. As part of the demands made by the SADL, the cage would always remain below ground, near the hostage takers, when not in use.

Dekins felt a sense of foreboding as the only sound in the air was the grinding clatter of ancient, groaning machinery, winching the weight of not only the caged elevator car but two thousand feet of steel cable. As the cage neared the level of the platform, Dekins, Gibbs, the South African soldiers, and some civilians who had been allowed passage beyond the police lines, began to peer over the edge of the sliding safety gates to see what might be atop the moving car's latticed roof. The darkness of the shaft obscured the emerging cage, but when the first rays of sunshine struck, its contents were unmistakable. There was a body riding slowly upward. It was a girl.

Among police and military troops hardened by years of atrocities committed on all sides of apartheid's wicked political shadow, there was nevertheless an audible, collective gasp that escaped from the crowd of onlookers. By the time the elevator cage had reached level with the platform, most shrank back out of revulsion, some reacting from the fear of beholding pure evil.

The girl was in her teens, not fully matured but with bare breasts that had promised further development. The girl's hair was bright blond, her skin very white, and her clothing, patches of which still clung to her body by her coagulated blood, had been ripped from her. Dekins had seen battle wounds in his career but nothing that equaled what the child had suffered. At a glance, it was clear that the girl's killer had placed a sharp object, possibly a trench knife or machete, across the bridge of her nose and eyes, then smashed down with great force, splitting her face in half. A second wound, a gaping cut probably made with the same instrument, ran down the length of her body as though she had endured a post-mortem examination. The flesh had been carelessly thrown back from each side of the deep cut, exposing her lungs, stomach and other organs.

All eyes turned away and few looked back. Dekins heard a noise from the throat of his colleague, Arlen Gibbs, but it was unintelligible. Only one set of eyes seemed unoffended by what they saw, and they belonged to Major An Louden. When he looked away from the corpse he focused purposely on Gibbs, silently accusing

the American of angering the butcher, Felinda. Flies had
begun to swarm around the body when Dekins opened
the safety gate and stepped onto the elevator car. He removed his outer desert jacket and draped it over the girl's
body, leaving only her legs protruding from beneath the
fabric. He retrieved a nylon map folder that had been left
by the body, and put it into his pocket.

"Major, get a medic team here, fast." Dekins almost
wished the indolent state policeman would refuse to
move so that he could have the pleasure of throwing him
bodily from the platform. But, without comment, the security officer moved to his own field telephone to make
the necessary call. There were already two ambulances
standing by. Within minutes medics arrived to take
charge of the desecrated body.

Pete Dekins sat heavily onto a canvas chair and
opened the map folder. Inside was two pages of lined
paper, written upon with ballpoint pen. The handwriting
was labored, untidy, as though the writer was either illit-
erate or English was not his native language. Gibbs read
over his shoulders.

*We have 51 prisons. Read ther names, daniell
huukin, reann, alic Willicas, recel austin, Juli
Denkums, Lorleen, D. Maffsui, J. Kettles, Racine
Pate, H. Record, J. Hubbel, Hetsi Gonzalas, Bishop
Kimo Jimini, Rob, Carol Herlift, Ron, Dorthy Man,
ben Levy, wife Woofie . . .*

The list continued on and ended with: *Now the
amerikans are niggers here. We will lern how the die
maybe.*

Kimo Jimini. The Anglican Bishop. Gibbs's mouth
went dry.

The telephone rang.

For long moments Gibbs could only stare at it, his arms at his sides, untrusting of what it might be if he lifted the loathed instrument. It continued to ring and, at last, Gibbs put the receiver to his ear.

"Yes?" he said.

"Did you enjoy our little gift? Eh?" the deep mellifluous voice of Walter Felinda rumbled up from the bowels of hell.

"Monstrous," Gibbs heard himself say.

"Yes? Monstrous? Yes, that is what you are to understand. You do not deal now with gay little people or white la-la girls, you see. I give orders, you carry them out. You understand now."

"Yes, of course, you are right," Gibbs said into the phone, ordering his brain to improvise with this madman. Gibbs had to assume that the murderer on the other end of the line put absolutely no value on human life and that his rational thinking process was starkly underdeveloped. "We will do everything within our power to keep the hostages from harm. Will you keep them safe for us, General Felinda?" Gibbs was careful to phrase his question so that it did not sound like a demand, but the first step in creating a set of quid pro quo.

"Of course they will be safe, Massah Gibbs. Put the government man on the phone," Felinda said.

Training, experience, and technique had taught Gibbs that under no circumstances would the hostage takers be allowed to speak with anyone other than the negotiator. Gibbs had discussed this with General Dekins and Pete had agreed without argument. Gibbs was about to make up an excuse for Dekins's unavailability but Felinda seemed to read his mind.

"Don' make me repeat myself, Massah Gibbs." The black man's voice dripped with derision.

"No, of course not. He's here on the platform. I'll get

him," Gibbs said. Covering the mouthpiece carefully with the palm of his hand, Gibbs said, "Better talk to him, Pete. Frankly, I think he'd kill again if you don't."

Dekins nodded and took the phone. "This is Peter Dekins."

"You know who I am?" the resonant voice said.

"Sorry, I haven't had the pleasure," Dekins said.

"I am General Walter Felinda. You have seen the list?" Felinda said.

"The hostage list? Yeah, I've got it," Dekins said.

"Believe me, Peter Dekins, I will kill every one of them with my own hands if you do not do exactly what I tell you. Understand what I say?"

"Yes. I understand."

"Do not in any way interfere with our supply of electricity or water. Anything at all happens, and I will slaughter your precious children. Do you understand that, Peter Dekins?"

"Yes, I understand."

"That is good. Save us time, and your blood. What rank do you hold in American government, Peter Dekins?" Felinda said.

"I, uh, work in the National Security Council. I am second in command," Dekins said, promoting himself by a couple of levels. There was enough hesitation on the other end of the line to cause Dekins to believe that Felinda was not sure, or possibly totally ignorant, of what the NSC was.

"Hmm. Security. You are a security man?" Felinda said.

Dekins considered his next answer carefully. The last thing he wanted to do was to anger Felinda by making him feel inferior, or that he, Dekins, was trying to intimidate him. "I am a brigadier general in the United States Army," he said and waited.

"Good. I am a colonel general. I outrank you, but at least you know how to carry out an order. I have an order for you now."

Dekins glanced at their recording machine to insure that they had sufficient tape to get all of the conversation. "General Felinda," Dekins said, "I must know the condition of the hostages in your care. Are they uninjured? Is there anything they—"

"And I must tell you that if you interrupt me again, I will send you another little present," Felinda shouted. His voice boomed so that Dekins had to move the ear piece away from his head. "Is that clear?"

Put off his pace, and frankly intimidated, Dekins could only say "Yes, go ahead."

"I am sending you another package. Not like the other," Felinda said, allowing a touch of evil into his voice. The elevator cage suddenly began to descend, activated from below.

Then there was a click from Felinda's telephone and the circuit was closed. Gibbs, wearing a headset to listen in on the conversation, glanced into Dekins's eyes and nodded his head. "Damn," he said softly. "This guy is way off the charts. My charts, anyway."

"Want the phone back?" Dekins said.

"No. Let's wait," he said.

Support had become slightly more easily obtained after President Elling got off the telephone with South African President Kwisi. A South African military liaison had been assigned to Captain Getts to provide him with whatever supplies or services he should request. So far Getts was satisfied. He had requested two tents, one to use as a command post, the other for him and his men to sleep under. In point of fact, Getts had no intention of allowing his men to congregate in a single, easily attacked

area. At night they were dispersed on the outside of the
perimeter fence around the mine. They slept on hard
ground, using natural cover and at times prism or ghillie
coverings. A second aircraft, a C-130, had brought three
DPVs (Desert Patrol Vehicles) completely fueled, armed
with two M-60 machine guns each, and powered by
200hp VW engines. Diving gear had been brought by the
same aircraft, not because its use was contemplated but
because it was better to be prepared than to need equipment and not have it. That equipment, plus communications gear, was placed in the second tent. Special
explosives and various ammunition were removed from
the C-130 at night and were already buried in "ammo
graves" and camouflaged.

The SEAL manpower Peach had brought with him in-
cluded six men, all in their mid- to late twenties. They
would be divided into three fire teams—or Tangos, for
short—of three each, including Getts and Peach. Tango
Two would operate with Getts, Cheetam, and Haskins.
Peach, who would lead Tango One, had Joe "Snake"
Chandel and Eddie Knowles on board. Rick "The
Viking" Heggstad would head up Tango Three with Dean
Banks and Waco Miller as his team.

Radioman PO First Class "Psycho" Cheetam was
under six feet like Getts, but wider in every respect.
Cheetam had sandy colored hair, freckles, and a disarming smile. He was a Phoenix, Arizona, boy who joined
the navy at the suggestion of his juvenile probation officer. Other than drink while under age, Cheetam had never
broken any serious laws except that he was much too
quick to use his fists for the liking of school officials and,
later, the police. He had a devastating impact with either
hand that Getts had first seen seven years prior in San
Diego, when Cheetam was a marine lance corporal fighting in the cruiser weight class against an army boxer. It

was really no contest and Peach, then a chief, casually mentioned to Cheetam after the bout that the SEALs could use another fighter, pointing out that any candy-ass can dance around a ring. Getts was sure that his presence, and his rank, kept Peach from an on-the-spot demonstration of Cheetam's right cross. Eighteen months later, Cheetam emerged successfully from BUD training and was assigned to SEAL Six.

Joe "Snake" Chandel was a baby-faced killer with morals. He had curly blond hair, a wide smile that stayed in place while he stuck a diving knife through an enemy's throat. Not a large man, Snake hated bullies with a passion and wanted to be a SEAL because they were always fewer in number than the big guys they took on. Snake loved to party, laughing till he cried and screwing till it wilted.

Waco Miller was a tall Texan who wore glasses and loved it when somebody tried to knock them off. He said his folks named him Waco because they were too lazy to look for a real name. But if that was true he did not inherit a lazy gene in his body. He got through SEAL training by wearing contact lenses and pure guts. He ran track at the University of Oregon but only after he couldn't make the football team at one hundred thirty-four pounds. He volunteered for SEAL training only because he thought they wouldn't want him. He once got arrested in Hawaii when the Samoan Marine Shore Patrol thought he was wearing the SEAL Budweiser illegally. One of the SPs spent four days in the hospital and the second refused to testify against Miller at a Captain's mass.

Steve "Short Game" Haskins was an oil field roughneck from California who woke up one morning able to hit anything with any kind of gun he ever held in his hands. At the age of six he performed trick shooting for visitors who only came to the small town of Taft because they had heard of him. He shot revolvers, auto-loaders, pistols, and rifles with rare accuracy. And Short Game never aimed: he just pointed. After enlisting in the Marine Corps, Haskins scored the third highest marks for shooting in the history of the Corps because, he said, "I wasn't really trying." He was kept at Camp Pendleton as a gunnery instructor, but soon grew bored and volunteered for SEALs. Bobby Getts never tried to teach Short Game to shoot the military way.

Eddie Knowles played defensive tackle for the Tennessee Titans in the NFL. He was selected to play in the Pro Bowl his rookie year, signed a three-year contract extension that called for a $1 million annual salary, then changed his mind one week prior to July summer camp and enlisted in the Navy with SEALs in mind. Asked why, Eddie said that he wanted a challenge.

Dean Banks was arguably the best striker of a baseball in the history of Iowa, minor leagues or big leagues notwithstanding. But Dean injured the rotator cuff in his right shoulder and figured he was too old to learn to throw left-handed, so he joined the navy to get free medical care. Sure enough, the navy operated on his shoulder and Dean learned to love swimming during his rehabilitation. When he won a $100 bet that he could swim farther underwater than a navy SEAL officer by the name of Derrick Argel, Argel talked him into joining the SEALs. "You'll love it," Argel said. "We just kind of lay around the beach in San Diego and get tan."

Each SEAL could shoot at the expert level and had an intimate association with things that go bang in the night. Running into a SEAL ambush team would be like hitting the wall at one hundred miles per hour. It would hurt like hell and you probably wouldn't walk away from the experience.

Getts and Peach occupied spaces around a table in the

CP upon which was spread a map. There were other maps, some rolled and some folded, in a portable cabinet in a corner of the square tent. In addition to the two SEALs, there were three other people. One was Neils Grunden, an aging mine engineer who had worked the Salisbury mine and probably knew it better than anyone alive. The second was a black man by the name of Gatiang, also aging, a one-time laborer in the Salisbury mine from age ten until forty. The third man was Richard Nemes, ambassador to South Africa from the Netherlands. Nemes was, Getts believed, about forty-two, with sandy hair and mustache, very quick of mind and an ability to say the right thing at the right time, then blend into the background when his counsel was no longer required.

Nemes had told Getts, General Dekins, and Arlen Gibbs that the Netherlands was in a national state of high apprehension about the Girl Scouts that were being held captive by an apparent madman. It was too early, he said, for his government and his nation to have learned the fate of the brutally murdered girl. The collective reaction could only be imagined as horrible shock, he said. Getts and Peach agreed. But what was to be done?

"You see, here," Neils Grunden said, moving his fingers along an engineering drawing of a network of tunnels under the very surface of the earth where they were standing, "these are horizontal branches of the Salisbury shaft, called 'drifts.' They follow veins to the south, here, and to the east and, here, to the west. They are twenty—"

"All with names?" Getts interrupted.

"Shafts have names, the drifts have numbers," the old engineer said.

"Okay, let's renumber them, Peach," he said, bending over the map to etch marks with a fine ink pen. "We'll keep it simple. N1, N2, for north, S1, S2, for south, and so forth. Got it?"

"Marks are good," Peach said, making notes on a clipboard pad. He would write down everything that was said of any import at the meeting so that it could be discussed and analyzed later with the entire Green Solitaire team.

"They all dead-end?" Peach asked.

"Yes, they stop," Neils replied. "The drifts go nowhere and intersected at the vertical shafts, Salisbury and Tauber."

"You mean there is a second shaft?" Getts asked.

"Yes, Tauber is on the lower side of the mountain, here." The engineer pointed to a place on the mine drawing. "But there is no access there. We filled it in at the top when we closed the mine."

"No way to get through it?" Getts pressed.

The engineer shook his head emphatically. "We blasted it. Probably twenty thousand cubic yards of rock between the adit and the drifts below."

"Okay. Tell me again about ventilation. How much of it was there, how did you get air to the miners?" Getts wanted to know.

"Hmph," was the cynical reaction from Gatiang.

Neils nodded his head in understanding. "There was never enough, ja Gatiang?"

"Never. It was hot, you know. Very hot. We never had enough good water, either. Always contaminated. And we fell often, but if we do not get up, our pay was less, so we moved rock with our hearts, not our muscles," Gatiang said. His manner was matter-of-fact, not accusing, and his eyes were steady.

"So what was your source of air?" Getts pushed. "It had to circulate."

"Well," Neils said, thoughtfully, "we pumped air from big diesel-driven compressors, but only to cool. There are two, still over at the sheds across the compound." He gestured toward the northeast side of the platform. The compressor shed was marked Bldg J on Getts's schematic of the Salisbury complex. "We kept pressures of about fifty psi on the delivery pipes at all times. It was all that we needed, and there was no return system required."

"Diameter of the pipes?" Getts asked.

"Forty millimeters," the engineer said.

Getts and Peach locked eyes. Peach shook his head. "First thing they'd think of. A dead man's switch," he said. Peach meant that if the SEALs pumped an odorless, tasteless sleeping gas into the ventilation system, the terrorists might have thought of it and figured out a way of setting off a device to either kill them all, themselves included, or perhaps seal the mine forever. "Besides," Peach said, "they're not using the air pumping system now and if they heard it fire up, we'd have fifty dead hostages to bury."

"I know," Getts said. "File it under plan Z. There's got to be a better way."

"No there doesn't, Skipper," Peach said.

"What?"

"I said no there doesn't. I mean, it might be impossible. All they need is one man to stay awake while the other one sleeps, and they could hold off an army with an M-60. That's a fact, Bobby."

Getts knew it was true. Richard Nemes knew it, and the terrorists damn sure knew it. But Getts had no intention of throwing up his hands and quitting. At that moment he could see Pete Dekins striding toward the CP from the rig platform. When the army general entered the tent he nodded at everyone inside, tried without success to muster a smile, then said, "Ambassador Nemes, gentlemen," he said to include Gatiang and Neils Grunden, "would you excuse us for a few minutes? I need to talk with Getts and Peach alone. I'll get together with you afterward."

"Developments?" Nemes asked.

"Yes, sir, in a way. I'll give you a full briefing later today," Dekins said.

After the three civilians had left the tent and were out of hearing range, Dekins slumped into a canvas chair. "We have their demands." From a slick, heavy gauge cardboard folder, Dekins removed a sheaf of papers to which he referred as he spoke with Getts and Peach. "They want a software program, SNIAD-98-116, Block IV Differential Global Positioning System, they want it compatible with the UK Sea Eagle system, and they want the APR99 Deviation Correction code."

"Shit," Peach said.

"What are you going to do?" Getts asked Dekins.

"You have any thoughts about how to get into the mine?" Dekins said.

"None that includes any survivors," Getts said.

Dekins looked again at the printed demands of the SADL. "Gibbs is talking to Felinda. Fucking madman," he said, under his breath. "We'll send this on to Washington but"—he shrugged—"nobody is going to authorize this kind of trade. Agree?"

Getts's eyebrows arched up.

"You think President Elling would give cruise missile guidance codes to terrorists?" Dekins said.

"I don't have an opinion on the matter, Deke," Getts said.

"Jesus Christ, Getts, come on," Dekins said.

Getts thought Dekins was probably correct but the president had sold the Chinese top secret government documents and hardware, why the hell not this? Besides, he did not want to think about fifty more dead hostages, especially killed in the way that Felinda showed he was capable of doing.

Before he could elaborate, the secure telephone, linked to a satellite array, blinked a flashing red light and simultaneously rang. Getts reached for it. "Captain Getts," he said into the mouthpiece.

"This is a National Security Council call from David Magazine, deputy duty officer Major Howard Marlantes speaking. Say your serial number please, Captain Getts."

Getts authenticated his identification by repeating his serial number to the duty officer.

"Operational code, sir," Major Marlantes said.

"Green Solitaire," Getts said.

"Are you alone, sir?" the duty officer asked.

"Negative. I am in the company of General Dekins and Warrant Officer Peach," Getts responded patiently.

There was a brief pause on the other end of the line while Major Marlantes referred to his Green Solitaire authorization list. "Very well, sir, stand by."

Moments later there was another audible click on the line and the new voice that spoke was easy for Getts to recognize. "Hello, Bobby. Dave Magazine."

"We have an extension for this phone if you want."

"Are you running hostage rescue, Bobby?" Magazine said.

"Yes, sir," Getts said.

"I'll talk to you but have Deke pick up. Ready?"

Getts made a hand signal to Pete Dekins who immediately picked up the phone extension. "I'm on," he said.

"Okay. Either one of you guys heard of Ron Mauser?" Magazine asked.

"You mean CIA Mauser?" Getts asked.

"The same," Magazine said.

Dekins nodded his head in the affirmative.

"He's Counter-Intel chief, I believe," Getts added.

"That's the same guy. Turns out he's down in your gold mine. And his wife is with him."

Chapter Three

Princess Melissa Witherspoon's Gulfstream V jet was passing through Flight Level 390 (39,000 feet) toward an en route cruising altitude of 42,000 feet, well above that at which most commercial airliners operate. The Gulf V could cruise at .8 Mach as she pierced the -40 degree air from England south toward the continent of Africa. Her flight deck crew, working with Heathrow Special Flights Office, had cleared the aircraft for overflight through sovereign airspace toward her destination of South Africa. It was not always easy. Prior to the end of apartheid, almost all African nations would refuse aircraft destined for S.A. safe transit, thus forcing those flights to fly a much longer way around Africa's Horn, then proceeding on a southeasterly heading.

Melissa's jet—and it was hers, not the property of the government—was configured for a flight crew of four and held room for as many as ten passengers. There was a sofa bed that occupied a port bulkhead, and a mahogany table toward the aft section surrounded by four reclinable chairs, which could be used for everything from dining to cards to business conferences. While not Spartan, the decor of the aircraft was not ostentatious. The only homage to her royal heritage was a family coat of arms countersunk into the top of knee-high cabinets that lined the aisle near the dining table. Otherwise, the jet might belong to a corporation that manufactured soap.

Taking space on the Gulfstream in whatever seat Melissa did not wish to occupy was Arthur Carlin, Melissa's assigned bodyguard. By what government department Carlin was paid, Melissa did not know or care. He was well over six feet tall and had legs like oak boles. She knew this because she happened to have seen a photograph of Carlin in a rugby uniform, taken while he was in school and later made a part of his military personnel file. She knew—also from the personnel folder—that Carlin was under forty years of age but his craggy face and massive hands made him seem older. She thought that while his girth was ample it was surely solid muscle and she felt perfectly safe in the company of the Yorkshire man. Looks were not everything in a male, Melissa knew, but Carlin was not a particularly engaging conversationalist, so while she spent many a leisure hour in his company, she was uninspired while protected.

"Are you hungry yet, Princess Witherspoon?" a young, brightly smiling flight attendant asked as Melissa rested her hands atop a leather note case, its zipper still fastened. It always bothered her to be addressed by her title by a contemporary. It made her feel cold. And kind of out of touch. But she realized that she did not have the luxury of being on a first-name basis with either employees or, she hated to admit, the general public.

"Not yet. Maybe a brandy. You're new," she observed.

"Yes, ma'am. Jeanelle was caught in Central America. Bad weather; hurricane, we're told. I'm filling in," the girl said.

To be called *ma'am* was uncomfortable as well, but Melissa didn't see an alternative there, either. "Ah. Well, I'm glad you're with us. It's a long trip. I hope I didn't disrupt your weekend plans," Melissa said.

"Not at all, ma'am. I'll just get your brandy," the girl said, starting to turn away.

"Oh, hell, never mind the liquor. I'll drink tea," Melissa said, remembering that she had reading to do.

"We have delicious scones aboard, if you'd like," the girl offered, her luminous smile brilliantly alight.

"Bring them on," Melissa said ruefully, knowing that the scones would find a permanent home somewhere on her flesh, no matter how microscopic the bulge, and that she would have to walk a thousand kilometers or row a boat across the Atlantic ocean to get rid of them. *Gluttony, thou art mine enemy.*

By the time the tea was placed at her elbow, Melissa had opened the case and put a folder in front of her. There were two files, both frustratingly thin, but she began rereading them. Was she, as Sir Hogue Ortwith argued, finding far too much portent in name and circumstances?

"That may be so, Hogue, but we're in the puzzle business, aren't we? I mean, did I read all of those spy books for nothing?" she had said to Sir Hogue who, upon his recent award of that title, relished its use. Still, he was not about to instruct a member of the royal family upon his own diaphanous claim to peerage.

Sir Hogue chuckled uncomfortably at his atypical employee's brand of humor and took the safest tact he knew. "Naturally I cannot categorically say that your suspicions are untrue. I am only pointing out that they are only that—suspicions. Russia is still a large country and its citizens now travel widely."

"With respect, Sir Hogue," buttering the old boy with her unique source of social margarine, as though he were one of her peers even if she was not one of his spies, "that is exactly the point I'm trying to make. Boris Eveshenko might still be in the cruise missile business, and because we know that he was, at least for a while, within a scant

three hundred air kilometers from the Salisbury mine in
South Africa, and that demands have been made upon not
only the United States but the United Kingdom as well
for cruise missile technology, the people and events
might well be connected." Melissa leaned back in her
chair, recrossed her legs, and waited impatiently for her
boss to respond.

"It has been years since Eveshenko has worked on
these threat systems—" he began.

"We don't know that," she interjected.

"—and he was just one of many technicians—"

"He was more than that. He improved their AS-15,"
she snapped. Melissa was no longer an obsequious employee tugging at her superior's coattails for a hearing.

Hmm, he thought. She was right about that. The AS-
15, or the Russian KH 55, as they called it, was very
nearly a parallel-quality product with the American Tomahawk. And he recalled that Eveshenko was instrumental
in making that upgrade to the formidable weapon that it
was. "Still," he said to her, "it does not follow that we
will submit to terrorist extortion. Nor will the United
States, in all likelihood. So we'll sit it out."

Sir Hogue smiled briefly but it was forced. He added
tentatively, "I simply cannot authorize your travel to
South Africa. In point of fact—"

"If you authorized anyone, it would be someone more
senior, isn't that so, Hogue?" she said.

He turned his palms upward in a helpless gesture,
wishing that he could have put them firmly around her
shapely neck. Princess or not, he gladly would have throt-
tled her to close her dilettante mouth.

"I have vacation coming," she said, rising from her
chair and turning toward the door. "I'll return in about
two weeks."

"We shall miss you, Princess—"

His words were cut off by the sound of his heavy paneled door slamming shut. "—Witherspoon, you bitch."

"Look at your clock, Massah Gibbs," the malevolent voice of Walter Felinda said over the telephone to negotiator Arlen Gibbs. "What time does it say?"

"Almost seven P.M.," Gibbs said in compliance.

"Make your watch say exactly seven—now. There. We have the same time. Now Massah Gibbs, I want you to call me back in exactly forty-five minutes. Do you understand?"

It was against everything any hostage negotiator worth his—or her—salt would willingly do to allow the hostage taker to dictate terms, no matter how small. The initiative must be on the side of the negotiator at almost any cost or the game would be lost. Tempted as Arlen Gibbs was to change the time of the call, however slightly, to get a toehold of control, in this case he dared not anger the madman below. Gibbs knew he would have to accomplish this delicate task sooner or later. But not now. "I can do that," he said.

The telephone line went dead.

Arlen Gibbs spent the next forty-five minutes pacing the service road to the platform attempting to collect his thoughts, considering strategies that would somehow turn the balance of power away from the monster beneath the earth into his own hands. He was repeatedly frustrated when he asked about the condition of the hostages. He needed to know if any of them required medical attention and he continued to press Felinda for answers. He wanted the terrorist to show some concern, no matter how tepid, to the feelings of those tortured souls he kept prisoner. But whenever Gibbs probed, Felinda either hung up or threatened atrocious reprisals. There was no need to convince Gibbs that he not only could but would use gruesome force. When he was away from the telephone, there was always someone who could answer a ring. Psychologically, in fact, it was better if someone other than he answered.

With one minute left, Gibbs walked steadily from the service road to the loading dock on the platform. He ascended three short stairs to the platform, and walked to the location where the telephone was kept in the shade. He took his usual chair, waving away one of the junior South African police officers present, and pushed the connect button.

The bullet, as it entered the side of Gibbs's head, was a high-velocity, 5.56mm load that was light and designed to expand upon impact. The entry hole was quite small but the exit wound was the size of a grapefruit, literally removing half of the FBI agent's head.

Getts, Dekins, and Peach, within one hundred yards of the telephone, were walking toward the platform when the single round was fired. They heard only the hum of the round and a slight crack as it exceeded the sound barrier, but did not see whence it might have come.

"Damn," Dekins said as he arrived on the scene and knew at a glance that his recently acquainted colleague was dead. Gibbs was a good man, a smart, hard worker who prided himself upon professionalism. He knew that Gibbs had a wife and two teenage daughters, neither of whom had finished college. He was disgusted with such a waste of quality life.

An ambulance, parked not far away, was already entering a periphery gate, its emergency lights flashing.

"Peach," Getts said when they had arrived on scene, "it had to be from that quadrant, over there." He motioned in a northeasterly direction, judging from Gibbs's position in his chair when he was hit. The terrain sloped at a gentle seven percent grade for a half-mile before the crest, providing a shooter with a clear view of his target.

Neither man spoke as they traced the arc the bullet must have taken before hitting its target. The bullet would have passed through Gibbs's skull, and they got on their hands and knees to look, beginning with the gore of what was once the FBI negotiator's head, then crawling right and left from the chair.

In less than two minutes they had the slug. Peach examined it closely. "Five point four five, or close to it. Maybe an AK-74," he said, describing the newer, smaller caliber weapon used by Russian assault troops, sometimes for sniping.

"Let's go get 'em," Getts said.

Peach spoke into his lip mike to his fire teams. "Foxtrot-Tango One, Two, and Three, Top Hat, report." Top Hat was the code word for Getts. Thus, the invocation of Top Hat stated that the order was coming from the unit commander. If Getts were to be killed or become disabled, Peach would assume the leadership position of Top Hat.

"Tango One, good to go." Peach recognized Snake's voice as it reported in.

"Tango Two, all set, Top Hat," Haskins said in turn, with Getts at his side.

"Tango Three, roger, Top Hat," Rick Heggstad's voice crackled over the airwaves.

"Break out the DPVs. We've got a CSAD mission," Getts said, referring to a combat search and destroy operation. "We're looking for a sniper, probably with support. Shot came from zero three zero, range approximately seven hundred. He's booked it by now. Tango One, sweep sectors zero to two-zero, Top Hat will take radials zero-two-zero to zero-five-zero. Tango Two pick up the skipper, Tango Three has the rest. Read back," Peach said.

"Get me first, Eddie." The radials to which Peach referred were 360 degrees of the compass, with Salisbury's tower as its center. Hence, by adding a zero on to each number, radial twenty-seven was 270 degrees, or directly west.

"Tango One has one-zero to your left flank to zero-two. Moving," reported Snake. The driver of the SEAL DPV had correctly understood his search area and was moving out to execute that mission. With him was Eddie Knowles. They would pick up Peach en route to their search area.

"Tango Two has one to two-zero," Haskins acknowledged. In the Three vehicle with Heggstad was Dean Banks, who manned the M-60 mount on the Desert Patrol Vehicle.

"Roger, Tango Three has the bottom, sweeping from zero-five. Moving," Heggstad said.

The SEALs wore desert camouflage uniforms, bush hats, face paint. Along with the DPV-mounted M-60 light machine gun, with a 7.62 cartridge load, each trooper carried an AR-18 assault weapon that fired the same round. It made good sense to Getts because it simplified ammo logistics. In addition, their Armalite "widowmakers" supported a forty-round magazine and, by taping three magazines together, each trooper had a quick-load capability that allowed him to put out a very heavy volume of fire. Zippered into a heavy but flexible carrying case was a Steyr Scout, a .308 ten-round capacity sniper rifle. The rifle and case were attached to Peach's DPV.

Each man also packed a SIG-Sauer P220, .45 model. Pistols are for close work and Getts knew from experience that a .45 would knock anybody flat on their ass no matter where the bullet hit them. The Green Solitaire team also carried night-vision glasses, starlight scopes on their rifles, assault knives on their legs, and maximum ammunition for each trooper.

In less than thirty minutes of searching, Tango One had picked up a track five kilometers from the Salisbury mine. "Top Hat, Tango One," Getts heard on his field radio.

"Top Hat," he responded.

"I think we've got 'em, Bobby," Peach said over the radio. He punched an ML (mark location) button on his GPS and, with his two troopers, waited in his DPV for the other two cars to reach his position by following a track and bearing on their GPS receivers.

"What kind of vehicle?" Getts asked Cheetam. Cheetam, who was standing on the right side of the DPV, squatted on his haunches looking closely at the tire marks in the red dirt leading from a road marked on their maps as Romeo Twelve. "Two ton," he said, "dual axle. And there's a scout car with it," he said, certain of his tracking divinations. "They left the road here, single file." Getts followed Cheetam's gaze westward. Getts referred to one of his several maps, spreading it out on the ground. The maps were specially modified with all landmarks, including secondary and tertiary roads marked to comply with their own code. The town of Sasolburg, for example, might be marked Sierra 9, while its highway may remain Romeo 26.

Referring to his map, Getts could see that the only populated area in the same general direction of the tracks was a village marked Elizabeth and the nearest road, unpaved, according to the map, was Romeo Four. Peering through his binoculars, Getts could see the village. Sweeping from side to side, he could see no vehicles of the kind that fit the tracks Cheetam found, nor were there any signs of people among the village's buildings. Strange, since he would have expected to see children playing and people going about their business in the middle of the day. Lowering his binoculars, Getts looked to his left and right to see that the other two fire teams had quietly taken up positions on his flanks.

Getts, in Tango Two, was 1.5 kilometers northeast of the village, less than one hundred meters from a bridge that covered a dry river bed. The river bed reached from the west, in the direction of a low mountain range, to the east, back toward the Salisbury mine. As he looked to the southwest, Getts's scan took in a thirty-foot-high water tank located approximately fifty meters from Romeo 4. Getts checked his six, the position behind him. On the north side of the river bed was a second range of low hills, the dry, rolling topography continuing a quilt-work of lesser channels. The north was dominated by a singular rock formation, about nine hundred feet high. The field of fire from that elevation would be advantageous, but too easily cut off.

Getts turned his binoculars back toward the village of Elizabeth. He could easily make out a gas station, which seemed to double as a general store. On the west end of town was a church and a second large building that might have been a meeting hall. There were three streets in the town, none of them paved, that serviced small but well-maintained houses. The town's houses were not laid out in square patterns but seemed to be located upon circular lots. Getts estimated that there might be as many as thirty dwellings, along with an assorted number of roaming livestock as well as their sheds and pens. There was a hill behind the village on its south side, very near the last row of houses, and about three hundred meters beyond was a large, dry lake bed.

"I want a prisoner," Getts said into his lip mike to the other fire teams.

"Aye aye," came one response.

"Roger," came the last team to report their understanding of the order.

"Tango One, clear the water tower," Getts ordered, knowing from experience that there were work ladders inside towers, and that they often made irresistible positions for snipers.

Tango One was nearest the tower. It had traveled parallel to Romeo 4 and was near the junction of Romeo 4 and the main street out of town. Waco drove the DPV right at the tower, circumnavigating the structure two times as Dean, carrying one of the M-60 guns in his hands, and Heggstad, looked up at the sides and top of the wooden tower. Heggstad, spotting movement on top, signaled to Waco to stop. As Waco braked the DPV to a halt, Heggstad leaped out, placed his AR-18 back in the vehicle and stuffed two extra grenades into a small canvas utility bag fixed to his web belt around his waist.

"Cover me," he told his teammates as he slipped the leather gloves he was wearing into his belt. Heggstad ran to the side of the tower and, without hesitating, began rapidly climbing the ladder. He reached the top in a matter of seconds. Before looking inside the tank, Heggstad looked down at Dean, who gave him a hand signal for all clear. Heggstad looked over the brim of the wooden water tank, then pulled quickly back as shots rang out from within the tank. Crouching to keep his head below the rim of the tower, Heggstad pulled the pins on the two hand grenades and tossed them backwards over his head. He immediately placed the insides of his boots on the edge of the ladder and, using his leather gloves to grasp the sides of the ladder, allowed himself to go into a controlled fall, speedily descending to the ground. He had barely landed and began to run toward the DPV when the grenades went off.

Staves, water, and fragments of wood sprayed in every

direction of the compass as the two grenades exploded almost simultaneously. Cascading to the ground with thousands of gallons of water and falling debris were two uniformed bodies. His .45 pistol in hand, Heggstad quickly ran to the bodies. As he bent over each, he could see that both were dead, one killed by grenade shrapnel, the other probably by the fall to the ground. The dead were both black, both in camouflage. A Vektor assault rifle lay nearby.

"Two T's down," Heggstad said into his lip mike, using "T" to identify terrorist. "Both dead."

"Roger," Getts said. "Tango One, block egress from the town. Tango Three guard our west—Tango Two is going in."

Getts received a pair of rogers as he nodded to Psycho Cheetam to move forward toward the village. When Psycho had arrived at a position of about four hundred meters, Getts gave an order to dismount. Getts and Psycho would advance on the town while Haskins remained on the twin M-60s to provide covering fire. Now on foot, Getts and Psycho moved forward, keeping low and twenty meters apart, running at various speeds, zigzagging, dropping to the ground, watching and waiting. They then moved in the direction of the town's gas station, AR-18s hot, safeties off. There was still no movement of people that the SEALs could see. The only sounds were those of chickens, dogs, and goats that voiced their disapproval of aliens approaching their town.

The sniper's shot, when it came, was muffled by a suppressor. The round caught Haskins on the left side of his vest. The bullet did not penetrate the vest but its kinetic energy broke two of Haskins's ribs and knocked him backward and to the side of his driver's seat. The impact also knocked the air out of his lungs and for several minutes he could only gasp and try to put aside the pain while he lay across the front seats of the DPV.

When there was no response fire from Haskins's M-60s, Getts guessed that the SEAL had been hit. "Haskins," he said into his lip mike. "Report."

Initial sounds coming from Haskins were strangled, unintelligible.

"How bad are you hit?" Getts said into his mike.

There was a pause while air returned to his lungs. "Okay. N-A-N," Haskins said through gritted teeth. No assistance needed.

"Did you see the gun?" Getts asked Haskins.

"Negative," Haskins grunted.

"Anybody?" Getts asked all units.

"Bobby, check the second house behind the gas station, on the roof," Psycho said into his mike. "A flash. Reflection in the sun, maybe."

Getts looked through his binoculars. There was nothing. But Getts had patience. After several minutes of waiting, his glasses trained on the roof of the house, he saw movement, then a brief ocular reflection.

"Got it," he said softly. "Reflection off a scope. Cover me." He rose to his feet and sprinted thirty yards before falling forward and rolling sideways as he hit, his head snapping back to focus on the sniper's perch on the roof.

Haskins sighted in his twin 60s on the same location while Psycho aimed his AR-18. As Getts rose to run again, both SEALs opened up on the target atop the roof. Steel jacket slugs striking the corrugated iron roof created an incredible din of noise as metal was ripped through by the parabellum rounds. After his teammates poured fire into the target, Getts paused to scan the roof, now some 150 meters away. As he prepared to rise again he heard a warning in his earphone, then more extended bursts of gunfire.

"Your one o'clock," Haskins said as he opened up on another house with his 60s.

"I got the one o'clock," Psycho said, swinging his AR-18 to provide suppressing fire on the window of the new threat coming from that direction, knowing that Haskins had to continue pouring fire on the sniper.

Getts no longer needed binoculars to see shooters materializing from windows and doors of houses throughout the village. Getts did not want to move Tango Three from their position where they could cut off retreat from the village, so he quickly opted for Tango One to lay down suppressing fire.

"Tango One," he said into his lip mike, "many Ts, I count nine. Hit their flank, Peach."

"Roger," Peach said, "we're moving in."

Peach turned to Snake and Eddie. "Let's roll 'em up." Snake pulled the DPV into gear, slammed the accelerator to the floor, reaching forty miles per hour in just six seconds as they sprinted from their stand-off position seven hundred yards away to the side of the church building in the village. Snake placed the vehicle in the shelter of the church and snatched an M-60 from one of the mounts while Eddie manhandled the other gun. The vehicle would always be in their sight while they advanced through the town; and anybody who attempted to reach it would be an easy target for the SEALs. Peach ran from house to house as Snake covered him with high-volume suppressing fire. Eddie then covered Snake as he leapfrogged Peach's position; Peach then covered for Eddie while he moved. In this way the SEALs moved rapidly under well-positioned covering fire.

Peach tossed a flash-bang grenade through the window of a house where he had seen muzzle flashes, then kicked in the flimsy door. Amidst screams of the black couple and their two children within, Peach immediately spotted the camouflaged gunman and gave him a quick three-round burst. The gunman took two of the bullets in his sternum, the third in his head. Peach knew that while the family inside would be dazed by the blast of the grenade, they would be uninjured. He stepped out of the door and raised his gun sights to cover Eddie's advance.

In crisp fashion they methodically worked their way down the town's middle row of houses, taking out Ts while leaving civilians unharmed. It became obvious that the cowering civilian population of the village were not supporting the terrorists willingly.

On the north edge of the village, Getts ordered Haskins to stay on the twin 60s while he and Psycho moved into the town. Haskins dropped the DPV into gear and roared smartly forward to reduce the range of his fire to approximately two hundred yards. At that range his M-60 fire would devastate anything in its path.

Dug in near the wreckage that was once the water tower, Heggstad alerted his team. "Vehicles, Deano."

"I got 'em," Dean Banks responded, turning his M-60s toward the two vehicles trying to break out of the village. One was a scout car, the second a two-ton double-axle truck. Dean could see that there were Ts in the back of the truck. His first order of business would be to stop them and he quickly locked in a set of MK 19 40mm grenade launchers.

The escaping vehicles were running through their gears, picking up speed, following the dirt road out of the village and heading almost directly at Tango Three's position. Dean calmly put his laser sight on the lead machine, the scout car, and when it came into comfortable range of about 200 meters, he fired. The armor-piercing grenade slammed into the car and exploded. The car and its occupants went up in a mighty roar followed by flames from the ignited fuel tank. Dean then turned his MK 19 toward the trailing truck.

"I want a live one out of there," Heggstad told the gunner.

"Understand," Dean said and shifted his aim at the engine section of the truck. He pulled the trigger and again there was another great explosion. But while the cab of the truck was blown apart, the rear of the truck was left largely intact. At the moment the grenade slammed into the truck, Heggstad was running toward the smoldering wreckage with Waco Miller following a few steps behind to provide fire support.

By the time the two SEALs had covered the sixty meters, the two surviving Ts had gotten to their feet. "Freeze, fuckers," Heggstad barked, motioning with his .45 caliber pistol for the Ts to raise their hands. One T slowly complied, now dazed, his camo suit shredded, while the second T dove for his Vektor lying in the dust. Heggstad beat him to the weapon and kicked it toward Waco who covered them both with his Armalite. Not to be outdone, the T reached into his boot and came up with a combat knife. He squared off to face Heggstad, the blade held low, his feet spaced apart, one ahead of the other in a professional fighter's stance. Heggstad, an expert martial artist, shot the T in the head with his .45.

"Damn, they're dedicated bastards." Heggstad turned to deal with the surviving T, now a prisoner of Tango Three. "You speak English?" he asked. The T did not respond, but his eyes did not show fear. "Well," Heggstad said, "Bobby can worry about talking to your ass. Move, asshole." Heggstad gave the prisoner a shove toward the DPV. While Waco maintained the T in his gun sights, Heggstad locked the man's hands behind his back with a set of plastic handcuffs.

"Top Hat, Tango Three, we've got a live one," Getts heard Heggstad report over the radio.

"Good work, Rick. Maintain your position on the road," Getts ordered. "Peach, where are you?"

"I'm south, behind the last house. Snake's with me and Eddie's got the DPV west of the town."

"Anybody see the sniper?" Getts asked all fire teams.

"Negative, Tango Three," Heggstad reported.

"No joy," Peach said. "He's not on that roof and there's nobody inside the house."

"Peach, can you see the backs of the other roofs?" Getts asked.

"Give me five," Peach said.

While Getts waited behind a wall of the gas station, Peach and Snake climbed the small hill behind the town. From an elevation of about seventy-five feet, Peach surveyed the village. "Top Hat, Tango One, still no joy on the shooter."

Shit, Getts said to himself and wondered where the shooter had disappeared to. As he tried to imagine where he would position himself if he were a sniper in this environment, the crack of a bullet passing through the sound barrier snapped by his ear. From the corner of his eye Getts saw Psycho's head jerk, his body spasm involuntarily. Getts leaped from his prone position, ran as fast as he could for several meters, then dove toward the unmoving body of Psycho. Another bullet smacked the ground near Getts. Getts sighted his AR-18 and fired several bursts to his left, over the blood-soaked body of his fire teammate. A very quick view of Psycho told Getts that the SEAL was dead, a hole in one side of his head, another, larger gaping exit wound on the opposite side.

"He's in the big riverbed, Peach," Getts said into his lip mike. "North of the dry lake. He got Psycho," Getts added.

"I'll get the son of a bitch," Peach seethed.

"Roger, Haskins and I will work down toward you," Getts said.

Tango One, and Peach's DPV, was closest to the dry lake. Not only was Peach's DPV in the best position, but Peach, an expert marksman, had with him the Steyr sniper rifle with a Leupold M8 scope. Getts was very aware that Peach was an accomplished, well-trained sniper and that he had a better chance of taking out another shooter with less risk of casualties than if the entire Green Solitaire were to engage the lone enemy. Getts placed his binoculars to his eyes, carefully sweeping the riverbed and the approximately 1,500-foot-high hill behind it. When there was no sign of the sniper, Getts hoisted Psycho's body onto his shoulder and rapidly moved toward their DPV less than forty yards away. Despite the extreme pain caused by his broken ribs, Haskins kept his eyes and gun sights on the direction whence the last enemy shot was fired. Getts placed Psycho's body into the rear of the DPV and covered his head with camouflage material. Responding to Getts's hand signals, Haskins put the DPV into gear and began driving slowly toward the rocky, dry riverbed.

Four hundred meters away, at their ten o'clock, they saw movement among a delicate mist of rising dust. Through his binoculars Getts could see that the stirring was caused by Peach and Snake as the two SEALs made their way toward the wadi by crawling on their bellies.

Another snap in the air signaled to Peach that the sniper had fired again. But the round was not in their direction. He and Snake moved forward with little more cover than basketball-sized rocks and occasional clumps of indigenous grass. Peach pointed to his eye and made a question mark with the same hand, silent language for "See him?" Snake shook his head, and using the tele-

scopic sight of his AR-18, scanned the area ahead, the dry
bed now only twenty meters from their position. Peach
could hear Getts's DPV despite its silenced engine as
Tango Two advanced down the bed, and knew that Bobby
was attempting to draw fire, or at least distract the
sniper's attention while Peach and Snake maneuvered
into position.

There was another snap as a round cut through the air,
this time just over Peach's head. The SEAL rolled right
and into a small defile. Snake likewise rolled over the
edge of the riverbed and into a shallow depression in the
ground.

Peach alternately crawled and rolled across the bed
until he found a large rock that afforded him good cover.
He used his 2.5x28mm telescopic sight to scan for the
sniper's position. He was ready. He nodded to Snake.

Snake popped up behind the protection of the rock and
dirt levee and laid down a series of bursts in the general
direction of the sniper. After firing most of a forty-round
magazine, Snake pulled back into concealment while
Peach watched. There, at a distance of about 600 meters,
Peach saw a flash in the bed. What he had seen was the
sun's reflection from the sniper's ocular sight, the second—and fatal—mistake made by the sniper this day.
Still, the marksman had not exposed his body and Peach
had no shot yet.

"Tango Two, he's in the riverbed. You got him
marked?" Peach said.

"Negative," Getts answered.

"He's six hundred meters west of Snake's position,"
Peach advised.

"He's good. I don't see him," Getts responded. "We
can wait 'til dark, get him with infrared."

Peach did not answer. He had his Steyr zeroed in on
the last location the sniper had occupied. If he had not

moved, Peach would make his shot. He waited. Snake was also silent, surveying the same location through his scope. Getts sensed that he should make no move without direction from Peach, who was initiating the attack.

The sun bore down from a cloudless sky, baking the SEALs, sweat oozing from every pore of their bodies. Yet they remained motionless, waiting for the enemy to make the first move, to raise a trace of dust, to make a give-away noise. Shadows cast by scrub bush or rounded riverbed rock moved agonizingly slow, while insects buzzed around the SEALs' heads, hands, and arms, biting infinitely small chunks of skin from their bodies. Insects, lizards, beetles, and curious rabbits emerged from holes in the ground, emboldened by the motionless men who stared, almost unblinking, across the kill zone in front of them. It was intense, uncomfortable, but the SEALs knew that sooner or later one side or the other would have to move, and it wasn't going to be them.

While Getts was waiting for minutes to pass, Peach was counting on the sun's changing position to move directly into the eyes of his foe. And, as shadows were beginning to grow, spreading out over the hard-baked soil, Peach saw the flash again. It was the sniper's scope and he was looking toward Peach's position—but Peach had the sun at his back. He adjusted his aim until his sight picture centered on the other sniper's telescope. The sniper had to be looking directly into Peach's own telescopic sight when Peach squeezed the trigger. The crack of his .308 caliber rifle rolled up and down the bed and echoed off the surrounding hills. The target in his sights instantly disappeared from his view and Peach felt, rather than saw, that the sniper was hit.

"This is Tango One. I think I got him," Peach said.

"We'll check it out, Tango Two," Getts said, his DPV circling from the south to approach the sniper's last position from his flank. Haskins drove fast, the rough terrain stabbing at his broken rib cage. Dust billowed up behind the DPV and Getts manned one of the M-60s as they neared the sniper's place of business.

They spied the prone position of the sniper, his weapon still pointing down the riverbed. Haskins carried one of the M-60s on his hip, supported by a strap over his shoulder, and kept a safe separation from Getts as the two SEALs approached. The sniper's camouflage ghillie suit was well made, as Getts suspected it would be, but he was no longer wearing his hat. The back of his head was nothing more than red pulp and white bone, the blood already drying on the hot ground. Flies lost no time clustering to the wound. Getts took the sniper's rifle from his hands and looked at its telescopic sight. There was a hole bored through the lens, front to back. There was now a dark void in the place where the sniper's right eye once was. Getts bent over the dead shooter and began searching his body for identification of any kind. There was a leather thong around his neck with two carved ivory figures, possibly good luck amulets, a pouch in a cargo pocket that contained scraps of toilet paper, a self-help medical kit—plastic for sealing sucking chest wounds, tape, a compression pack—but nothing with a name on it and no pictures.

"Tango One, you got him, Peach," Getts said into his lip mike. "One hell of a shot." Indeed, Getts had not seen one quite like it before. "Make sure you search your Ts for ID," he added, doubtful that anything of value would be found.

Waiting at a discreet VIP parking ramp for Melissa's Gulfstream V's door to open was Her Majesty's ambassador to South Africa, Hillary Leach, his wife, his aide, and a number of mid-level South African officials, as well as bodyguards sufficient enough to fill a dozen limousines. Most wore civilian clothes but there was a contingent of uniformed S.A. Army. All stood respectfully waiting for the princess to deplane. When she at last stood in the doorway and beheld her nonofficial welcoming committee, she almost fled back into the interior of the airplane. But, her frustration mounting, she descended the stairs briskly and scarcely smiled as Leach stepped forward.

"Welcome to South Africa, Princess Melissa. I am Ambassador Hillary Leach. I hope your trip was not overtiring, but anticipating that it was I've taken the liberty of making ready the royal suite at State House."

"Thank you, Mr. Leach, but I am not tired. Please thank these people on my behalf and ask them to go about their business," Melissa said.

"Er, may I present my wife, Ermine—"

"Mr. Leach," Melissa interrupted, "I'm sure that your wife is a lovely thing and under other circumstances I would be honored to meet her, but I am here to work, not socialize. Arthur," she said to her bodyguard, "have the crew put our bags into that car." She pointed to one of the black sedans. "You drive."

Ambassador Leach fell into step with Melissa as she began walking toward one of the parked cars amidst gaping mouths and fretting officials.

"But Princess Melissa, I sincerely hope you do not intend to drive through the countryside unescorted. I would be—"

"I am not unescorted," she said, nodding over her shoulder at Arthur. "Mr. Carlin is more than capable of looking after me."

"Yes, I'm sure, but this is not England, Madam." Leach's voice dropped to a conspiratorial tone. His well-trimmed mustache seemed to sag over his lower lip, causing his shadowed mouth to resemble a small, dark cave. "The citizenry is not, ah, stable, shall we say? Strict order does not prevail everywhere in this country and, well, I am directly responsible for your safety." Hillary Leach had broken into a more profuse sweat than the warm weather should have caused.

"You simply must take our security officers with you, wherever you are going," Leach beseeched.

"Must?" At times like this Melissa cursed the day when her forebears had become mixed up with royalty. Freedom came in many forms and she was damned if she would give away hers and be coddled like a breakfast egg. She was committed to her work, as she saw it, and it was much more important than the pomp of minor state officials.

"Please, Madam," Leach anguished.

Melissa fought off her frustration, trying to put herself in the poor man's shoes. Arthur Carlin was holding open the door to her chosen car and their baggage had been loaded.

"Very well, pick one of your people to drive the car," she said.

"Your Highness . . ." Leach began, but withered like his sagging trousers under the heated glare of Princess Melissa Witherspoon. "Of course, Madam."

The man who took the wheel of Melissa's limo was Sergeant Maury Fletcher of the Royal Marines, though the princess was not interested in learning the man's name. Sergeant Fletcher, thirty-one years of age, was among the best trained and most dedicated members of Her Majesty's service and could be counted upon to handle any assignment with confidence. Melissa was sure such was the case—wasn't it always?—but she was anxious to leave the sweltering city and get to the Salisbury mine.

"How far is it to Elizabeth, Arthur?" she asked her stoic bodyguard as their car left the city of Johannesburg and passed into the environs.

"About forty-five kilometers, according to the map, ma'am," Arthur said, turning slightly in his seat to address Melissa.

"Thirty minutes," the sergeant said in response to Arthur's querying glance.

It seemed to take far longer. Melissa *was* tired, a truth she had denied to Ambassador Leach, and she dwelled between wakefulness and an overpowering tug to close her eyes and sleep as the car rolled along. Suddenly she felt herself pitching forward as the car unexpectedly braked. She immediately became fully alert.

"What's happened?" she demanded of Arthur.

"We'll know soon. Stay in the car, please, ma'am," her bodyguard said.

Melissa could see a kind of roadblock ahead, with three vehicles crossing the road, two of them damaged and charred by fire, the third, a squat, strange looking thing, like a dune buggy with guns. There was an armed man in dark sunglasses dressed in desert camouflage uniform and floppy hat. He held up his hand, ordering them to stop.

But the sergeant stopped on his own terms, well short of the soldier, giving himself ample room to maneuver the car, even spin it around in the middle of the road if need be. Arthur opened his door to step out of the car and slipped his small, easily concealed Ingram submachine gun into shooting position if it was needed.

"What's the trouble?" Arthur said to the uniformed man, whom he could now see had camouflage paint on his face and carried an AR-18 assault rifle. Arthur's trained eye could see other commandos, if that's what they were, backing up the man in the road. It was no time to start anything as he and Sergeant Fletcher were at a slight disadvantage in firepower. Still . . .

"The road's closed, sir. Turn around and take another route," Heggstad said.

Arthur could see a fourth uniformed figure sitting on the ground well off the road, this one a black man, his hands and feet tied.

"There isn't another direct way, mate. Looks that we've got plenty of room to get around your bang-up, here," Arthur said, his Ingram tracking the tall soldier behind the car door.

"Close your door," Heggstad firmly ordered the bodyguard, "and find another way around."

Princess Melissa's safety was of paramount importance here, Arthur was aware, but his warrior spirit pushed him hard to resist a threat, real or implied. He could teach this young man a thing or two. It was Arthur's feeling that Sergeant Fletcher was no amateur in this business. The Royal Marine remained silent but ready. He was armed and knew how to handle a car, that much was clear. While Arthur considered his next move, however, the issue took a completely unexpected turn.

The limousine's rear door flew open and Melissa Witherspoon stepped out of the automobile onto the dusty road and fixed Heggstad in a withering eye lock.

"And just who, pray tell, do you think you are talking to?" she spat at the SEAL. "I am Her Royal Highness, Princess Melissa Radford-Gayles Witherspoon, Duchess of Kent, Countess of Beaumont. I order you to get your filthy gun out of my face and let us pass!"

"I'll be goddamned," Heggstad mumbled. "Top Hat, Tango Three," he said over the air.

"Go ahead, Three," Getts acknowledged.

"I got another live one. I'm having trouble holding on here," Heggstad said.

"Understand. We're on our way, ETA six," Getts said, motioning to Knowles and Haskins to spare no speed and mount up and drive to the water tower complex and relieve Tango Three. As the two DPVs roared ahead, bouncing wildly over rugged terrain, Getts spoke again into his lip mike. "Tango Three, say your situation. Can you hold?"

"Roger, Skipper, Dean is holding his dick, so is Miller, and my chops are busted," Heggstad's voice responded.

"Are you under fire, Heggstad?" Getts asked, thoroughly confused by Heggstad's unmilitary sitrep.

"Negative. I'll just wait until you get here, sir," he said.

"Hey, Rick," Waco Miller said to Heggstad, "I think you're supposed to curtsy."

"Lady," Heggstad said, ignoring his dive buddy's suggestion, "you're not going down this road unless it's back that way. And you, Bigfoot. Put that lettuce grinder back under your coat where it came from."

For the very long count of ten seconds it was a toss-up whether Arthur would pull the trigger or Heggstad would. Melissa, however, had heard about all she could take.

"Why you wretched sod, when your government hears from Her Majesty's prime minister the result will be an international embarrassment, and you will spend the rest of your life behind bars for assaulting a lady of the court!"

Even Heggstad, fearless in battle, clever as a mongoose eyeing a snake, understood that he may be facing a problem he couldn't solve with a three-second burst from his assault rifle. He was about to call to Getts when the skipper's DPV arrived on scene in a cloud of dust. Immediately behind him, his DPV skidding to a halt alongside, was Tango One. Getts dismounted and moved to Heggstad's side. "What's up, Rick?" he asked.

Before Heggstad could respond, Melissa resumed her harangue, now directed at Getts. "Ah, more savages. Are you the one in charge of these . . ."—she flipped her hand dismissively toward Tango Three—". . . people? You have uniforms and carry guns, so I suppose you are some sort of military contingent?"

"Yes, ma'am. Captain Robert Getts, United States Navy," he said, politely.

"How lucky for America. In that case will you kindly tell your soldier there to stand aside and let us pass!" Melissa said, the only person not sweating despite the heat of the afternoon.

"And you are?" Getts asked, recognizing that the two men in her car were professional bodyguards of some kind. It was his wish to settle the issue with as little fuss as possible.

"As I have been trying to tell this mechanical ingrate, I am Melissa Radford-Gayles Witherspoon, and I am traveling on official business of Her Majesty's government—"

"She's a princess," Heggstad interjected to Getts.

"And these are your . . . escorts?" Getts asked.

"They are," Melissa said dryly.

"I'm sorry, ma'am, but my men were ordered to stop all traffic on this road. We've just had an assassination nearby and one of my men was killed. Of course you can proceed," Getts said.

Melissa took in a deep breath, her mouth open. The word *assassination* was in itself anathema to her; one of the most traumatic events of her life was the murder of her great uncle, and the word sparked a special fear deep inside her. And the loss of this young officer's man must have affected his entire unit. She exchanged a quick but knowing glance at Arthur, who had returned his Ingram to its place under his jacket. He lowered his eyes in silent acquiescence.

"I am very sorry to know that, Captain," Melissa said, her voice heavy with fatigue and now remorse. "I know I speak for Arthur and Sergeant Fletcher, as well, when I tell you that we are saddened by the loss of one of your men."

"Thank you, ma'am. Can we help you get to where you're going?" Getts said.

Melissa was aware of still another set of eyes on her, those of the tall American commando with Getts's attachment. He had tanned skin, brown eyes, dark hair, and a presence that made her feel like her clothing was being removed from her body, item by item. She looked suddenly at Peach who, unblinking, equal to her challenge, continued to disrobe her in his mind. The corners of his mouth twitched slightly upward, hoping that she was sharing his thoughts.

"Well, ah, that's kind of you, Captain Getts," she said, struggling to disengage from Peach's focus, attempting to control her environment as she was used to doing throughout her entire royal life. "We're going to, to . . ."

"The Salisbury gold mine," Arthur put in, helping HRH in her sudden loss of memory.

"I see," Getts said, considering for a moment. "Then your official business involves the hostage situation?"

"Yes, it does," Melissa said, regaining her balance. "And you, too?"

"Yes, ma'am. If you want to follow us, we'll make sure you get there safely."

Sergeant Fletcher joined the three-car caravan, led by two DPVs in front and one in back, for the short run back to the Salisbury mine. The trip was uneventful, and while the fire teams field-stripped their weapons and cleaned them, Getts arranged for Psycho's body, now zipped inside a heavy plastic bag, to be taken immediately to the Johannesburg airport where a SPECOPS support aircraft would fly it back to Little Creek. Psycho would be buried with full military honors by his brothers in arms.

The body of FBI negotiator Arlen Gibbs would also make the journey home.

Chapter Four

Several floors below ground level of the White House, President Elling, Vice President Spencer McGraw, National Security Advisor David Magazine, and Colonel Dick Meier occupied the smallest of the two secure conference rooms within the White House situation room. Colonel Meier was deputy director of DRSO—Defense Reconnaissance Support Office—and was an expert on cruise missile guidance systems. The South African terrorists' demands were a long stretch from the interests of the vice president's office, but President Elling had the feeling that maybe he should be prepared to spread around the blame in case something went wrong in the decision-making department. Furthermore, McGraw's avuncular approach to the press might later be of help in spreading oil over troubled waters. In fact, Les Elling would have included several more people in this group but for David Magazine's insistence that the "need to know" be restricted to a very small number.

The train derailment and kidnappings had been front page news and prime television coverage for three days now, and the collective world population was waiting with bated breath for the president's move. Due to events beyond his control, Elling had usurped South Africa's authority over the bloody incident by sending American special warfare personnel on scene to take charge. In the

process he had snookered himself before knowing that
there was very little chance of rescuing the hostages. In
fact, the president of South Africa, Rtou Kwisi, had been
quietly rubbing his hands with relief that his own commando units, Recce One and Recce Three, only had to
stand by and sympathize.

Elling's head ached. He disliked ingesting medicines
of any kind, but tonight he had taken a prescription pain
pill that he hoped would allow him a full night's sleep.
He rubbed at his temples as David Magazine continued to
outline the terrorists' demands.

"They asked for SNIAD-98-116, Block IV Differential Global Positioning System software. They even included the APR99 Deviation Correction code," the NSC
advisor said, referring to notes. "That's incredible. I
mean, it isn't some uneducated backwoods revolutionary
with an AK-47 trying to extort money from Uncle Sam.
They obviously have help from a very sophisticated
source."

"But everybody has a cruise missile," McGraw said,
struggling to stifle a yawn. "What, twenty-six countries
have their own models? Some have more than one," he
said as he reached for a chrome coffeepot in front of him.

"That's true, Spencer," the NSC chief agreed, "but
there are cruise missiles and there are cruise missiles.
What makes ours better than all the others is our guidance
systems. That's what these people are demanding."

"Yeah, well, let 'em ask," McGraw said. "We sure as
hell aren't going to start paying off terrorists, are we? I
mean, that was an issue settled a long time ago, I
thought."

There was silence in the room for several minutes.
While Magazine had much more to say, he chose to wait
for the president to present his view. Elling looked
around the table as he blew air forcefully from his lungs.

"Girl Scouts," he said, then shook his head in resignation. "Can you imagine? This monster Felinda murdered a Girl Scout. Fourteen years old. Cut her up into pieces in front of her mother's eyes." The president shook his head again, his eyes closing tight as though to shut out the horror from his mind. "And he has ten more. Can you believe how this is playing around the world?"

Nobody at the table spoke.

"And," the president went on, "there are seven inner-city kids from America down there in that hole. All minorities."

"Plus Ron Mauser and his wife," McGraw reminded the president.

"Oh, Jesus, as if this nightmare weren't bad enough, we've got Mauser to think about."

"Ask yourselves how this administration is going to be viewed if we don't get the hostages back. Those poor souls in that damn pit are depending on us to get them out."

The president picked up the full cup of black coffee in front of him but put it back down when he realized it had turned cold. "I'm not saying we should give away our national secrets under threat. I'm not saying that at all. I'm just asking you to think of the big picture."

"You don't mean, Mr. President," David Magazine said, "that this country would trade away its military secrets to terrorists?"

"Goddamn it, I didn't say that, David. I just want you to remember that there's a political side to all of this. Give me a clean cup, Colonel. Right behind you, there," the president said.

Colonel Meier, a tall man with a long reach, grasped a fresh coffee cup from a silver tray on the counter behind him without leaving his leather bound chair. He passed it wordlessly to the president.

Magazine sighed. "The terrorists killed the FBI negotiator. Shot him through the head at long range."

"Oh, no," McGraw said, rolling his eyes.

"When did this happen?" the president wanted to know.

"About eight hours ago, sir. We don't know why it happened. His name was"—the advisor glanced again at his notes—"Gibbs. Arlen Gibbs. Maybe he did something to anger this Felinda guy, maybe Felinda was just trying to make another strong statement, whatever. Captain Getts and his SEAL group pursued the sniper and several other terrorists to a nearby town. There was a fire fight. One SEAL was killed but our guys killed nine of theirs including the sniper. One prisoner taken."

"Get Bobby Getts on the phone when this meeting is over. I want the name of his man that was killed. I'll talk to his family myself," the president said.

"He'll appreciate that," Magazine said.

"What's the prisoner telling us?" the president asked.

"He's being interrogated now," Magazine said.

The room was silent for another minute while the president and vice-president digested events. "At least there's one thing I feel okay about—Getts. And Dekins. Is Pete all right?" the president asked.

"Yes, sir. He's taken over communicating with the terrorists in the gold mine. Getts is running the SEAL team. They're waiting for our decision now," Magazine said.

The president raised his coffee cup up but did not touch it to his lips while he pondered. "Okay, what do you see for options?"

Magazine nodded toward Colonel Meier. "Colonel Meier knows as much about the military application of our cruise missile guidance systems as anyone. I'll let him sketch it out."

Meier leaned forward in his chair. His head was small

for his body and his eyes were dark and sunken, which conveyed a somewhat desperate appearance even when no such condition existed for the air force officer. He seemed older than most bird colonels, and the president idly wondered why the man was not wearing a star or, if not that, why he was not in a civil service position. Meier's voice was soft as he spoke and the president found himself straining to hear the colonel's words, delivered in an almost slurred speech.

"We use GPS in our CALCMs and their variants now, Mr. President. That's global positioning system, angulations from satellite clusters. We also use TERCOM—Terrain Contour Matching and digital scene matching systems. The missile's radar can follow the contours of the ground and follow any kind of a mapping scenario we put in it. Problem is that it gets a little tough to do in a desert where the terrain can change. Like shifting sand dunes. So we put the two systems together. GPS sends the missile to a particular map coordinate on the face of the Earth. So many degrees and minutes of latitude, so much longitude—"

"Yes, I understand that," the president said, interrupting.

"Well, sir, we don't want other countries to copy that. We don't want them to use our satellite navigation signals in their missiles if they're launched against us, so we put into our software a thing we call the Differential. The Differential is contained in a Deviation Correction code. So our satellite signals received on the ground by someone else, say North Korea, won't help them navigate their missile unless they also have the Deviation Correction codes," Colonel Meier said, his large hands forming shapes of globes, missiles, and satellites.

"Okay. So?" the president asked.

"I think we could give the terrorists the SNIAD-98,

but we corrupt the deviation code. They couldn't guide a canoe across a lake with it," Meier said, allowing himself a tight grin.

The president glanced at McGraw, who returned his eye contact. While there was a certain appreciation for what the air force colonel was suggesting, the president asked the inevitable question.

"All right, let's say we did this. How long does it take them to figure out they've been had?"

"Ah, that depends, sir," Meier said, his eyes rolling upward while he calculated. "In the first place, we need to encrypt the entire program. That isn't easy, and the code the terrorists insist we use allows us to say it is taking us longer to get ready, but NSA could do it in about twenty-four hours. Give it another eight hours to corrupt the deviation codes. Then we send it out. The time it takes for the terrorists to figure out they've been dicked depends on their equipment, how good their computers are, but most important, how good their personnel are. Once they get it to run, they've got to test it to know whether or not it will work."

"Okay," the president said, showing an edge, "so let's say the people at the other end know their stuff. How long?"

Colonel Meier shrugged. "Could be twelve hours, could be a week. Maybe they never pick up the corruption patterns."

"Let's say at the end of three days," the president said, turning to David Magazine, "they find out they've been screwed. What happens to the hostages?"

No one around the table wanted to look the president in the eye.

"Here's all we can do," David Magazine said to Pete Dekins and Bobby Getts via the WHCA (White House

Communication Agency) scrambled line. "We're going to send them what they want per their instructions. It's going to look like the real thing but we're going to put a bug in it."

Neither Dekins nor Getts responded immediately. They were sitting inside a mobile field headquarters, which, with its two double beds, also served as a place to sleep and eat for command personnel. It had been flown out from Pope AFB in North Carolina on a C-5A along with other equipment. Getts would not sleep in the luxurious accommodation, preferring to spend his nights on the ground with his men and taking his turn standing perimeter guard. But he admitted to Dekins that it was one hell of a relief to have a secure communication facility within easy reach. Atop the roof of the HQ caravan were two satellite communications dishes, capable of handling seven hundred UHF and VHF frequencies. And there was an obvious advantage in having a place to spread out maps and set up an RC-2400 computer.

"Understand," Dekins said into the telephone mouthpiece. "I suppose you've talked about what happens when the Ts find out the software is unserviceable."

An ensuing silence on the other end told Getts all he wanted to know. He shuddered inwardly. "Well, that's it from here," Magazine's voice continued, lacking enthusiasm. "Any contingency plans you folks are proud of?"

"Negative. We're still trying to do homework, but it's hard," Dekins said.

"The president is sorry about your KIA," Magazine said. "We'll contact his family."

"That's good. Thank you," Getts said from his extension.

At that moment there was a single knock on the door of the HQ.

"Come," Dekins said.

The door opened and Snake walked in. With his blond
locks curled up under his bush hat, his quick smile and
gleaming teeth, Snake could still pass for the star of his
high school water polo team in Kentucky. Snake always
appeared to have just heard a joke or was about to tell
one, and he was grinning from ear to ear as he said,
"Rhino wants you back on the phone, General. He's tired
of talkin' to me. Hollerin' his ass off for General Dekins."

"Rhino?" Getts asked while Dekins replaced his telephone receiver in its fabric box.

"Yes, sir. I figure ol' Felinda's fat and looks like a
rhino. Course I don't tell him that when I'm spellin' the
general," Snake said, his grin widening so that his eyes
were almost hidden behind freckled cheeks.

"I'm on my way," Dekins said over his shoulder to
Getts, who was still on the live connection with Washington, D.C.

"Dave," Getts said to Dr. Magazine, "we'll be back in
an hour, maybe two."

"Roger. Good luck," Magazine said, then rang off.

Getts did not believe in torture for more reasons than
one. It was his experience that no one being tortured could
stand an infinite amount of pain and would invariably talk.
But when the prisoner talked, he—or she—may tell only
what the torturer wished to hear, not necessarily the truth.
Of course it was possible, even likely, that once the prisoner began talking under torture, he would speak the truth.
But the torturer could never be sure. Some governments
fared well using the combination of a skilled interrogator
along with selected methods of physical and mental tor-
ment to gain the intelligence they sought; France and Israel
being prime examples among Western nations who routinely employed these techniques against terrorists, crimi-
nals, and other enemies of their states. But as a matter of

personal ethics, Getts chose to use a more civilized method of obtaining information from a prisoner—that of intelligent questioning.

The technique was a method first employed in known history by the Greeks in the Peloponnesian wars and raised to an art form by the British in the twentieth century. Dutch Colonel Oreste Pinto, who served with British MI5, was personally responsible for the capture of a dozen highly trained German spies who attempted to take up residence in England during WWII. Pinto simply asked questions of the detainees, analyzed their answers, and asked more questions until their real identities became obvious.

Among prerequisites of the questioner are that he have a vast knowledge of information relating to the subject matter that he is interested in extracting from the prisoner inside his head at instant recall. He must know his geography well, including an intimate familiarity of cities and their streets in Europe, Asia, America, or Africa, depending upon those locations in which the prisoner claims to have traveled. He must be skilled in more than one language if he is to understand the nuance of the prisoner's thought processes in play during the questioning. He must be a superb reader of body language so as to be on the level with a champion poker player.

These kinds of interrogators are rare, and they are usually well known among intelligence agencies around the world. Getts was painfully aware of his shortcomings, but he saw no other options. Among others who were aware of Getts's limitations was General Johannes Boord who, through his adjutant Major An Louden, had demanded that the prisoner Getts had captured at Elizabeth be handed over to his office. Getts refused. The issue of jurisdiction was clearly on Boord's side, Getts admitted to himself, but the SEAL leader did not trust General

Boord at all and did not for a minute believe that information extracted from the prisoner by Boord would find its way back to Green Solitaire. So, at the risk of causing another political imbroglio for his country, Getts had ignored the general's demands.

It was late at night that Getts chose to question his prisoner. Walter Felinda was only human and his circadian clock would, Getts hoped, make the terrorist tired enough to sleep. That way Pete Dekins could sit in on the questioning while Snake monitored the telephone connecting the hostages to the surface.

Also present was Peach, skilled himself at extracting information from prisoners but not always using his skipper's cerebral technique. The venue for the questioning was the mobile HQ. Neither Peach nor Dekins would question the prisoner, but would instead pretend to occupy themselves with paperwork in an adjoining space, as though the prisoner was of little importance.

While SEAL Waco Miller stood guard outside, Getts poured two cups of coffee, Dekins and Peach preferring to drink water. Getts placed a cup on the counter near the prisoner, whose name they learned was Jku.

"Did you get enough to eat, Jku?" Getts asked the terrorist who sat in front of him in a straight-backed wooden chair. Jku did not immediately speak, which was not a surprise to Getts though he knew from Heggstad that Jku spoke English.

Jku allowed the lids of his eyes to nearly close as he contemplated the coffee. Getts waited, anxious to hear whatever information Jku could tell him but unwilling to appear eager. While he waited, he considered what he saw before him. Jku appeared to be quite young, possibly fifteen or sixteen. He was not tall, shorter than Getts, but had more meat on his bones than most young African men from conflicted nations. His eyes were clear and his deep ebony skin showed no signs of disease or infection. This told Getts that the lad was well cared for by whatever kind of paramilitary organization he belonged.

"Yes," Jku said, opening his eyes, engaging Getts squarely, without fear. He took a tentative sip of the warm coffee.

"We have plenty. You'll have more in the morning. And all you can eat." Getts paused but Jku had nothing to offer. Yet. "You work for Sergeant Felinda? How long, now?"

Getts purposely reduced Felinda's rank to provoke a reaction in Jku.

"Felinda is a general. General Felinda, we call him, and he is."

"Who is we?" Getts asked, conversationally, and sipped at his coffee.

Jku considered for a moment, then said, "We are freedom fighters. We hate you."

"Let's see," Getts said, pretending to refresh his memory from a piece of paper he took from his shirt pocket. "You are SADL, the South African Defense League." He replaced the slip of paper into his pocket.

"Yes," the young man said. Then he corrected himself, "No. Not defense."

"I'm sorry. What, then?" Getts said.

"That is not your business."

"Democratic League?"

"Yes."

"Ah. Thank you, Jku. And the people in your league, they are democrats?"

"Yes."

"How many democrats in your league?"

Jku considered for a minute. Getts did not think Jku to be an accomplished liar, but that the young terrorist was calculating what Getts might believe. "Thousands," he said while nodding his head for emphasis.

"Are you paid for your work?" he asked.

"That is none of your concern."

"Well, it's too bad you're not being paid for your work," Getts said, allowing his eyes to disengage from Jku's for a half moment.

"But we—"

Getts waited in vain for the rest of the rebuttal but none came. "Felinda was nothing but a sergeant before you met him," Getts continued. "He was not a good field leader. See what happened to you today? All were killed, except you."

When there was no response Getts said, "More coffee? Coca Cola? I think I'll have one, too," Getts said as he moved two steps to reach a refrigerator. He removed two of the distinctive red and white cans of cola from the fridge and placed one in front of Jku and resumed his seat across the table from the young prisoner. For several moments it seemed that the prisoner would reject the cold refreshment, but after licking his lips a few times, he reached over and quickly opened the can and took a long drink from it. Still, he said nothing.

"Jku," Getts said, "if you tell me what I want to know, I will try to help you. You are guilty of murder. You and your friends have kidnapped innocent civilians, some of them you have killed. You also killed an FBI agent—a man who works for the American government. So you could go to jail for the rest of your life. Even hanged. Did your leader tell you this?"

Fear stabbed at the young Tutsi's eyes like a bright light. He blinked nervously, placed a hand upon his forehead, and shook his head as though two parts of him were warring against each other.

"White people, they our enemies. One day, you will all die—in Africa," Jku said.

"No we won't, and you know it," Getts said, simply. He watched Jku's eyes as they avoided his and looked around the HQ.

"He is keeping all of the money, you know," Getts said, then enjoyed a long swallow of cola.

Jku's attention once again became focused.

"That is a lie!" Jku said, passionately.

"He's received hundreds of thousand of dollars to equip his men and to pay wages to his fighters. Are you one of his fighters? Has he paid you?"

As Jku's lips compressed and his blink rate increased, Getts saw that a vein on his neck began to expand and pulse.

"Your leader expects to make millions of dollars from America. That's why he wrecked the train and took our people. Is he going to give some of it to you?" Getts said, smiling.

Jku clenched his teeth and did not speak.

"You are from Burundi?" Getts pressed. Slowly the young warrior nodded his head.

"Tutsi?" Getts said, knowing that Felinda held a major part in those tribal wars, and easily recruited young killers, like Jku, from that area. Only seven years ago the Tutsi had slaughtered more than one hundred thousand Hutus without making any excuses for their atrocities. One year later, the same group of Tutsi tribes added another two hundred thousand victims to their score of dead, men, women, and children hacked to death, shot, strangled, drowned, and burned. Young children were introduced by their elders to the joy of genocide, later to be armed with more efficient weapons and harnessed for use as commercial terrorists. The death toll was now in the millions.

Again Jku nodded his head.

"The man who led your squad of fighters. He's dead now because we killed him. What was his name?" Getts asked.

When Jku hesitated, Getts said, "If you cooperate with us, we will be your friends. If you don't talk to me, we will hand you over to the South African police. You wouldn't like that."

After long minutes of deliberation, Jku lowered his eyes again, but spoke: "Dtrakka."

"Dtrakka," Getts repeated. "Was he close to Felinda? Were they friends?"

Jku nodded again. "Yes. Good friend."

"All right. Jku, I have several questions for you to answer for me. If you get them all right, you will earn five thousand American dollars and you will be set free. You can go home to Burundi or anyplace else you want to go. You will have plenty of money to travel."

Getts began writing on sheets of notebook paper. "How does Felinda communicate with his men in the field, like you and Dtrakka? How did he pass on orders?" he said aloud as he wrote.

As the young Tutsi opened his mouth to speak there was a loud banging on the door of the HQ, and voices raised. Getts could make out Snake's distinctive voice as he warned whoever was making the outside noise that he was to stand away from the HQ. Peach got to his feet and stepped outside.

General Johannes Boord, his bemedaled uniform veritably glowing with gold trim, silver braid, and colorful garrison hat, pulled his lips back in what he offered as a smile at the appearance of Peach in the doorway. "Ah, you weren't *all* asleep, then?" Boord said, sarcasm dripping from his tongue. Boord had, standing behind him, several dozen South African police officers, none of which, Peach could see at a glance, were among the well-trained commandos of Recce One or Three. And at his elbow was his adjutant, Major An Louden.

"Just turning in, General," Peach said. "What can I do for you?"

"What can you do for me?" Boord said, again using biting sarcasm. "Not much, I'm afraid. No matter how hard you tried, Mr. Peach, you couldn't do much for me. However, you *can* bring out the terrorist you captured today at Elizabeth. At once, please."

"Sorry, General, we're talking to him now. Why don't you call us in the morning and we'll make an appointment for you to stop by at a better time."

Boord's smile widened as his eyes turned to ice. It was as though he wanted a refusal from the American SEAL. "*This* is the better time. I have a writ from the federal magistrate in Pretoria ordering you to surrender your prisoner forthwith. If you do not, I cannot guarantee your safe conduct in South Africa."

"Is that a threat, General Boord?" Peach said.

"Yes. You have—" Boord looked at his watch. "Five minutes."

Peach glanced at Snake Chandel out of the corners of his eyes. He knew that Snake's AR-18 was off-safety and set for full auto fire. And he knew that the other SEAL fire teams would have dispersed to cross-fire positions out of sight of General Boord's policemen. He was not concerned about who would win a fight, and he knew it would be brief. But there were other issues involved.

"Stand by, General," Peach said, then opened the door to the HQ and walked in, closing the door firmly behind him. "Did you hear that?" Peach asked Getts.

"Some of it. He wants Jku, huh?" Getts said.

"He's got a piece of paper with him. No doubt it's the real deal," Peach said, stealing a glance at Jku. The young man seemed to get smaller, his shoulders hunched into a defensive position. His eyes shifted nervously from Getts to Peach and back again. "He's got some troopers with him, none we can't handle."

Getts considered for a full minute before turning to Pete Dekins. Getts raised his eyebrows in question.

"We have to let him get away with this, Bobby," Dekins said.

"He's our prisoner," Getts said, his jaw muscles flexing.

"I guess it's a matter of jurisdiction. We're in their country. We have no authority of any kind. Certainly not judicial. If we get into a pissing contest with the South African government it's all over for the people down below."

Getts rose from his seat and crossed the room to speak to Dekins in a whisper. "If we give him this kid, we won't see him again."

"You don't know that," Dekins said.

"I know it."

"That's an emotional judgment, not a military one."

"I can think of a hundred reasons to keep Jku with us. The brass dictator out there can go fuck himself," Getts said.

"Sure, but we don't have a legal right. Bobby, we can't go to war with the whole country. And that's what we'd have to do. Turn him over. That's an order," Dekins said.

Getts straightened and turned to the door. He could not look Jku in the eyes. Getts opened the HQ door. Only a few steps outside, General Boord sat on a camp chair, casually flicking at night-flying insects with his riding crop.

"General Boord, will you come in?" Getts said.

Boord nodded to Louden, who stepped forward. Getts stopped him with an upraised hand.

"Just you, General. I won't turn him over to anyone else," Getts said.

With studied reluctance, Boord rose, shot a cuff beneath his impeccable uniform sleeve, and stepped inside the HQ, Getts following behind. Boord did not deign to inspect the prisoner, but merely took in his presence in a casual, disinterested appraisal of the mobile HQ.

"I suppose this is he," Boord said. Turning his head slightly toward Jku, he said, "Stand up. You'll come with me."

"Stay where you are, Jku," Getts said. The youth settled back into his seat. "I want a receipt," Getts said, sliding a piece of blank paper and a pen on the tabletop toward the South African policeman.

"Ridiculous," Boord sniffed.

"Sign for the prisoner or he goes nowhere," Getts said implacably.

Boord shot a glance around the room. Seeing no effects of his own powerful government position on the faces of Dekins, Peach, or Getts, he reluctantly scribbled a few words on the paper and signed his name.

Getts looked at it. "Date it," he demanded.

Clearly angry now, Boord added the date, then glared at Getts. "You're a disgrace to your uniform, Captain," Boord spat. "If you were under my command I would break you. I've dealt with men like you and before I was through with them they cried like babies for their mothers."

"Jku is under your protection, now. I intend to continue my interrogation of him tomorrow, and he better be in good shape and able to answer questions," Getts said.

After Jku had walked down the two steps from the HQ, Boord turned once more to Getts. "No one instructs me in my duties, Captain, least of all you."

Chapter Five

The bottom of the gold mine was like a scene from hell, Dorothy Mauser thought. Although there were electric lights strung above the drifts it was always dim. Along the walls were widened diggings where the miners had followed the veins that ran elusively through dark, hard rock, carving out what appeared to be rooms. The rooms, called drifts, were accessible only by stooping over as the roof of the diggings and floor of the drifts converged. The rooms were dark, illuminated only by the secondary scattered light from bulbs in the drifts.

The air they breathed was thick and oppressive, made repulsive by rotting food waste and body effluents discharged by captives and jailers alike. While there were countless miles of drifts, the terrorists did not regard calls of nature important enough to take them far from their central positions near the main vertical shaft of the Salisbury mine. They likewise refused to allow their hostages to travel any greater distances. Indeed, the guards would often get very close to the women—and girls—laughing and pointing to them as they squatted among the rocks of the dimly lit drifts. Mortified in their public embarrassment, they would often return to the group fully enveloped in tears. Dorothy's heart went out to them.

What almost broke Dorothy's indomitable spirit was watching Danielle Hüüken as she exhibited the aftershock of watching her daughter carved up with a machete. The event, required by Felinda for all to watch, shocked the entire assemblage of hostages to the very cores of their souls. If Dorothy had been horrorstruck into insensibility, she could only guess at what Danielle must have endured at the murder scene.

They were not denied food or water. Dorothy tried in vain to get Danielle to eat but she would not take even a morsel. Dorothy made sure the Dutch woman drank water; at times Dorothy would physically force a crude cup to the woman's lips, like hydrating a frightened animal.

Ronald Mauser had cried out, lunging at Felinda who wielded the ghastly knife, but was restrained by a number of terrorists. Dorothy and the others—certainly Ronald— were aware that Felinda was using horror as a weapon of control. But it worked. They were terrified that the madman would give a hellish order and others would be raped or tortured or worse.

Dorothy sat close to Ron, tending the deep abrasion he had suffered at the hands of the terrorists. She had kept it as clean as possible and saw that it was healing without medication. She could not see all of the approximately fifty hostages but made an effort to keep Danielle within her range of vision. She was certain that the Girl Scout leader would, sooner or later, do something foolish. "I think she is suicidal," she said to Ronald.

"I can't blame her. God, to watch while . . ." His voice trailed off and his head shook in disbelief.

"Why us?" Dorothy asked.

Ronald shrugged. "We're Americans, I guess. Those kids from the inner schools. Black America will want answers to whatever President Elling does. And the girls from the Netherlands will also intensify international public opinion, put heat on our government to come

through. No one wants to see little girls murdered."
Ronald almost spat the last words, bile rising in his
mouth.

"So what do they want? Money, I suppose. That's what
everyone wants." Dorothy gently leaned her tired head
against Ron's shoulder as she interlaced her fingers with
his.

"I guess so. I don't know," Ronald said.

"I'm sorry I got you into this, my love. We could have
gone anywhere else," she said, squeezing his hand
tightly. Ironically, it was Ronald who suggested that
Dorothy would enjoy seeing the wild animals in South
Africa but she did not want to remind him of the fact.

"It wouldn't have mattered. They're everywhere, these
people." Ronald placed his head gently against Dorothy's
and closed his eyes.

He might have drifted into an uncomfortable sleep, but
for suddenly snapping fully awake to a sharp pain in his
right shoulder. He realized that he had been kicked backward by one of the uniformed kidnapers.

"Stand up, Ronald Mauser!" Felinda bellowed into his
face. "I know who you are, now. On your feet, Mr. Shit."
The soldier with Felinda grabbed Ronald by his jacket
lapels and shirt front and pulled him roughly from his sitting position on the hard ground.

"Leave him alone!" Dorothy exclaimed, jumping to
her husband's side.

Felinda pushed her back down, but with a surprising
lack of force, Dorothy thought.

"He's done nothing! Nothing to you," she said, fighting back tears of rage and frustration.

"It's all right, darling. Don't worry. We're just going to
talk." Before Ronald started to walk away with Felinda
and the uniformed terrorist he leaned down to his wife.
"Dorothy, please don't worry about me. He won't harm

me in any way. I promise you," he said in a whisper, then
kissed her cheek.

But Dorothy knew better as she watched while her
husband was literally dragged away from her. The
butcher Felinda had somehow learned that Ronald was a
CIA officer, and she knew that he would be brutalized because of it. And she also knew that their government
could do nothing whatever to stop it. Though she tried to
erase the image from her mind, she knew that she would
never see her husband again. As she broke into uncon-
trolled sobs, in the deep recesses of her heart she wished
that her husband would die suddenly, without pain, by a
divine hand.

"I've come a long way to tell you about a man called
Eveshenko," Melissa said to the American SEALs and
General Dekins. "He is a Russian nationalist and he is involved with this terrorist kidnapping. Boris Eveshenko is
fifty-two years old, married to a woman age sixty-four,
has two grown daughters and a son who died at eighteen
serving in the Russian–Afghan wars. The boy was a con-
script. I have no information about what Boris felt about
his son's death or about his military service. He had lived
with his wife in Kirov. The Peroskov military assembly
plant shut down in 1995."

"What did they make at the Peroskov plant?" General
Dekins asked.

"The Peroskov complex fabricated exotic metals for
high performance aviation and space vehicles," Melissa
said, brushing stray hair from her eyes, hardly glancing
up from her notes. "It was very reluctantly closed down
by the Russian Defense Ministry and was among the last
of its kind. Well, closed down is the wrong word, I'm
afraid. Portions are still at work, mostly involving R&D.
One of their projects is an air-superiority fighter. I can get

you more information on that if you wish, but it doesn't seem to be germaine to the issue we're facing now. But Peroskov is important because it is also doing work on a new breed of cruise missile and we think Eveshenko was working on that."

"Jesus Christ," Getts said, wanting to stand up and pace but remaining in his seat because of the confinement of the mobile HQ. "The Russians are behind all this?"

"It would seem that way, except for some dots that don't want to connect," Melissa said. "You see, Boris Eveshenko dropped out of sight for almost two years. Then, in 1997, he offered his services to your country. To Lockheed Aircraft, as a matter of fact." Melissa looked up from her notes and directly into the eyes of Peach. The SEAL very much liked what he saw and Melissa recalled his look when she first spied the man at Elizabeth. Again, she could feel a slight increase in body heat. And she thought that she might be coloring just a shade of crimson.

"What did he offer to do?" General Dekins wanted to know.

"Boris had been a critical designer of the Russian AS-15. They call it KH 55. Before he did his magic to the AS-15 it was just another piece of pipe with an engine attached, but when he finished it was almost the equal of your Tomahawk. With one vital difference."

"The guidance system," Getts suggested.

"That's right, Captain," Melissa allowed herself a brief smile. She was, in fact, inwardly pleased that these professional men apparently took her logical conclusions with the same gravity as she.

"So Lockheed turned him down," Dekins said.

"Yes. He left the United States and we lost track of him—not that we were terribly interested, really—until two weeks ago. A Boris L. Eveshenko was arrested in

Gaborone, Botswana, one week ago. The man had killed a mother and a child driving his vehicle while drunk. He did not spend the night in jail but was almost immediately bailed out. No charges are pending, as far as we know. This leads me to believe that somebody with powerful influence in the government of Botswana is protecting him. Asking myself the rhetorical question of why anyone in Africa would want to rescue a Russian cruise missile expert from jail, this all would have remained a complete mystery were it not for the current hostage crisis that we find ourselves in now. In fairness, I might add that my department head at MI6 does not agree with me. I have traveled here out of personal conviction that I am correct."

It was 0310 local time and Melissa was beyond exhaustion. Because of jet lag, she was keeping her eyes open strictly from the adrenaline that she could feel racing through her system. She knew that once she closed them it would be for a good, long, sleep. She reasoned that the men in the mobile HQ must have been in-country long enough to have overcome the physiological changes of global travel. They showed no sign of particular weariness or loss of attention. It did not occur to her that special warfare personnel trained very long and very hard to control precisely those body urges. She would have been surprised at how long the SEALs and General Dekins could go using only moments of sleep garnered whenever opportunity allowed.

"The Russians?" Dekins said, turning to Getts. "Is that how you see it, Bobby? They're looking to upgrade their guidance system and this is how they're going about it?"

Getts placed his hands behind his head, interlocking his fingers, and allowed his eyes to drift toward one of the ventilation inlets in the roof of the HQ. "Doesn't feel good, does it?" he said.

"What do you think, Peach?" Dekins said.

"Well, sir, I don't see how my job description changes, here. My function is to get the hostages out of that hole in the ground. Alive. I don't see that knowing who's behind it matters."

An uneasy quiet settled over the group while Peach's words sunk in. Getts had the feeling that Peach might be right, at least in the short term, which is about all the hell that matters in a hostage situation. They weren't there to do research on national foreign policy. Getts, like Peach, was itching to engage the enemy and shoot their god-damn asses off. But he had never run into a brick wall—or a rock pit—like this. If there was ever an assault-proof fortress, these bastards had it.

"Okay," Dekins said, "let's suppose the Russians are calling the shots. Some diehard Reds back in Moscow are looking to upgrade their cruise missile threat, and this certainly seems like a cheap and fast way to do it. If that's the situation, and I don't say it is, what do we do about it?"

"Has your government sent out the software codes yet?" Melissa asked.

Dekins's eyes caught Getts's, and for a moment both men were considering the level of security of those present. Then, having made the decision that Melissa had done all of the sharing to this point, he nodded his head. "It's encrypted, per their instructions, and the material will be put on the Internet in about—" he glanced at his chronometer, "—seven hours."

"You're not giving Felinda the authentic information, are you?" she said.

This time all three men exchanged surprised looks. Their collective respect for this woman of royal birth moved up several notches as Dekins grappled with what he felt he could share with her. He decided that caution was required before bonhommie. "As far as I know," he said, "Felinda will receive the entire GPS guidance system, including TERCOM/DSMAC."

If Melissa believed it or not, she did not let on. "Does Felinda know your progress?"

Minutes later Getts rang the telephone line that tethered him to the kidnappers below. "General Felinda," he said into the mouthpiece, "this is Captain Getts. Are you there?" For several moments there were eerie sounds of breathing that filtered through to Getts. He pressed the receiver closer to his ear. "Is that you, General Felinda?"

"I am here. Who are you?"

"I'm Robert Getts, United States Navy. General Dekins is busy and asked me to call you and pass on information."

"The news better be good. I am in the mood to kill hostages. If you give me provocation, they will die," Felinda said.

The matter-of-fact tone of Felinda's voice sent small chills up the spine of the battle-hardened SEAL commander. "The news is very good for you. The National Security Advisor has agreed to place the guidance system software you requested on the Internet. The encryption is almost complete and it will appear on line within twenty-four hours," Getts said, trying to gain more time.

"Twenty-four hours is not what I demanded! Do you hear? I want it sent out immediately!" Felinda shrieked into Getts's ear. "I called General Dekins twenty minutes ago and he was not there. I demand he remain by the telephone when I call!"

"You killed his man who stayed by the phone. There is a hell of a lot of work for the general to do so you can get what you want. He can't get it done sitting around waiting for you to call," Getts said rationally.

"I order you both to stand by! The codes will be released in one hour! I am prepared to kill all of the hostages. *All* of them, and you will not like how they will die!"

"General Felinda," Getts said, his voice calm and easy, "you almost have what you want: the guidance codes for the Tomahawk missile. No other man in the world has been able to do what you have almost accomplished. Surely a few more hours doesn't mean anything to—"

"Do not patronize me, American fuck-ass!" Felinda screamed, interrupting Getts. "Do you want these people dead? Is that what you want?"

Well, Getts thought, I'm not scoring big on psychology. "Okay, General, let's do it your way. If you kill the hostages I'm going to dump ten thousand gallons of high octane aviation gasoline down this mine shaft, then I'm going to drop a lighted flare down the hole and burn you into toast. You want to fucking kill somebody, then let's do some *real* killing, starting with your sorry ass!"

The ensuing silence was interrupted only by the hammering sound of Getts's heart pounding out of control inside his chest.

"You are not talking to a man who knows fear. I am Zulu. You have heard of us. Fear does not touch our lives. I know you are trying to be brave but you have not made me tremble, which was your plan," Getts heard Felinda say, but Getts heard enough quaver in the terrorist's voice to know that he had, indeed, touched a nerve. Every man and woman has a point where the organism requires self-preservation. Getts knew that Felinda's brain had attained that place.

"I understand. We're moving ahead as fast as we can. We want our people out of there," Getts said.

"By midday tomorrow," Felinda said, his voice regaining confidence in his position of power.

Getts quickly considered. He could live with a difference of four hours. It was a face-saving bone for the terrorist and easy for Getts to give. "Very well, General."

The sun was beginning to light the eastern sky when Melissa was gently shaken awake by Peach. HRH had simply dropped from exhaustion upon one of the beds in the rear of the SEALs' HQ, and she had slept soundly in her safari clothing. She was warm to Peach's touch, and he would have much rather joined her in the sack rather than forcing her out of sleep and into harsh reality. "Rise and shine, Princess," he said. "I hate to do it, ma'am, but we need you right now."

She was quickly alert, though she rubbed her eyes free of sleep.

"Perfectly all right, Peach. Call me Melissa, for God's sake, not Princess. Where are Arthur and Sergeant Fletcher?"

"They did a five mile run this morning, then they had breakfast with us. I think they're just waiting for you, now. General Dekins wants to talk to you, if that's all right," Peach said.

"Of course. I'll just wash up quickly," Melissa said as she swung her legs over the edge of the bed and stepped into the small but efficient toilet.

When she emerged, looking amazingly attractive and clear of eye, Getts, General Dekins, and Peach were standing at the central table in the HQ's kitchenette. On the table was an array of food, including coffee, tea, pastries, toast, and fresh fruits.

"Good morning," Getts said. "I hope it isn't too early for you, ma'am."

"Of course not. It's just that I'm usually asleep. God, how do you people do it? Don't you ever close your eyes?"

"The code will be out this afternoon, Melissa. We have to make some moves," Dekins said.

"I understand," she responded, sitting down at the table. The three SpecWar men took their seats after her. Melissa poured herself coffee as each person at the table helped themselves to the fare.

"About Boris Eveshenko," Dekins began. "Is he capable of analyzing a guidance system for ALCMs or SLCMs?"

"I don't know that, General," Melissa said, spreading marmalade on toast. "We do know that he designed them so I would assume that he could."

"Let's skip the formalities. Call me Pete, Melissa."

"We think you're right, Melissa," Getts said. "We think we can't afford to gamble that he *couldn't* analyze the software. Or at least supervise the job. Otherwise, why would he be here in Africa? That's also assuming, of course, that he's connected with the kidnappings and the ransom."

"Yes, yes, I think that's the safe way of looking at it," she said.

"Well, then, I think we're all in agreement," Dekins said, glancing quickly around the table, then settling his focus back on Melissa. "Do you know exactly where Boris Eveshenko is now?"

"At this hour? Do you mean besides Gaborone?" she said, swallowing her toast awkwardly.

"Yes. Is he still in Gaborone and, if so, where?" Dekins asked.

"We, ah, made no attempt to run a current address check on Boris so the easy answer is no, I don't know. But I would assume, since we're now in the assumption business, that because the ransom from the kidnapping has not yet been paid, he is probably still here. Or there, if you prefer. In Gaborone," the princess replied.

"Do you have any knowledge of how he's traveling? I mean, what about security personnel?" Dekins asked.

"We know that he's not alone. Otherwise, how would he have gotten out of jail so fast? But an armed escort? I shouldn't think the man would want to attract attention," the princess said.

Dekins nodded. "That's about how we see it. I'm sending two men up there. I want them to try to find Boris. I'd like to send more people but I don't have any to spare. I think if you went to Gaborone with them, you might be able to help."

Melissa almost spit her coffee back into her cup. "Me? Well!"

"I can't make that an order, of course. But we've talked about it among the three of us and we think you could provide cover for our small team." Dekins, suddenly aware that he was asking a member of the British royal family to launch on a mission that could easily become dangerous, said, "It could be risky. You have every right to turn us down."

"Oh, no, I think it's a brilliant idea. I'm flattered that you would include me in your plans." Melissa took a deep breath, then looked Dekins squarely in the eye. "General Dekins—Pete—I'm really an amateur at this business. I think you know that. Honesty compels me to say that I would rather die than mess up your mission," she said, smiling winsomely.

"Well, then, if you're only worried about messing things up, you leave that part to us. We think that a man and a woman moving about town like tourists wouldn't attract attention. To provide cover, you might ask around about an acquaintance that you met in Europe who said he was planning to stop in Gaborone. Of course you'd have to play that by ear when you got there. Walk around, feel out the town, do whatever you feel comfortable with in order to find Boris. We'd have our people nearby, including your own, if you agree. Every man we have counts, and your people are more than capable of handling the assignment," Dekins said.

"Arthur and Sergeant Fletcher? Certainly I agree. And who else?" she said.

"Warrant Officer Crosley, here," Dekins said. "Peach, if you don't mind using his cover name. And we'll send another SEAL. A South African Airlines plane will depart Jo'burg at 0800 this morning, and arrive in Gaborone about 0930. It's two hundred air miles. You'll have to make your own accommodations at Gaborone. You might act like it was a spur of the moment trip. Okay so far?"

"Yes," Melissa said, nodding her head in what she hoped was not a display of overenthusiasm.

"I don't know what travel documents you have with you, Melissa, but we've borrowed a passport from a South African patriot whose name is Wanda Layden. She will wait forty-eight hours before realizing that her passport has been stolen, and will then notify police." Dekins pushed across the table a blue booklet with the gold seal of the South African state on its cover. "There is no visa stamp required for Botswana from South Africa, we're told. If anything goes wrong, just use cash to buy your way out of the problem. Peach will never be away from your side, and he is an expert at settling misunderstandings." Dekins did not go into detail how Peach settled conflicts.

"Well, then I suppose we should get going," Melissa said, turning first to Peach then to Getts, holding her hand out to Dekins, who smiled warmly as he shook it.

"We more than appreciate your willingness to do . . ." Getts almost said *a dirty job* but finished with ". . . what could become messy. We know you understand that there are always risks with this kind of thing." Getts and the others waited for her response. Had HRH even hesitated, they would have drawn up new plans.

"I appreciate your concern, Captain—Bobby—but I wouldn't pass up a chance to play the part of a spy for all the money in the world. I just hope I don't hash it up." She tried not to beam. "By the way," she said, "no reason, is there, to let anyone know about this little adventure? Even when we've finished."

"Melissa, you have the natural instincts of a spy," Dekins said.

Even in the early hours of the day the winds of the Kalahari desert had begun to boil up from the floor of Botswana, making the airplane's approach to the city's international airport extremely bumpy. Peach and Eddie Knowles were used to rough rides of all kinds, including in airplanes. Eddie, a man of wide shoulders, long trunk, shaved skull, and chubby cheeks, scanned a tourist guide to Botswana as the turbo-prop commuter violently pitched and rolled its way toward the airport ten miles out on final approach. Arthur and Maury seemed equally unimpressed with the low level turbulence and gazed absently out of their respective windows at the sun-browned ground below. Surprisingly to Peach, Melissa seemed as unaffected as any of them, remaining cool and very calm at a time when some passengers might think the wings would snap off from the fuselage.

Arthur and Eddie were the first to descend the aircraft's self-contained steps that folded down from the cabin. They stayed near the luggage compartment while the ground crew arrived with a small tug and baggage trailer. The plane was only half full so that their extra-heavy fabric duffle bags were easy to see among the other passengers' bags. Sergeant Fletcher went directly to the terminal and the baggage carousel while Peach and

Melissa walked together. Their luggage, containing a modest amount of arms and ammunition, was never out of their sight.

All five traveled in casual clothing, khakis being de rigueur, worn in the form of unisex safari jackets, pants, shirts, and hats. The plan was for Peach and Melissa to move about town as a couple, while Arthur and Eddie would take turns being inconspicuously nearby. Peach and Melissa employed a taxi in front of the airport and gave the driver instructions to take them to the best hotel in Gaborone. The driver spoke and understood English well enough. Peach knew by experience that if he did not negotiate the fare before entering the cab, he would no doubt be scandalously overcharged. Peach put up an uninspired objection to the driver's suggestion of five American dollars only for the sake of appearances, but the driver quickly retreated to two and a half. Peach, not much interested in either quote, agreed.

Although Gaborone was the capital city of Botswana, few of the streets were paved. The highway from the airport was one of those few, but it was apparent that any infrastructure that required government money not directly related to mining or manufacturing was spent grudgingly. Dust from constant desert winds flowing along the Tropic of Capricorn painted everything with a dull coat of grime. Most of the black working population tended cattle—the country's leading commodity after nickel, manganese, and chromium ores—the herds mostly owned by joint families of the same tribe. Goats or sheep were second and third among livestock following beef and dairy cattle, and they mingled among chickens, all with noses and eyes close to the ground scrounging for anything edible.

Botswana was landlocked and suffered for millennia from a scarcity of water. What small rivers and large ponds served the population also provided breeding grounds for all description of bacteria and viruses, including malaria and Hepatitis A and B, the B strain hyper-endemic to the state. Peach and the others knew, from a fast but efficient briefing by one of the South African policemen who traveled frequently to Botswana, that most forms of food served in hotels of the city were safe to eat, but that one should avoid street vendors at all costs and never drink any water that did not flow from a city spigot. And never, under any circumstances, swim in Botswana's rivers or lakes lest one became included in the national statistics that showed forty as the average age of death.

Their cab driver stopped in front of the Imperial Hotel, an aging monument to the past British empire. It had a massive portico entrance with eight white Doric columns supporting a wide architrave, below which were four mahogany doors with huge polished brass latchings. The Imperial Hotel was a six-story white wooden building, which to the eye of a romantic, would have been mouth-watering. But Peach made a mental note to insist on a ground-floor room which was easier to exit during fire. He could feel Melissa smile even before he looked her way. As they walked across the thinning crimson carpet in the cavernous main lobby, she marveled at the care the owners had placed in the hotel's maintenance. Paint was lavishly used as protection against a ravishing sun and abrasive, wind-driven desert sands.

Constructed near the turn of the twentieth century, the hotel's rustic interior would not disappoint an afficionado of Victorian Britannia. Period furnishings in the lobby had not fared as well as the rest of the building, but the owners had made an effort to keep it all reasonably upholstered and replaced with complimenting pieces when necessary. Doors leading into the large dining area, as well as those going to a bar and lounge, were paned French glass.

"Shall I get one room or two, darling?" Peach asked in a perfectly clear voice as the day manager waited their registration.

Melissa regarded Peach for several moments, then said, "I'm over my hay fever, I think, Peach. Of course I might still snore."

"Your snoring has never kept me awake in my life," Peach said, then turned to write the name of P.R. Diehl—mister and misses—onto a registration card. All of the Green Solitaire team members had access to genuine passports and identification certificates—drivers licenses, credit cards, library cards, and other pedestrian items that anyone might carry—should there be a need to travel clandestinely. These documents were kept in a secure metal attaché case signed for and maintained by Getts.

"We want the best room in the hotel—on the first floor, that is," Peach said.

"But of course. We have a suite that I think the lady will find very comfortable. You may look at it first, indeed," the clerk beamed.

"No need," Melissa said. "I like surprises."

"Passports, please," the clerk said, bowing his head in apology for having to ask.

Peach reached into his pocket and produced his passport. Before handing it to the clerk, however, he inserted a $20.00 bill. "My wife lost hers when we were on safari. Won't be a problem, will it?"

The clerk's eyebrows raised and he exposed a set of healthy teeth and gums. "Of course it's no problem, sir. We understand. Room 1012. I will have a boy help you with your—bag," the clerk added, looking over the counter at Peach's single but large duffle bag.

"Tell you what, here's a dollar tip for the boy and I'll carry my own bag," Peach said, taking the key from the clerk's hand. Peach and the other SEALs usually carried American dollars as well as the local currency—in this case the Botswana pula and the South African rand.

"By the way," Melissa said to the clerk, "Peach and I met a very nice man in Rome who asked us to look him up when we got here but I can't think of his name. Oh, it's so embarrassing. Darling, do you still have his card?"

"No. I thought you had it," Peach said, playing along.

"Well," she said to the concierge, "he was Russian. He tells wonderful stories at a party. Tall, dark hair . . ." Melissa paused to give the desk man a chance to think.

"Forgive me," the clerk said. "I do not know the gentleman."

"Well, let us know if you see him, will you?" Peach said, turning toward a door leading off the lobby.

"Lunch is served between twelve and three o'clock," the clerk called out to his newest guests' retreating backs, but they did not seem interested in food.

They had no trouble finding their room. The door opened into a large enough living room, which contained two overstuffed sofas facing each other across a central coffee table. A window was located directly across the room from the door and it was sufficiently large to let in all of the light needed for either day or night. It was curtained with heavy, sun-resistant material with beige velveteen coverings atop. There was a bar in the living area, Peach noticed, but investigation proved that it contained no liquors of any kind, and no faucet was provided for water.

There were two bedrooms—with doors attached—each of which contained a double bed. Peach and Melissa made eye contact but looked away without comment. Melissa opened the window drapes and looked out over part of the city of 150,000 people, which simmered during the heat of the middle of the day. Most of the build-

ings in town were made of a kind of adobe covered with
heavy whitewash, not unattractive for the geography,
Melissa thought. She could see two other distant buildings, which were unmistakably hotels of some kind, and
she wondered why their driver had chosen this hotel to
bring them rather than any of the others. It did not occur
to her that the driver was no doubt paid for each of his
fares who registered at the Imperial Hotel. Instead, she
was grateful that the cab driver discerned that she—and
maybe even Peach—would find the place quaint.

"Last case scenario," Peach said as Melissa splashed
water on her face from a bathroom basin, "is that I go to
the police station and ask questions about a Russian who
got busted for a hit and run. I don't want to do that but if
everything else fails . . ." He shrugged.

"If it comes to that, I'll go ask the police. I can claim
to be an angry mistress or something," she suggested,
wiping her face. She wore little makeup; a touch of red
for her lips, a bit of coloring on her eyebrows. Peach had
thought that she used mascara but upon closer view he
could see that her green eyes and dark lashes needed no
help. Peach noticed that Melissa had removed some of
the jewelry that she had been wearing when he first met
her on the road to Elizabeth. Then she wore four rings, including two that were large gems, an expensive watch, a
diamond broach, and a gold bracelet. Apparently she became aware of what that kind of walking treasure meant
to a population of have-nots, because on the current trip
she wore a relatively inexpensive watch, no bracelets,
one ring and plain earrings. No more than any European
and American would display on an African tour.

Ed Knowles, Maury Fletcher, and Arthur Carlin registered an hour later. Knowles's passport listed his name as
Edward Rollo. They listed their occupations as engineers

and paid three days in advance in South African rand. After routinely checking for ways into and out of their rooms in the event of emergencies, they also scanned for listening devices, tested locks on the doors, and retrieved the weapons from their bags. One by one they discreetly assembled in Peach's room.

"I don't see Boris changing his drinking habits just because he happened to run over a couple people here in town. So we're going to check every bar in town." Peach produced a street map and photocopies, which he handed to each man and Melissa. "It isn't the biggest place in the world, so we'll divide it into two teams. We can forget most of the city because it's pretty much a shithole that Boris wouldn't hang out in anyway, so we'll look at the high-rent districts first. All the hotels, restaurants and bars. We don't have com out here unless we wear harnesses, and that ain't going to cut it," Peach said, referring to assault transceivers worn under balaclava face masks. Nor did they have microwave receivers for cell phones. Peach carried a TS-300 scrambled satellite telephone that would keep the team in touch with Getts—or if need be, Washington—but it was the size of an attaché case, weighed twenty-eight pounds, and would only attract attention if used in public, so it would be left at the hotel.

"We're going to have to use the local phone system. Eddie, you work with Fletcher. Arthur will stay with us— but you don't know us. Got it, Arthur?"

"Right on, Peachie," the Englishman said, eliciting a grin from Peach. He would provide backup for them in case of a threat, but would not position himself close enough to give the game away.

"Call the Imperial Hotel if you make contact. Tell the concierge that you would like to meet Mr. Rollo here, in the bar, at whatever hour you say. Melissa or I will check for messages all day and night. If we find Boris, we'll leave the same message for you. In any case we'll meet back here at 2400 hours. Questions?" Peach asked.

Maury Fletcher spoke. "Any way to communicate if we need help?"

"Not unless you can think of one," Peach said.

"I'm not going to be arrested here," Fletcher said, calmly but firmly.

"Understand," Peach said. "Either way, we may not be able to pull you out. Or you us. Want out now?"

"Not me. I'm just tellin' *you* what happens to *them* if they try to take me down, mate," the Royal Marine said.

After a moment of mutual consideration, Arthur Carlin said, "My duty is to the princess."

"We know where your first duty goes," Peach said.

"No, it is to the group, here, Arthur," Melissa interjected, her chin rising. "I don't hold that my safety transcends group integrity."

"My lady . . ." the bodyguard began.

"I am one-fifth of a single unit," Melissa said, eyeing Arthur sternly. "That is an order."

"Yes, ma'am," Arthur said, solemnly and proudly.

"The encrypted software goes out on the Internet at 1200 hours local time. We need to locate Boris before then," Peach said. "All right. Let's hit this town and do it hard."

Each man took from his baggage the weapons he might need on the street. Heavier ordnance remained behind in the suite.

When Ronald Mauser was allowed to return to his wife his clothes were torn, blood staining his shirt and jacket in several places. His left cheek was lacerated under one eye. He walked stooped at the waist, his right arm clutching his ribs. Dorothy rushed to his side and helped him gently to the ground, first removing his jacket then rolling it for a pillow to place under his head. "That filthy animal!" she seethed. "Oh, God, Ron, what did he do to you?"

Ronald forced a thin smile. "Nothing. I've had worse fights when I was a kid." He patted her hands. "Really, darling, I'll be just fine in a few minutes. Wind knocked out of me, that's all." He stilled her probing fingers, resisting her attempts to locate sources of leaking blood. There was no medication to treat his injuries, anyway, and they both knew it.

She rose from his side, found Walter Felinda and, facing him, cursed him roundly and demanded water for her husband so that she might clean his wounds. Surprisingly, Felinda did not strike or berate her. He merely nodded to a subordinate and turned his back on her. She got the water without protest.

Despite the early hour, they searched every bar for the Russian. Some they merely stuck their heads into—the crummiest, black-only bars—while more upscale locales received more of their attention. They would order a drink, look around at the clientele, and always ask the bartenders if their new friend, Boris, had arrived in town.

Melissa, insisting she would attract less suspicion than a man, visited the local police headquarters and spoke with a desk sergeant. A plainclothed officer was called from a rear room when Melissa invoked the name of Boris Eveshenko. Melissa told the detective—if that's what he was—that her girlfriend in England had tried to call Boris here in Gaborone, but his number had changed. Since she was traveling through with friends, Melissa thought she might look him up.

Melissa had made the amateur's mistake of trying to sell a complex story. The cop was not buying. And it was

Melissa of whom the police became suspicious. She was
required to produce her passport. She flashed Wanda
Layden's documents which passed the detective's
scrutiny. She was questioned about how she had arrived
in Gaborone, with whom, and why. She felt increasingly
helpless, vulnerable, and alone as she strained to keep her
stories straight, even while realizing that the backwater
policeman from Botswana was not the most sophisticated
interrogator in the world. She could feel herself perspiring, her hands wet and clammy. In desperation she remembered the advice given to her by Bobby Getts, who
had told them to extract oneself from problems with
money if possible.

She dug into her fabric purse and removed a handful
of rand notes and thrust them at the menacing policeman
in front of her. She apologized for taking up official police time on a matter of only personal interest, she said.
She was quite thoughtless. She hoped that the banknotes
would serve to excuse her. And if, by chance, the officer
should happen to run into Boris again, he might call her
at the Imperial Hotel.

Without counting the bills, the policeman nodded his
head reluctantly. He grunted toward the door, indicating
that Melissa was free to go. She reached for the passport
on his desk and tried not to run as she fled the building.

Eddie found one of three auto repair shops around
town that had repaired a Mercedes automobile within
days of Boris's killing the mother and child at a bus stop.
The repair shop manager no longer worked there but one
of the employees, for the price of what was probably a
month's labor, told him that the car was brought into the
shop by a man who was not from the city, and was picked
up and paid for by the same man. He was black, the repair
man said, and he carried a gun. The repair man thought
the man was a policeman, but not from Botswana.

From where, then? The workman shrugged. South Africa, he thought.

The five of them had all walked the downtown area of Gaborone twice, through the main market square, over dusty roads, appearing as inquisitive tourists. They had hired taxis to "sightsee" the entirety of the town, making short work of the more degraded living areas, reasoning that Boris would not live or labor in these slum conditions. They concentrated instead on the upscale residential neighborhoods that offered gated protection for high government employees, mine and factory supervisors, and the like.

They found women digging ditches, kiosks in the marketplace selling tourist curios as well as food. The train station, with its corrugated roof and iron pipe frame, provided relief from the sun during daylight hours and attracted masses of insects to its fluorescent overhead lights. Peach doubted that Boris would leave town by train, anyway. After learning that Felinda had succeeded in getting the missile guidance code posted, he would probably want to leave town as quickly as possible.

It was almost midnight when Melissa pointed out to Peach that they had not eaten since that morning when they were still in the SEAL HQ at the Salisbury mine. Peach was keen, alert, and wound up tight. He wanted action but it was eluding him. He did not want to stop the hunt—and could not—but he also needed to think. It was almost time to rendezvous with the others. "Maybe we can scare up some food at the hotel," he said.

The interior of the Elephant Bar at the Imperial Hotel might have been decorated by someone who had worked for Trader Vic's; lots of bamboo masks—probably made in China from wood or plastic—and painted in bright, uniform colors. Bows, arrows, and spears were fastened to the walls and photographs of big-game safaris were plentifully allocated for each wall and tacked across the wall behind the bar. A mindless mix of salsa and jazz on a tape, worn so that it alternately faded and surged in the background noise of conversation, the clattering air conditioning unit, and the buzzing electric insect killers that had long ago lost the battle. The bartender's name was Trami, according to the plastic pin tag on his shirt. It was a different man than the one Peach and Melissa had queried the previous midday.

Trami served drinks to three other men who occupied bar stools, and dispensed orders to a cocktail waitress who moved among another dozen patrons who sat at tables. Peach ordered a beer and was surprised when Melissa asked for Irish whiskey. Peach tipped the girl two dollars in advance and said that they were hungry and wanted to eat. The cook would be on duty for two more hours, the waitress said, but the demand for dinner was great and she was not sure what was left. Melissa informed her that she didn't care what they ate and that she should just bring whatever was available. And would she ask Trami to bring their drinks?

"We're looking for an old friend who may be in town," Melissa said to Trami when he arrived at their table, forgetting their cover story that they had only recently met the Russian, "and we wondered if he had been in here recently. His name is Boris. He's Russian. Tall man, like Peach, here, but thinner."

The bartender pursed his lips and shook his head slowly. "No. Do not know him." Trami's eyes arched to the top of his head as though there was more to say but, after a moment, turned on his heel and went back to the bar.

"Have I been excess baggage on this mission?" Melissa asked Peach.

He regarded her for a long minute. "Yeah. If we didn't

have to drag you around we could have put the arm on somebody by now. Stuck a gun up their asses and pulled some triggers. We'd have got some answers, then. Know what I mean?" Peach put the bottle of beer to his mouth and inhaled half of its contents.

Melissa's eyes went wide open, her mouth falling agape, her hand holding the neat whiskey returning to the tabletop. "Well," she said. "I dare say that I . . ." She then realized that her leg was being pulled. "Oh, hell, Peach, you don't really think I let our side down, do you?"

"No. You're terrific," he said, absently picking the label off of his beer bottle.

Melissa drank from her own glass, enjoying the burning sensation of the Irish whiskey, but her eyes fixed on Peach, not yet convinced that he wasn't yet again putting her on. "You're not just saying that?" she said.

"Matter of fact we've got an exercise scheduled next month in Belize. We're going to lock out of a sub and do some underwater work. You're welcome to join the crew," he said.

"Well, that's very kind of you. And I do enjoy a swim. I'll give it some thought," she said.

Now it was Peach who was not sure who was pulling whose leg.

Dinner arrived. On a large single plate were overcooked yams, pocket bread, a broiled meat of some kind, cheese, mushrooms, and hummus. They ordered red wine and were served a surprisingly tasty bottle from the Stellenbosch region. They had scarcely gotten into their late-night snack before a second bottle was required. "Well, it tastes better than water. Anything does," Peach said as he gulped it down.

"You don't like water?" Melissa said, clearly surprised.

"Nope. No taste. I drink it only when there's nothing else left. Better lay off the cheese," he said.

"Have you tried it?" Melissa wanted to know. "It's goat, of course, but it's tart and very good."

Peach shrugged. "Suit yourself. Stay away from the mushrooms, too."

"You think they might be poisonous?" she asked.

"Possible. But even if they're not, there isn't any food value in a mushroom. Nada," he said, emphatically.

Peach motioned to the waitress.

"More wine?" Melissa said.

"Paying the bill. We're still working," Peach said.

"God, you're not going to get some sleep?"

When the waitress arrived Peach asked her about a tall Russian named Boris.

"Yes," the waitress said as she placed the drinks on the table, "I know him. He drinks vodka." The waitress tried to smother a chuckle, but said, "Bad, very bad kind. Cheap, you know." The grin remained on her face.

At that moment Trami arrived with his tally from the bar.

"I thought you said you didn't know Boris?" Peach said, careful not to frighten the small man.

"His name is not Boris," Trami said, holding out his hands, palms up.

"Yes," the waitress said. "Not Boris. His name is Geary. He says that it is. Russian, anyway."

"Where can we find him?" Peach said, producing more cash from his pocket.

Trami and the waitress exchanged looks, then shrugged.

"He comes in here, though?" Melissa said, trying to shake the effects of the wine from her head.

"Yes," Trami said, "but not tonight. Ah, he lives . . ." The bartender closed his eyes trying to think. "In a house with another man. Maybe two other men, there." Trami pointed vaguely in a southern direction. It was the "affluent" section of the town.

"Just two men? Do they come here together?" Peach wanted to know.

"Hmm. Not always same men," Trami said, thinking hard. "Sometime two others. Always somebody with him."

"Do you know the name of the street?" Peach said.

Trami made sure he had pocketed the cash Peach offered before shaking his head in the negative, then he left. Peach made sure that the waitress received her fair share of compensation for confirming that the Russian was in this town by leaving her a generous tip, as well.

Minutes later the rest of the detachment arrived. They only made eye contact, then exited the bar to meet in Peach and Melissa's first floor suite.

Peach was pacing the floor at 0200 hours local time. "He would need a modem. Not hard to get," he said. "Two phone lines, at least two computers."

"Yes," Arthur agreed, seated on the overstuffed chair in a far corner of the living room. "One to do the decrypting, another for downloading and analysis."

"So?" Melissa said, placing her hand on her forehead. She felt uncomfortably warm in the room. She turned up the control of the inset air-conditioning machine. The others paused in their conversation as she crossed the room in front of them. She appeared to be somewhat distracted, a fine sheen of sweat now covering her face.

"Are you all right, ma'am?" Arthur asked.

"Yes, of course. Too much grape, that's all," she said, sitting again.

"So," Arthur said, continuing his line of thought, "if I had as much at stake as Boris has, assuming he's connected to this criminal enterprise, I wouldn't want to rely upon the local telephones here in Botswana. Has anybody tried them lately?"

Everyone agreed that telephone service in the country was at best problematic. Nor, for that matter, was electrical power all that consistent.

"So I think we should look for a receiver," he said.

"He'll want one with reliability," Peach said, nodding his head vigorously. "A satellite telephone."

"With a generator running in the background?" Eddie Knowles asked.

"That would damn well nail it down," Peach said.

"So let's look," Arthur said. "The neighborhood isn't that big."

And it wasn't. "The village," as the locals referred to Gaborone's elite dwellings, encompassed an area of about two square miles, involving approximately a dozen streets.

Pete Dekins and Bobby Getts were not asleep but were sitting with their alpha brain waves at low power at 0215 local time when the WHCA line buzzed. "Dekins," the army general answered into the mouthpiece. After identifying himself and stating that he was in the company of Captain Getts he was asked to wait while David Magazine came on the line.

"How's it going, Pete?" the NSC advisor said into the scrambled instrument. Magazine had, of course, been briefed on their plan to locate Boris Eveshenko in Botswana and, if possible, to turn him.

"We just talked to Peach," Dekins said. "They know the subject is in town but they don't know exactly where. They're going out on a recce as we speak with a better than even chance of finding the man tonight."

"Can you reach them right now?" Magazine demanded.

"Maybe." Dekins's senses—and Getts's—suddenly sharpened.

"Call 'em and tell them to stand down."

Getts, listening in, reached for the TS-300 and quickly punched in the correct digits. He could hear the TS-300 at the other end ringing.

"Captain Getts is calling them now. What's up?" Dekins asked the NSC chief.

"Couple arguments going on here. First one is, the NSA code mavens are saying that nobody is going to find out they've scrammed the codes until the guidance system is put into the missile and fired. In argument one, if the NSA people are right, the Ts get fooled and let our people go. That's how they think it will go down. But the other side of the argument is that this guy Eveshenko isn't chopped liver and the bad guys wouldn't bother having him in the game if he can't tell the difference between a ball and a strike. So if you lay hands on him and he doesn't roll over for us, they kill the hostages. Got the picture?"

"Understand," Dekins said as he turned toward Getts, who was holding a telephone to each ear.

"Peach?" Getts said into the second phone, "Bobby. All your people with you?" After a pause Getts simply said, "Stand by."

Getts nodded to Dekins. "They were just walking out the door when we caught 'em."

"All right," Dekins said to Magazine in Washington. "We called them back. What's next?"

"We wait," Magazine said.

"How long?"

Dekins could hear a long sigh escape from the NSC advisor. "The code went out a couple hours ago. Your

Russian is probably working on it now. I guess we wait until he comes up with a yea or nay."

Dekins remained silent for what seemed to be several minutes before he spoke again. "I don't like that decision. I think we should take him out now. Tonight. I like our chances that we can turn the son of a bitch."

"The president has made his decision," Magazine said.

"They'll kill the hostages," Dekins said.

"Maybe not."

"I want a finding by the president with his signature. Send it by fax," Dekins said.

"Sorry," Magazine said, "can't do that."

"Yes, sir, so am I," Dekins said and replaced the phone in its cradle.

While Getts was explaining the stand-down order to Peach, Dekins scribbled with an ink pen on a piece of notebook paper. At its end he dated it and signed it, then passed it to Getts. Getts scanned the paper but pushed it back toward Dekins. It was an official order from Dekins to Getts ordering him to have his men stand down from the apprehension or interference of one Boris Eveshenko in the conduct of his affairs, whatever they may be and however hostile to the interests of the United States of America.

"I don't need this," Getts said.

"Put it in your dispatch bag. If this bastard operation goes the way I think it's going to go, you could get your ass chopped off. They're setting us up for it," Dekins said.

Getts wordlessly tore up the order.

"Don't give me any of this 'we're in this together' shit, Getts. I'll need a character witness at my court-martial and I don't want the prosecutor to find out how dumb you really are," Dekins said.

Chapter Six

It was Bradley Wallis's first visit to the private dining room of Goldman Sachs. A nearer office to the H. P. Carlisle Foundation would have been on Pennsylvania Avenue in Washington, D.C., but Leon Manton's office was located at the firm's original location in New York. While Bradley stretched his legs out on the Persian rug in the foyer of the dining room, he noted with interest some of the artwork on the walls. There were oils of several varieties, including a portrait of Marcus Goldman, who founded the firm in 1869. There were several lesser-known paintings by well known masters such as Degas, van Gogh, and Lefrait. A company with a recent third-quarter net earnings of $638 million on assets of $29 billion could afford to squeeze a bit of art into its budget. Wallis leaned forward to study "The Ailing Pig" by Lefrait when he heard a familiar voice behind him.

"I should have known you've kept up your interest in art forgeries, Bradley."

Wallis turned to view a man several inches taller than his own five feet nine inches. Leon Manton's once thick, tightly curled brown hair had thinned considerably since Wallis had seen him last, leaving only a fringe above the ears. The broken cartilage in Manton's nose expanded a bit, lending the man behind the visage of a one-time pugilist. Wallis noted with shared pride that Manton's

midsection was still lean, his body athletic as he moved
lightly on the balls of his feet. Leon Manton was, by Wallis's attempt to estimate, in his seventies. And the mind
behind the fighter's nose did, indeed, fear no peer.

"Leon," Wallis said, taking Manton's extended hand,
"how wonderful you look. God, I feel virtually bed-
ridden standing here next to you."

"You look good too, Bradley. You still work out every
day?"

It was true that Wallis was careful about his diet and
made a point to walk at least two miles a day, but he had
long ago lost his love of violent exercise. "I still keep my
black belt current. Tournaments, you know."

Manton's face suddenly sobered. "Good grief, I had no
idea you were a martial arts expert! And still at it? What
kind of belt, Bradley?"

"The kind that holds up my trousers. I was fifty years
old before I realized that a karate chop wasn't a cut of
meat," Wallis deadpanned.

Manton threw his head back and laughed heartily as he
put his arm around Wallis's shoulders. "I haven't seen
you in thirty years and just realized how much I've
missed you. Come on, Bradley, let's have something to
eat and catch up."

Neither man ordered a drink before their meal but, at
Manton's urging, enjoyed a glass of red French estate
wine with their food. They had been seated at a quiet window table at 1:30 and by 2:45 almost everyone had left
the room except the two of them, each sipping Spanish
cognac and reliving the Cold War.

"But you retired before our side won," Wallis was saying.

"Quit," Manton corrected.

"I thought you were a career man. Right out of college
and into the service."

"Not directly. I came here first. I had four years of German and French at Penn State figuring to get into international finance—more just to get in on the free travel, I think—and applied here." Manton rolled his eyes skyward for a moment at the memory. "I was twenty-six and living in Berlin when I was asked to take on another line of work."

"Full time?" Wallis asked.

"No," Manton laughed again. "In addition. I never slept. Looking back on it now, I lost the woman I loved most in life because I couldn't find time to take her out."

"Who?" Wallis asked out of curiosity.

"Her name was Gerry Owens. You didn't know her," Manton said, leaning back in his chair.

"She married someone else?" Wallis said.

"A school teacher. The great sorrow out of a life of very few regrets. Ah, well. And how is Hildy? Well, I hope?" Manton said.

"Passed away twelve years ago. Cancer," Wallis said, concealing any trace of the heartsick loss he still experienced at the mention of her name.

"Sorry to hear that, Bradley," Manton said meaningfully. The tall investment banker swirled the remaining cognac in his glass for a moment, then lifted his eyes to meet his old friend's. "So, I know you love me and miss me, but I sense that you need something besides a bowl of French onion soup."

"I'm with a research organization in Virginia that caters to a specialized customer," Wallis began, trying not to sound portentous but unwilling to disclose too much.

"The H. P. Carlisle Foundation," Manton interjected smoothly.

"Yes. How did you know?" Wallis said, intrigued.

"Your major customer is the government of the United States of America and several of its more exotic intelligence gathering agencies. Like the NRO, for example," Manton said, leaning back in his chair as he watched Wallis's face change from surprise to amazement to apprehension.

"This isn't exactly fair, Leon. I thought you were out of the game," Wallis sputtered.

"I am. Do you think civilians aren't connected? The government doesn't exist in a vacuum, old pal," Manton said, clearly enjoying himself.

Wallis lowered his voice as he leaned over the table nearer the tall businessman.

"What you know about me is . . . well, Leon, very secret. I must say that I—"

Manton reached across the table and, touching his friend's forearm, lowered his own voice for theatrical affect. "I have no secret information, Bradley. The H. P. Carlisle Foundation is in the public telephone directory. I merely guessed that if you were still a spook, so was the Carlisle Foundation, and if it was, one of the agencies you might work with or for was the NRO. It was a guess."

Manton watched with continued amusement as Wallis's pallor turned from gray to crimson. "If you were being interrogated by the other side, you would be on your way to a firing squad before you finished your drink." Then Manton's face sobered. "All right, Bradley. I'm sorry for that silly joke. Tell me what I can do for you. Please."

Thoroughly relieved to be off the hook, Wallis downed the rest of his cognac but allowed his voice to remain subdued as he spoke. "The country is in a hostage crisis."

"South Africa," Manton said crisply. "It's all over the news."

"Exactly. The kidnappers are asking a ransom that is

substantial. A military secret's involved. I'm afraid I can't tell you exactly what it is."

Manton waved a hand in the air, dismissing his need for that detail.

"But the terrorist's enterprise is large, a very expensive operation. There has to be an additional payoff to these people in money. Dollars, francs, deutschmarks. Something. And in large quantity. We also believe the money may be paid by various third-world governments, nations sympathetic to, shall we say, terrorist activities. That could be half the nations on earth, of course."

"Some more than others," Manton interjected.

"Of course. It seemed to me that you—or Goldman Sachs—might put an ear to the ground for us. Moving money is, after all, your business," Wallis suggested.

"Hmm. We're not the only people who watch cash flow around the world. And, frankly, what you might perceive to be big money is hardly a fraction of the electronic funds that circle the globe in twenty-four hours. It's damn like looking for the proverbial needle, Bradley."

Wallis leaned back in his chair, falling silent.

"Still," Manton said, reflecting again, "I do the *New York Times* crossword puzzle every morning."

Wallis opened his eyes wide in question.

"I sometimes—right in the middle of the thing—ask myself why I'm addicted. The answer is that I don't know why I'm addicted because if I knew the answer to that, I could get alcoholics off the sauce and get my sister to kick her forty-year cigarette habit. I do the crosswords because I enjoy it. Just like I enjoy helping you. When do you need a response?" Manton asked.

"I think you know we're racing the clock," Wallis said.

"And those people down in the mine are going to die. You know that, don't you, Bradley?"

*   *   *

That night Melissa was sick. It was in the early morning hours that she collapsed to the floor as she staggered
toward the bathroom in their suite, her stomach erupting
its contents onto the carpeted floor. By the time Peach
picked her up and carried her to the edge of the toilet
more bilious material, including the evening meal, passed
back through the route it originally went down. It could
have been anything in the food, Peach knew, and he was
not surprised that the offending bacteria affected Melissa
and not him. He had virtually every immunization known
to man, while it was likely that Melissa had not. He used
two full-size bath towels to clean up the vomit on the
rugs, after which he washed the towels thoroughly and
used them again to scrub the stain on the rugs, then
washed the towels yet again.

When it seemed Melissa had regurgitated everything
from her insides, he cleaned her face and hands with a
dampened washcloth, carried her into her bedroom, and
laid her carefully on the bed. He rinsed off the toilet bowl
and cursed himself for not bringing one of the SEAL
medical kits with him.

Melissa had been sweating, and she stifled moans of
cramping pain, so Peach removed her well-soiled khaki
blouse. Underneath she was wearing a black bra that she
completely filled out. He looked at her for an extended
moment, debating whether respect for modesty was a legitimate trade-off for medical requirements. Postponing
that decision, he unfastened her fabric woven belt, and
unzipped her trousers. As he moved to her feet and
began to pull them down, he was struck by Melissa's
well-maintained legs, a perfect match to her small waist
and ample breasts. He considered removing her black
panties—a lacy match to her bra—but realized that
doing so would have served no other purpose than to

provide pleasure for himself. Instead he threw back the bed covers and pulled only the sheet over her.

Melissa grunted something that was unmistakably a thanks, but she was hurting too badly to make a real presentation of it. Peach wrung out a fresh washcloth with cool water and began to slowly wipe her face, head, neck, and back. Melissa moved her hand to touch one of his. He easily enfolded hers in his, squeezed it, and sat quietly on the edge of the bed.

In the next hour Melissa made two more trips to the bathroom to sprawl over the edge of the toilet, but each time nothing came up. He was there each time to help her back to the bed, wiping her face and her arms with a cool, damp cloth. Peach was certain that Melissa was suffering from nothing worse than food poisoning, and that her discomfort was aggravated by liquor and exhaustion. But he acknowledged to himself that if she did not improve dramatically in the next couple of hours, he would call Getts and have the skipper choose a safe doctor to rush to her side.

When daylight arrived, Melissa was sleeping soundly, sans her bra which HRH had removed herself during a lucid moment during the night. Peach was still at her side, awake, and he did not close his eyes while she performed the strip. Then her head fell back onto the pillow and she fell asleep once again. Peach personally delivered her soiled clothing to the services desk and told the head of housekeeping—an eager-to-please young man—that the clothes needed to be personally tended, cleaned, ironed, and delivered to the room within two hours. And gave the man a generous tip.

Peach then called his men together for a meeting in Eddie's room where the portent of Getts's stand-down order was discussed. The two sides to the issue of whether to take Boris down, or allow him to analyze the guidance system code in the hopes that he would miss the intentional errors built into it by the NSA, was clearly understood by everyone in the room. But no one, not even the two British servicemen, was under any illusion about what would happen to the hostages if and when the ruse was discovered. Peach and the others would, until further orders from Getts, continue to gather and refine intelligence about Eveshenko and his bodyguards.

"Arthur," Peach said to HRH's official protector when the meeting was completed, "Melissa's sick. I think it's only an upset stomach from something she ate, and she's asleep right now. For security reasons I don't want to call a doctor from around here, or anywhere else, unless I have to. But I'll do it if she isn't better real quick. Trust me on this one?"

Arthur's first reaction to Peach's news—a look of alarm—was replaced with thoughtful concern. "Stomach pains, you say?"

"Yeah. She puked her insides out a while ago. Like I say, I'm pretty sure it was something she ate. Nothing like appendicitis."

Arthur nodded. He respected the commando's lay assessment of the princess's medical condition as an informed one. "I'm sure you are as concerned with her continued good health as I am. You'll keep me closely informed?"

"I promise," Peach said.

"I should also tell you," Arthur said, his demeanor quite weighty, "that I am aware that Her Highness's, ahem, room arrangement here is dictated by the covert nature of our mission, and that the royal family would not be pleased if such sleeping arrangements were made for any other, ah, reason."

"Want me to tell her that?" Peach wanted to know.

"Not necessary, Peach. I know my duty. That's all."

"Right on, old top," Peach said without a smile.

When he returned to their room Melissa was still sound asleep. She was no longer sweating and seemed to be resting comfortably. He could have left her alone without worry but decided to spend some time nearby, anyway. He removed his bush boots and stretched out on the sofa in the living room and closed his eyes.

Early morning was spent locating the house in which Boris Eveshenko was residing and, presumably, doing his work. It turned out to be a four bedroom, two bath house on Safari Street, the last address on the end of the block. The discovery was a no-brainer for Eddie Knowles and Maury Fletcher, who drove a rented car around the village until they spotted the two new, oversized microwave receivers fixed to the roof of the house. To make sure, they surveilled the location from both the front and back of the house. A number of what Eddie believed were security personnel—five of them—departed and returned to the residence before noon. Eveshenko himself left the house at about 1600 hours, and walked around the neighborhood in the company of two security men who tried to act casual as they trailed behind. He walked for approximately thirty-five minutes, after which he returned to the house, still accompanied by his security detail.

For the balance of the day Eddie and Maury, later joined by Arthur, kept a surveillance on Eveshenko's residence from a discreet distance. They continued to note who came and went, choosing to remain afar until night fell and they would be able to perform a much closer inspection in an environment in which they were most effective: the black of night.

Getts traveled to Pretoria in a rented civilian car. With him were Snake and Dean. The three wore camo uniforms, Getts having decided that khaki attire might seem too formal. He wanted to keep the retrieval of their prisoner as low key as possible. All three wore 9mm HKs in shoulder holsters. Snake and Dean stashed AR-18s with extra ammo in the trunk of the car just in case.

At the headquarters for state security police, Getts made his request for the prisoner named Jku, taken into custody by General Boord two nights earlier. The OIC, a white uniformed captain by the name of Kleider, informed Getts that no such prisoner had been registered in the past two days. After checking his computer files once more at Getts's request, Captain Kleider still came up empty. Getts requested an interview with General Boord.

"I am sorry, Captain Getts," Kleider said, "but I am unable to make that arrangement for you. Perhaps if you write a letter—"

"I don't write letters," Getts snapped. "Get the general on the phone. Right now."

Kleider's face set into concrete. "The general does not wish to speak with you, Captain Getts."

"How do you know that?" Getts demanded.

"Because those are his orders." The Afrikaaner gritted his teeth.

"He's already given the orders, eh? Because he knew I'd come because he had my prisoner. Isn't that right, Kleider?"

The security officer turned crimson, caught in his own snare. "Good day, Captain," he said to Getts.

But Getts had something to add before leaving the premises. "I've got a message for General Johannes Boord and it comes from Captain Getts of the United States Navy. Tell that faggot son of a bitch you work for that I'm not going to send him a Christmas card this year."

Getts turned on his heel.

Before he had reached the exit door in the lobby of the building, Getts was stopped by a uniformed guard who politely asked if he would be kind enough to wait for General Boord. Always suspicious, Getts was glad he had brought fire support, outgunned though they would be. The South African general would not dare risk a fire fight in his own headquarters if it could be avoided. Would he?

Getts had waited near the massive glass door, per request, for less than a minute when an elevator door opened. Out stepped General Boord, in full bemedaled uniform and accompanied by a single staff officer. Getts glanced quickly around for hidden threats.

"Captain Getts," Boord said cordially, but not extending his hand. "I was just now informed that you were here."

"Doesn't matter, General. I got the message you left with your flunkie downstairs."

"I think there has been a mistake. Of course I expected you to come for that man—what was his name? Jku? But I could have saved you a trip. I have all his information for you."

"That so?" Getts said, surprised at Boord's matter-of-fact cordiality.

"Yes. We questioned Jku. That is, one of our interrogators did. But he knew nothing of any value to us. We even offered him bribes." Boord laughed. "I was pleasantly surprised that the young man was so cooperative with us after that. Well, I suppose he surprised you, too, when you questioned him first."

"He wasn't candid," Getts said. "Not at first, anyway."

"Exactly. In any case, we sent him on his way. The old bus ticket home. He was damn happy to see the last of us. And of you, too, he said."

Getts thought this was probably true. A youngster in

search of adventure learns the truth when the tide of blood rises to his ankles. "Where does he live?"

General Boord turned to his staff officer, hand out. The junior officer immediately produced a manilla envelope and placed it into Boord's hand. Boord, in turn, handed it to Getts. "It's all in there. His full name, his tribe—Tutsi, his village in Burundi, even his family name. His mother is still living. I've included a synopsis of what little information he gave us, useless as it is. You're welcome to it. And I want you to call if I can help you any further."

Getts could not think of anything more that he could have wanted. "He was in good health when you let him go?"

"Indeed. In fact he was almost flippant as he boarded the bus. He insulted one of my escort sergeants," Boord said, a tight smile on his face.

"Okay. I guess that does it," Getts said.

As he passed through the great entrance door and descended the steps to his waiting car, General Boord called out: "Captain Getts."

Getts turned.

"Please don't take me off your Christmas card list. I'm afraid it would ruin my holidays." The general laughed aloud.

At 2200 hours, Eddie and Maury were surprised when Boris came out of his house and opened the attached garage door. One of the men assigned to protect Boris followed the Russian and for a few moments the two men engaged in animated conversation, their voices rising as they exchanged heated dialogue, apparently over who was going to drive the car. The bodyguard seemed to win the argument, sliding behind the wheel. The driver started the engine but did not put the car in drive until three more men joined them, taking places in the rear seat. Eddie and

Maury followed at a safe distance as the Russian's car drove less than two miles into the heart of Gaborone. The car parked in a location near the Imperial Hotel. Boris Eveshenko stepped out of the car and walked directly into the hotel, followed by his retinue of bodyguards.

Meanwhile, Melissa was walking around the room barefoot, clad only in a nightgown and a lightweight robe, her initials embroidered over a breast pocket.

"I'm starving," she said to Peach.

"You just ate," he said from the living room sofa.

"Two hours ago," Melissa said, pouting.

"Well, it won't hurt you to miss a meal. Your legs are a little chubby," he said.

"Liar!" Melissa said, her mouth falling open in mock astonishment.

Peach shrugged.

Smiling widely, Melissa sat down next to Peach, close enough to cause the SEAL to shift his legs. "I'm fat? Is that what you think? I can't believe you said that!"

"What? That you're a swine?"

"Yes. You're a commoner and I have no interest in what the common people say. Least of all a—what do you call yourself? A seal?"

"Yeah. And I think you love SEALs because we can swim faster and deeper than anyone alive, and we're smashingly handsome."

"And you're conceited beyond belief!" she exclaimed.

"Confidence, my lady. As a matter of fact, I'll bet your heart is beating just a little faster than it was a while ago. Right? That's because my animal magnetism is starting to have an effect on you. Here, let me feel."

Peach took Melissa's hand and pretended to take her pulse.

"Yep," he said, "it's that special thing that SEALs have. If we're anything in the world, we're not common."

As he spoke, their eyes locked. He moved his head closer to hers, until their noses almost touched. He could feel the warm sweetness of her breath mingling with his. Then their lips touched. They kissed again, tenderly. Their arms encircled each other, feeling content for the moment, holding the other.

"Fat legs?" she said. "You were just trying to get a reaction from me. My legs are just right. You saw them last night."

"I had no choice."

"You left my panties on," she said.

"I don't take advantage of helpless ladies."

"I'm not helpless now."

Melissa's hands moved about Peach's body, exploring under his shirt, quietly marveling at the man's large and hard body. She kissed him fully on the mouth again, becoming impatient. She suddenly shivered as Peach slid his large hand under her robe, moving down her nightgown and onto bare leg. He moved slowly until his fingers rounded her wonderfully firm buttock. She gasped with delight, her mouth nipping at the small of his neck.

By unspoken consent, they were about to move into one of the two bedrooms when there was a sudden knock.

"He's downstairs. In the bar," Eddie said through the partially open door.

"Boris?" Peach said, surprised. "I'll be right down."

"I'm going with you," Melissa said.

"You feel well enough? As a matter of fact, he might be a lot friendlier to you than me," Peach said.

"Give me a minute to put something on," Melissa said, walking quickly to a dressing area that afforded privacy.

The fact that it was Saturday night must have accounted for the larger than average crowd. In place of the scratchy music tape was a live four-man band consisting of an electric piano, drums, a guitar, and a horn. Neither

Melissa nor Peach recognized the tune the musicians were working on, but the group seemed to be able to maintain a regular, almost danceable beat. Peach made brief eye contact with Eddie who stood at one end of the bar, his size fourteen foot parked on the brass rail, and with Arthur and Maury who occupied a small table at the rear of the room. An anxious maitre d' rushed a table out of storage, along with two chairs, and draped a white cloth over it for his guests, who to him looked important.

Peach was keenly aware of the stares Melissa attracted from everyone in the room, not only because she was a fair-skinned European a long way from home, but because she possessed sensuous appeal by any standards of beauty. He found himself immensely enjoying the feeling of HRH on his arm.

Peach caught Melissa's eye and nodded in the direction of another room connected to the main bar. When the door opened and a waiter passed in or out, card players could be seen sitting around a table, chips at the elbow of each man. Peach ordered whiskey and soda, which was served in separate glasses, from the same waitress who served them the night before. Melissa was tempted to register a complaint about her food poisoning, but abandoned the idea before it was born on her lips. Instead she asked for ginger ale, hedging her bet against a gastrointestinal revolt.

"Sorry we got sidetracked," Peach said to Melissa over the noise of the band, looking around the room for any sign of Boris.

"Not half as sorry as I am," she said, looking directly at Peach.

After their drinks had been placed on their table, Peach rose from his chair. "I'm going to get a cigar. Be right back."

He walked over to the bar, found a space near Eddie

who made no attempt to acknowledge Peach as he stood waiting for the bartender.

Barely nodding toward a nearby door, Eddie lifted a bottle of beer to his lips and said, "He's in the card room."

"I saw it," Peach responded sotto voce.

"Two bodyguards here, two inside," Eddie added after another pull from his bottle.

Peach asked for a panatela cigar from the bartender. He lit it, and found it surprisingly tasty. Normally, he could take cigars or leave them, but if he was to play cards, he wanted the stogie for a prop.

"Why didn't you buy me one?" Melissa said as Peach returned to the table.

"You like these things?" he said with arched eyebrows, offering Melissa the stogie to taste.

She elegantly drew off the cigar, holding it in her slender fingers. He wondered if anything, worn or touched by her, could look bad.

"Of course. I think they're rather sexy, don't you?" she said.

Looking into her flashing eyes, a wisp of her auburn hair across her cheek, Peach had to will his mind back to the job at hand. "He's in the card room," Peach said, casually eyeing people around the room. It wasn't hard to recognize the two bodyguards in the main room, one seated at a table against the far wall, one standing near the main door. They were African, Walter Felinda's SADL soldiers. They wore inexpensive lightweight sports jackets to cover obviously suspended Uzis. Their dark glasses, at night and indoors, hid their eye movements— a legitimate application—but made them look slick, not an accepted practice for real pros in their line of work.

Peach and Melissa finished their drinks then, as the waitress stopped again at their table, Peach smiled expansively and gave her a two-rand tip. "I see there's a card game going in the next room. I like cards. Suppose my lady and I might take a seat in there?"

The waitress's brows knit. "Oh, sir, ladies are not allowed. Never in the room with cards."

"Well, then," Peach said, rising and extending his hand to Melissa who stood up with him, "the men inside are about to get the first real treat of their lives." Peach led the way toward the card room while every patron in the Elephant Bar stared in disbelief. The excitement was palpable as he opened wide the door to the card room and stood aside allowing Melissa, wearing a dazzling smile, to precede him.

Peach quickly counted nine men, distributed like fog-bound icebergs through the smoke of cigars and cigarettes in the room. Six of the men sat around the only card table in the room while three others looked on, either standing or sitting in comfortable chairs, built high enough to view the game. The room was mahogany paneled and decorated with the mounted heads of several trophy animals and a number of erotic pieces of art. Far from being embarrassed, Melissa moved immediately to inspect the renderings with great interest, turning to smile at Peach. Those at the table had stopped playing, turning in their seats to gape at this elegant, rare phenomenon in their midst. One of the men, unmistakable from the others, was Boris Eveshenko.

An almost frantic, highly agitated maitre d' rushed into the room, bowing in front of both Peach and Melissa but firmly shaking his head and wagging an extended finger. "No, Madam, please, you must leave. No ladies allowed. Not allowed, please go!"

"I'll have the usual, scotch and soda," Peach said to the maitre d'. "Bring Melissa some ginger ale."

"Thank you, no, sir, the lady is not—"

"Do it right now," Peach said, with an edge to his

voice. "And bring these gentlemen whatever they want and put it on my bill. I think they need help swallowing." Peach smiled.

The maitre d' stood, confused, looking for direction from those at the table.

"I won't ask again," Peach said with absolute confidence and authority.

The maitre d' bowed again before scrambling from the room.

Of the three nonplaying spectators, two were carbon copies of the other pair of bodyguards in the main bar. Peach watched them carefully out of the corner of his eye as he addressed the players at the table.

"I see you're playing poker. I can't resist a poker game—"

"Because Peach knows I love to play," Melissa interjected, swaying toward the table's edge. "Now which one of you handsome men will offer a lady a chair?" she said, standing at Boris's elbow.

"You must allow me," Boris said, rising to his feet and moving his chair so that Melissa had room between him and a Japanese man who, despite his first nervous reaction, could not take his eyes off of Melissa. She beamed back at him from on high.

There were, at first, mumblings and murmurings around the table as Boris, still standing, pushed a chair comfortably under her and did not sit again until she had rewarded him with another mile-wide, flutter-eyed smile.

"And the buy-in?" she asked the black man who appeared to be the house dealer.

"Two hundred, lady—"

"Melissa. If I am to win all of your money, you should at least call me by my first name."

The players glanced at each other, then chuckled as

they turned their attention back to their cards and their chips.

"Very good, Melissa," the dealer said. He then briefly introduced the other players. She made no attempt to remember their names, save one. Boris Eveshenko.

When the Russian gave his name, one of his bodyguards quickly leaned over his shoulder and whispered excitedly into his ear. Boris, waving his hand at the man, screwed his face into a frown of disapproval, as though the bodyguard was bothering him unnecessarily. Clearly, the bodyguard did not like the idea of Boris's real name given out.

"We play American-style poker here," the dealer went on. "Five card stud. White chips are five rand, reds are ten, blues are twenty-five."

Peach opened his wallet and arched an eyebrow at Melissa.

"I think four hundred will do very well, darling," she said. "It looks like a friendly game."

While the game commenced with Melissa the newest player, Peach quietly gave instructions to the maitre d' to keep the glasses at the table full.

Steve Haskins was on hostage phone duty at the derrick when the line exploded into life.

"General Dekins! General Peter Dekins! Answer me, you American fool!"

"This is Steve Haskins, speaking. General Dekins is away from the phone. Can I help—"

"Get off, you silly fool!" Walter Felinda screamed into his mouthpiece, splitting the otherwise quiet of the night. "I want Dekins—no, do not bother. I will send for him myself." The line clicked dead. Haskins hung up his end of the com line and, double-timing to the mobile HQ, knocked on the door. It was opened immediately by Getts.

"What's up, Steve?" Getts said.

"Felinda just called up, screaming his ass off. Going nuts. Wants to talk to Dekins, then he says no, he doesn't want to talk to Dekins, that he's going to send for him himself. That's the way he put it, Bobby."

"Right, we're coming."

Dekins and Getts were only a few steps behind Haskins as the petty officer retraced his steps to the brightly illuminated derrick platform. Dekins grabbed the hot line and buzzed below. There was no answer. He buzzed several more times but still received no answer.

As Dekins and Getts stood on the platform, discussing what might be going on inside Felinda's enraged mind, the elevator ominously began to grind its way upward.

Down below it was a horror. Ronald Mauser dragged Dorothy away from the butchery but not before she saw one boy and three girls, all black, part of the inner-city tour of Africa, literally torn from the grasp of their chaperones and hacked to pieces with machetes. It was murder in the basest, most primitive form that Dorothy could imagine and it shocked her mind with such force that she fell to one knee and struggled for breath. Even as Ronald pulled her away into one of the side rooms, they could hear the screaming from the mouths of not only the victims, but from the throats of the killers, whose animalistic growls permeated the mine chambers with depraved evil.

The machetes were viciously swung again and again, reducing four young people from their human forms into piles of scrap meat before being then tossed onto the elevator carriage. The button was pushed and the grisly pile of bloody flesh and splintered bones started upward.

Dorothy was beyond tears, a kind of quiet hysteria having gripped her as Ronald held her tightly to his chest, rocking back and forth. Bishop Kimo Jimini staggered nearby, one hand gripping his bloody arm. Dorothy and Ronald reached for him, pulled him down into their space, and looked at the wound he was holding. He was cut to the bone—trying to stop the slaughter, he said in a disembodied voice—but was tossed aside. Whatever drove the terrorists, they certainly did not fear God's wrath, and they clearly did not fear the bishop.

Dekins and Getts had seen dead people before: victims, martyrs, soldiers blown to pieces. But never had either man seen such determined savagery as they stared down at the human gruel that covered the floor of the elevator cage. Although it was impossible to tell, they would later learn that they were looking at very young adults, Lorleen Steed, Jason Kittles, Josey Hubble, all fifteen years of age, and Racine Pate, sixteen, removed from the face of the earth by a mad executioner.

The sound of the hostage phone was surreal in its muted, almost dignified ring in the midst of carnage. "Dekins! Dekins!" Dekins heard even as he lifted the handset to his ear. "Are you there?!"

"I'm here, Felinda," Dekins said, making no pretense of adding the title of general to the name of a bloodthirsty killer.

"You lied! You tried to trick me. Now you see what you have done? I do not bluff. I am not a man to be trifled with. I am going to kill all—"

"Hold on! Wait a minute. I don't know what you're talking about. You've murdered innocent children. The world is watching what you do here, Felinda, and it looks to us that you don't have control over your own men."

"I have control. Perfect control! I told you what would happen if you tried to trick me!"

"Calm down. We're not going to get anywhere if you scream at me. Why did you kill these people? You promised me that you wouldn't—"

"Don't tell me to calm down. The code you sent was no good. It doesn't work!" he screamed at the top of his voice. "These people will pay!"

"How do you know it doesn't work?" Dekins said.

"I know! Do you think we are fools?"

"We did not try to trick you. We sent you the correct code in good faith. There must have been a mistake in the transmission," Dekins said.

"Do not lie! How can there be a mistake in sending a message? Huh?"

"It's easy to make an error when we are turning a complicated software formula into CPLEX crypto. You should know, being a military man, that linear optimizers are very easy to screw up," Dekins lied.

There was no response for a long moment while Felinda pondered what Pete Dekins had told him. Dekins was hoping—counting on—that Felinda had no real experience with or knowledge of cryptography. In point of fact Dekins knew that a CPLEX form was used to encode the software for use on the Internet. That was a requirement made through Felinda himself but it was obvious that Felinda had neither the equipment nor training to do more than pass on the demand without understanding what it had meant. Someone else, not Felinda, was behind the terrorist plot.

"Yes," Felinda said grudgingly, "I know that."

"Then you have to give us a chance to get it right. We're cooperating. We're doing what you've asked us to do, but you've got to stop killing innocent people right now," Dekins said.

Again there was a pause in the conversation while the terrorist considered his options.

"Very well, I give you six hours," he said.

"Not enough time. We've got to go over the whole code system again, find out where we made the mistake and then correct it. That's going to take twenty-four hours working around the clock."

"No! Not another whole day! You must do it faster," Felinda said, but lacking his earlier strong passion, Dekins thought.

"What's one more day? You're getting everything that you want. We'll try to do it in less time but I'm telling you in all honesty that it might take that long to do the job right. We don't want anyone else hurt."

After a silence, Felinda said, "Very well. Twenty-four hours. If it isn't right then, I kill them all. We can strike again, you know. More hostages are easy for us to take," the terrorist said chillingly.

"I understand," Dekins said.

"General Dekins."

"Yes?"

"This man, Mauser. We have him, you know."

Dekins gripped the telephone tightly, controlling his response only with great effort.

"Mauser? I don't know him," Dekins said.

Dekins then heard a soft, rumbling laughter. "Oh, yes, you know him. CIA. I catch you in another lie. I will not kill him quickly. He will beg his god to die before I allow it. Do you understand, Dekins?"

"We've been through all that. There is absolutely no reason—"

The line went dead in Dekins's hand.

Getts had given orders to have the hacked-up bodies removed from the platform. As medical personnel from Johannesburg's coroner's office began the grisly task, the two SpecWar men used the WHCA secure line to call Washington and fill them in on the latest events.

"Any suggestions?" David Magazine said to Getts and Dekins. "We're damn sure not going to give that maniac the real deal."

"Hell, we know that," Dekins said. "Just wait twenty-three hours and send it out again. We're working on something from this end."

"Want to tell me what it is?" Magazine said.

"I'd rather have you trust us on this one," Dekins said.

"Okay. We don't have any fresh ideas anyway. God, I don't know how we're going to tell the families of those kids. Do you have a positive ID on them, yet?"

"Negative. And to tell you the truth, I don't want to know. Not right now."

"Okay, Pete. Good luck," Magazine said.

"David?"

"Yeah?"

"He knows who Ron Mauser is," Dekins said.

"Jesus."

"I don't see how it changes anything, do you?"

For several moments the Washington end of the line was silent. "I feel like a high school freshman standing by with my thumb up my ass while my buddy is getting the shit kicked out of him by the school bully. I'd rather take the beating myself," Magazine said.

"I don't think you'd want to take the one he's going to get," Dekins said and signed off.

Dekins turned to Getts. "Call Peach. Tell him to go to make his move on Eveshenko. You know how much time we've got."

"Roger. I'll crank him up."

Minutes later there was a telephone call put through to the concierge at the Imperial Hotel. A message was left for Peach that he should immediately call his brother,

Bobby. A bellboy was dispatched at once to the card room.

Having given Peach his orders, Getts turned to the engineering map of the mine on the table inside the HQ. He studied it once again, familiar with every detail having already pored over it countless times and many hours. There was something niggling in the back of his mind that wouldn't go away. Part of it he consciously knew: that every box had a way in and a way out. Nothing was impervious to a determined enemy. And he was the enemy. There was a way in if he could just visualize it. The longer he studied the map the more focused his mind became. After thirty minutes of staring at the diagrams and geological delineations, a kind of rush swept over him. He sat down on the padded cushion, his hand shaking as he reached for the telephone. He called Neils Grunden, the mining engineer who had been requested to stand by his home telephone. Grunden answered after the first ring.

"I'd like you to come here to the mine right away," Getts said. "Bring any kinds of drawings or engineering reports with you that you think we don't have here. And I want you to call the hydraulic engineer you had on staff before you closed."

"He wasn't on our staff," Grunden interjected. "He was a consultant. He's no longer alive, I'm afraid."

"Then get me the name of his firm and the names of any hydraulic consulting companies in South Africa. How about the universities? Their geology departments?" Getts asked.

"Yes, that's a good suggestion. At Cape Town there is a good man by the name of Penay. We used him before, as I recall," Grunden said.

"You call him and I'll have him picked up and flown here," Getts said.

"Right. I'll get on it immediately."

*   *   *

To take his mind off of current events, Bradley Wallis had been rereading *The Corridors of Power* by C. P. Snow and had fallen asleep, his glasses still perched on the end of his nose, his head resting at an angle against a wing of his large upholstered chair. Despite the lateness of the hour, the central communications room had put through a call to him on his restricted line and its softened ring startled him awake.

"Wallis here," he said groggily into the mouthpiece.

"Good evening, Bradley. Leon Manton. I didn't expect you to be in the office this late. I should have known better."

"I'd like to report that I've been working feverishly but in fact I'd fallen asleep. Happens more often than I'd like to admit. How are you, Leon?"

"Fine, thanks. I'm calling from a telephone that our company regards as clean. How about you?" Manton said.

"Yes, you can talk. What's up?"

"I may have something for you on that little matter we discussed the other day. Now, this may be nothing at all, Bradley, but I think I'd like to tell you what we know and let you try to fit it into your picture—or throw it away, of course."

"Yes, of course," Bradley said.

"There is a diamond buyer in Antwerp who is of questionable reputation. His name is Majiah and he is by way of Bombay, where he supervised a diamond cutting and polishing enterprise before he began trading. He was never a huge success as a buyer or seller, either in India or in Europe. We have clients in that business, of course, and it is in our interest to know who are the good ones and the bad ones."

"Certainly," Bradley said, indicating that he understood the subtleties of Manton's information.

"Within the last one hundred days Majiah has been buying a great deal of high-quality diamonds."

"From DeBeers?" Bradley asked.

"Yes, and from Russia. Russia is a very big player in the diamond industry, as you know," Manton said.

"Hm."

"What is of interest, it seems to us, is twofold. The first is that Majiah is selling at a very small margin and, in some cases, at a loss. Unusual, even in a sloppy trader like Majiah. Second, we are not able to determine where the man is getting his capital to stay afloat in a business that seems to be running at a considerable volume."

"And what volume might that be?" Bradley asked.

"We don't know exactly but it has to be in the several hundred million dollar range. It seems to us that the man is laundering money. Majiah is getting all of his financing from a single account in London. The bank is privately owned, very substantial, good reputation."

Interesting, Bradley thought.

"It is *Banco el Merced.* Do you have all that, Bradley?" Manton asked.

"Yes, but—"

"I'm going to give you a number. It seems to me, Bradley, that you'll want to know who deposits money into one of those accounts."

"Ah. Not easy to do, Leon," Bradley mused aloud.

"No, you're very right about that. Still, I recall that you have friends who are very good at that sort of thing. Well, just a thought. Might all mean nothing."

Bradley thanked his old friend and hung up. His next telephone call was to the NSA.

Chapter Seven

Getts was with Steve Haskins and Snake Chandel. His men were taking turns cleaning their weapons, making sure that only one rifle and one machine gun was broken down at any time, leaving the others ready for action. With Peach and Eddie in Botswana, Snake was the lone Tango One man remaining for their quadrant near the mine's perimeter. Getts assigned to himself the task of relieving Snake. The added pressure was something Snake accepted gladly, almost preferring it, it seemed to Getts. Snake was a born scrapper and long odds didn't mean a thing to him. The only thing Snake craved, aside from sex, was ammo.

Getts was looking on in interest while the fire team took apart and cleaned or replaced certain parts of their DPV—air filter, oil level, spare tire, repair kits—under the light of gas-fueled lanterns, knowing that the machine's battle-readiness could mean the success or failure of any part of their operation.

"Steve," Getts said to Haskins, "you and Dean go through our diving rigs today. Make sure it's all there. Also make sure nobody knows what you're doing."

"Aye aye," Haskins said. Their equipment was covered by a heavy tent with a locking mechanism on the entrance flap. The tent could be cut through, but it would not have been easily done. Though the tent itself was inside the fenced perimeter of the mine platform, the SEALs didn't trust the local police or the people that they continually allowed to pass through the restricted zone.

"Bobby." Getts heard his name spoken through his command radio, which was attached to his belt and clipped onto his shoulder strap.

"This is Bobby," he returned.

"Major Louden wants to talk," Waco Miller—pulling platform guard duty—responded into his radio.

"On my way," Getts said and began walking toward the platform less than one hundred yards away. As he neared the platform he could see the form of Major Louden, framed in halogen lighting, step down the short ladder to the ground and walk forward to meet Getts.

"Captain Getts," the security police officer said in an austere greeting.

"Major," Getts said in return.

"I am very sorry that you have lost more people to the terrorists," he said.

It was a formal, almost pro forma, condolence but Getts felt that the security officer meant it.

"Thanks. I'm sorry, too," Getts said.

"I know that sympathies are not of much use. You haven't had much of an easy time here, but not all of South Africa is unsympathetic. We have seen our share of terror," Louden said.

"Well, if you feel so bad about it, we could use a couple of trucks, two ton or better," Getts said.

"Anything else?" Louden asked.

Getts studied the man for a minute, then said, "Yeah. I got a whole list of things."

"Then give it to me."

"Thanks, I will," Getts said, then waited for Louden to get to his point.

"Captain, the boy Jku . . ."

"Yeah?"

"He is not alive," Louden said. The security police officer hesitated, waiting for a response from Getts. When there was none, he continued, "He was not put on a bus to go home. He was taken to a place in Soweto, to a large house with a basement. It is a location left over from the bad days, and it was supposed to be destroyed but it still exists. The boy was tortured there and he died."

Major Louden's eyes started to fall in shame but he raised them level again to match Getts's heated gaze.

"General Boord?" Getts asked.

"Yes. The general . . . ah, let us say he enjoys his work. He is a specialist, one might say. The boy was brave but he told what he knew very quickly. General Boord, however, was not content. He continued for thirty hours. If you don't mind, I won't be specific," Louden said.

"What would happen to you if the general knew you had told me this?"

Louden allowed the corners of his mouth to flick upward, but it was a wan attempt at lightness. "Nothing good, I should think. Good-bye, Captain," Louden said, then turned toward his government car, which was parked inside the perimeter fence.

There was a brain-saturation point for every human being, Getts knew. It came when the nervous system was overcome with raw input and could no longer make an emotional connection to that stimulus. Getts had spent a good part of his adult life dealing with continually rising levels of inhumanity, and the information about Jku was only a single addition to his current list of horrors. He should have been able to deal objectively with the information that one more person had been tortured and murdered. It happened several times every day somewhere in the world. But Getts was close to overload and he deeply felt the loss of the young Tutsi who thought he was soldier material. As Getts went about accomplishing the requirements of his immediate tasks, in the back of his mind he had connected Johannes Boord as the evil mind that made all of this monstrous plot possible. There was no doubt in Getts's mind that Boord had murdered the Tutsi boy to keep him from talking.

His sense of justice outraged, Getts vowed to himself that General Boord would pay the price.

Melissa had not done well at the poker table, but she had invested the room with a special charm and humor the likes of which had not been previously experienced by her fellow players. Peach even believed that at one time, all of the gamblers had folded their hands in order to give her one of the pots—in the form of encouragement—as she held two pairs, fours and tens. It was not a huge pot, to be sure, but others, including Boris, were as happy as she as the princess raked in her winnings.

"Am I ahead, now, darling?" she disingenuously asked Peach, who was standing on the far side of the room.

"No, sweetheart. You're way behind."

The cards came around again, one down, the second up. Melissa had an ace showing. The next highest card up was a king. It belonged to Boris. Melissa looked sideways at the Russian and batted her eyes.

"I have two aces, Boris," she said, "but I'm only going to bet ten rand because I don't want you to fold."

"I am not going to fold. Not with a lovely lady sitting at my elbow. I bet fifteen rand. Another drink? Please allow me," Eveshenko said.

"Thank you," she said.

Melissa, as any poker player will do, watched Eveshenko's face as he reacted to her play. Her aim was not to win the hand but to see inside the man. What

was apparent on the outside was that Eveshenko was a
middle-aged man with a gaunt, prematurely lined face
who got that way thanks to too much vodka and by enduring incredible stress. He had most of his hair left and
it was only lightly sanded with gray. He was probably a
handsome man in his youth and it made her wonder why
he would have married a woman twelve years his senior.
When he smiled she could see that his teeth were well
tended. As a total package Melissa thought the Russian
would have been interesting even if she did not know his
background.

To give Melissa the space that she needed to work on
the Russian, Peach feigned disinterest in her, concentrat-
ing instead on drinking champagne and talking with another spectator. One of the two bodyguards likewise
turned his attention away from the SEAL in favor of
watching the game. The second bodyguard, however, sel-
dom took his eyes from Peach.

"Are you from South Africa?" Boris asked Melissa.

"America," she said. "Los Angeles."

The Russian's eyes lit up with momentary delight but
then his eyebrows cocked. "But you sound British."

"Oh, yes, I am originally from Britain but now I'm an
American."

"Ah, that is interesting. I would like to see Los Angeles," Eveshenko said.

"Well, if you ever get over there, give me a call. I'm an
actress, now."

"Really?! An American movie star, here at my table! I
am enchanted," he said, a huge smile now permanently
affixed to his face.

"Well, not really a star, Boris," Melissa said, "but it
won't take me long. And you shouldn't take too long, either," she said playfully, leaning into him flirtatiously and
knocking him slightly sideways—much to his delight.

"And you? Where are you from?" she said.

"I am . . ." Boris flicked a quick look over his shoulder at one of his bodyguards, his voice lowering conspiratorially, "a citizen of the world."

"Ah," she said, regarding him with great interest. "How fascinating! International high finance? An arms smuggler? Oh, please, do tell me."

"I, uh, no, I am an engineer," he said, struggling to maintain the sense of intrigue that seemed to light up the beautiful woman at his elbow.

Melissa received another card from the dealer and, reaching for her glass of champagne, knocked it over.

"Oh," she said to the attentive waiter who quickly sponged the green felt table, "I'm so sorry. I'm tired of champagne," Melissa said to Boris who had bought the last two rounds. "But it is my turn to buy," she said, fumbling with her purse.

"No, please," Boris said, "allow me."

"I think you've had enough to drink," Peach said into Melissa's ear but loud enough for Boris to hear. "And you've lost too much money."

"I'll decide how much I drink. And whose money is it, anyway? When was the last time you worked?" Melissa turned and winked at Boris.

Boris, unsure about insulting the large man who was either Melissa's husband or—hopefully—only her boyfriend, turned his eyes back to his cards.

"Hey, suit yourself. We have a big day tomorrow. I'm going to bed," Peach said, dismissing Melissa as an object of his interest and leaving the room.

Boris, relieved to see the two separated so conveniently and with so little effort, continued to play his hand, with no rational thought behind his bets. His chips slowly disappeared, as did Melissa's, until both of their piles were almost gone.

"Well," she said, turning her face toward Boris's until their lips almost touched, "tell me how a man like you came to a place like this. I mean, it's such a dusty little country. My fiancé thinks he needs to prove his manhood by chasing elephants. But you don't seem the type to waste time on safari." Melissa's smile almost snow-blinded the Russian.

"I am ah, shall we say, on business," Boris stammered.

"Engineering business. Hmm. That's too bad. I was hoping that you had lots of time. To play."

"I play," Boris said, and swallowed hard.

Everything about the house, from a security proposition, was counterproductive. There was heavy vegetation, which included banana trees in the back yard, a germander plant that attached itself to the walls of the house and its two-door garage, hanging lines of potted ivy-leaved geraniums native to South Africa, thickly leaved fire thorn trees on two sides of the house, and rose campion along the east wall where the front door of the house was located. While the owner, or former tenant, had enjoyed the wild colors of vegetation planted and tended carefully to flourish in the sunny climate he had also afforded a trespasser perfect cover.

By the time Melissa had allowed Boris to talk her into visiting "his" abode, Peach's detached team had thoroughly checked the house for audio and motion sensors, infrared detectors, and circuit alarms. The first three items were lacking entirely and the circuit alarms were easily bypassed by the simple method of cutting the electrical feeds to the central power pole. There was no battery backup, revealing a sophistication that this house and these terrorists-turned-security-men-in-Botswana lacked. Electricity in that part of the world was problematic in any case, so that when the lights winked out—and the SEALs were inside after disarming the alarm system—the neighbors might not have even noticed.

There was the problem of a fifth security guard left inside the house while the others accompanied Boris into town. Synchronized to the second with Peach's watch, Eddie easily picked the front door lock at the same time that Peach turned the tumblers on the back door. In less than one minute, both men were inside. With the house entirely black, Arthur remained just outside the house, covering Peach's entry—just as Maury covered Eddie as the SEAL stepped inside the front door. Peach moved like a shadow to one side, holding himself motionless against a hallway wall that led toward the kitchen. He flicked his eyes up and down, and from side to side, using his peripheral vision to enable him to see down the hallway, all the way to its end.

He listened intently. In the utter blackness he heard the sound of a dog barking at an outer fringe of the neighborhood, an answering bark nearer, the delicate footfalls of a cat treading on dry leaves outside the house, the tick of a spring-wound clock in the living room, and the almost inaudible tremble of a dislodged bubble in the hot water heater. He controlled his breathing so that the beat of his heart and his respiration did not adulterate his strained auditory system.

Peach's feet told him that the house was built on a concrete slab. He guessed that the carpet, if there was any in the house, would muffle almost all movement. He waited, hoping that the fifth man would move across a wooden floor covering or that his body would somehow come in contact with the smooth plaster walls of the house. Peach held his silenced 9mm H&K in his left hand leaving his right free. He had trained himself to shoot at the expert level with either hand equally well. He and his fire teams had spent countless hours inside block houses, in pitch darkness, training to shoot from a crouch, their weapons in the hip-firing position, discerning their targets unerringly by sight or sound. The practice paid off in real combat situations like this in lives saved or lost.

Peach knew that Eddie, according to plan, was standing or crouching silently at the other side of the house. Each movement was choreographed so that one SEAL did not hit another because a man was somewhere other than where he should have been. The security guard *had* to have heard the SEALs picking the locks. He would have to investigate. His communication to the outside, at least by telephone, had been cut. If he raised his voice to speak by radio he was a dead man. So Peach and Eddie waited. They would wait as long as ten minutes. If their target had not yet revealed himself, it was Peach who would go hunting while Eddie remained in his position as backup.

The seconds ticked by into minutes. As his hack watch approached eight minutes and forty seconds, Peach began to plan his stalk. A slight breeze began to blow through the partially open back door, confirming, if the home guard did not know before, that at least one other person was in the house with him.

Then Peach saw it. A barely discernable movement of a figure—a man in a crouch?—briefly shadowed in the faint ambient light of a dining room window. Then it was gone. But Peach knew where the man would have to step next in order to reach his own position in the kitchen.

In two silent strides, Peach traveled a corner of the kitchen and took up a position on a wall that separated him and the last apparent position of the guard. Again, controlling his breathing, Peach waited. His enemy made the mistake of leading with his weapon hand around the corner of the wall. Peach struck down hard on the man's wrist sending his Uzi, its stock folded, clattering onto the floor. Snapping his right hand into the man's exposed larynx, Peach cut off any sound the man might have made while at the same time sending a paralyzing shock through his entire nervous system. As the man futilely flung his arms outward in a mindless move to fend off his attacker, Peach snapped another fist into the man's neck directly under his ear. The guard was dead before falling to the floor.

"Clear here," Peach said in a hushed voice to Eddie in the other room. Leaving the body where it had fallen, the two SEALs now turned their attention to clearing the rest of the house. With Arthur and Maury now inside and watching their backs, the house was swept in less than a minute.

Satisfied that the terrorist had been dispatched without creating a messy pool of blood and scattered flesh, the body was dragged to a bedroom and left behind a bed.

Peach and the others then set up the house for the expected arrival of their next guests. Peach, Eddie and Maury took cover outside, while Arthur remained inside. Then they waited.

"I really shouldn't be out this late with a man I just met," Melissa said, feigning the effects of liquor, most of which she only pretended to drink while pouring it into potted plants during trips to the ladies room. "It isn't that I don't trust you, Boris, but these men are scary." She waved her hand airily at the silent black men also seated in the car.

Boris, his head thrown back as he laughed, said, "Yes, sometimes they scare me, too. But we are going to forget them, eh?" he said, nuzzling his mouth near Melissa's ear.

"All right," she said as the car slowed near the house

on Safari Street, "but we're only going to have one drink.
Peach will wonder where I've gone."

"He didn't seem that concerned about you at the club,"
Boris protested lightly.

"He usually isn't. But he worries when we travel together. He's a very, very nice man," she said.

"He is not as handsome as you are beautiful," Boris
cooed.

"You think I'm beautiful? Why, thank you, Boris," she
said, turning her head as he moved his lips toward hers.

The driver of the car, whom Melissa knew was named
Kaara, gave orders to the three men in the rear seat. He
honked his horn twice, then once—obviously a signal—
before he pulled into the driveway and waited for the
garage door to open. It remained closed.

When Kaara spoke in his native language to the men
in the back seat, the three immediately stepped out of the
car, one walking toward the garage door, the other two toward the front door. While Melissa did not understand his
words, it seemed to her that Kaara was concerned that the
yard lights were out and that the garage door was not
opening. One of the bodyguards opened the garage door
from the outside, then stood aside while Kaara pulled the
Mercedes inside and shut off the engine. Boris opened the
passenger side door, stepped out, and helped Melissa out
of the car. Kaara then opened his door and put his feet
onto the cement floor. He uttered two more curt words to
the guard who opened the garage, but the man to whom
he spoke was no longer there to hear them.

Kaara repeated himself, becoming instantly alert when
there was no answer, and withdrew the Uzi that hung by
a strap inside his bush jacket. Carefully, as though treading on broken glass, Kaara slowly moved toward the spot
where, moments ago, one of his men simply disappeared.
Kaara called his name, listened for a response, then

snapped off the safety of his Uzi as he unconsciously crouched and swung around the side of the garage. As he turned sharply around the corner, a nearly invisible loop of piano wire dropped over his head from the eaves above, and pulled tight. Kaara emitted a faint gurgling sound as Maury tightened the garrote still more, cutting through his windpipe and larynx. The terrorist's Uzi clattered onto the concrete driveway.

The first of Boris's bodyguards to open the front door and walk inside had little reason for alarm: he had not seen or heard anything that caused him to be suspicious. He flicked a wall switch once, twice, three times. But the house remained shrouded in darkness. The second T hesitated at the threshold. "I will see about the lights," he said to his companion, and turned away from the front of the house to walk to the rear of the property where he knew there was a fuse box. The sound of his own movement brushing against the foliage near the walls masked the carefully placed footsteps of Eddie Knowles as the muscular SEAL locked a powerful forearm under the T's chin, exposing his throat to a sharp dive knife.

"Is something wrong?" Melissa heard Boris say as the single remaining bodyguard, his eyes wide, called out for his comrades, who did not answer. Realizing he was the only man on his side left alive, the T dropped his Uzi and sprang through the open front door of the house, past a momentarily distracted Arthur. If the T got away he would get word back to Felinda—and the hostages would die.

"Get him, Eddie," Peach called.

The T, wearing lace-up leather shoes, lit out down the residential street, his leather soles slapping noisily upon the few paved streets in town. Eddie had no trouble keeping the man in sight as he began the chase seventy-five yards behind the T from the elite residential community into the town of Gaborone. Eddie was wearing a light-weight outdoor shoe made of synthetic materials and rubber soles. While not specifically designed as a running shoe, it provided enough comfort and protection for the SEAL to sustain a rapid jogging pace indefinitely. Eddie was grateful for the fact that SEALs, like most SpecWar personnel, maintain long runs as part of their weekly exercise regimens. His breathing settled into a smooth rhythm, his heart rate rising to about 120 beats per minute. At his current level of physical demand, he knew he could last for hours.

Not so his quarry. The T bodyguard was energized by fear, which, while an excellent motivator, interfered with the body's physiology. His breath came in gasps, his lungs demanding more oxygen, but his nervous system was overpumping adrenaline to every part of his body. The flooding of sensory information and adrenal acids caused the man's knees to weaken and fear caused his blood vessels to constrict rather than flow more swiftly. Saliva, pouring into his throat, slopped into his windpipe and he gagged, creating an even more critical need for oxygen already in short supply.

Eddie saw the man dart to the west, down a darkened street a block from the main avenue. As Eddie turned the same corner, he glimpsed his prey turning back to the south, now running through the low rent part of the business section. There were sewing shops, butcher stores and kiosks, all closed because of the late hour. Eddie was gaining on the T who, almost stumbling, turned yet another corner to the west and headed toward the railroad tracks. As Eddie jogged into the alley where the T had darted, a snap pistol shot narrowly missed his head. He could feel the movement of warm air and sensed the whirring of the bullet as it passed by his ear. Instinctively he flattened against the wall of a cement block building.

Eddie could see the muzzle flash of the T's semiautomatic pistol. The T had made the amateur's mistake of choosing the wrong side of the building from which to shoot. Situated on the left side of the alley, a right-handed person would have to expose a good part of his body in order to aim and fire. Eddie jumped across the narrow alley—to the same side as the corner the T was firing from—to force the man to reveal still more of his body if he was to have any chance at all of hitting his target. Eddie, keeping flat against the wall, silently moved down the alley closer to the building's edge, and waited. From the corner of his eyes he could see curious, even frightened eyes poking out of windows, looking to locate the source of the gunshots. Eddie knew that he had to finish his assignment quickly before the police arrived on the scene.

The T had not made a move yet. Eddie quickly spun around the corner of the building and spotted a dark hand holding an equally dark semiautomatic pistol. Instinctively Eddie grabbed for the gun just as it exploded. The round passed under his palm but opened a gash under his forearm. The pain was a shock but Eddie resolutely twisted the gun downward and jammed his own H&K hard against the T's chest. He rapidly pulled the trigger three times.

The T had barely fallen to the dirt when Eddie put one more between his eyes to make sure. Using a different route, Eddie walked calmly back to Safari Street.

With Getts and Pete Dekins in the HQ were two other men, Neils Grurden and Abraham Penay, the hydraulics consultant from Cape Town. Penay, Getts guessed, was in his late fifties, only a few inches over five feet, but was an active and forceful person who seemed to know exactly what he was talking about. His voice resonated from his rotund body with the timbre of an opera singer, a mop of hair falling into his eyes as he shook his head for emphasis.

"As a matter of fact," Penay was saying, tapping a cross section of the Salisbury mine with a mechanical pencil, "I rendered an opinion years ago about closing down number five drift here, on the north side."

All eyes followed the engineer's pointer to one of eight drifts splintering off from the Salisbury shaft.

"Because of water?" Getts asked.

"Yes. We were—ah, rather they were—two thousand feet down on the main shaft from the top of the mountain, give or take fifty feet. That is, from the top adit's elevation. All of this area, I'm sure you are very well aware, is about two thousand eight hundred feet ASL—above sea level. The water table is about two thousand one hundred feet, or roughly equal in depth to number five drift." Dropping his pencil and fixing his thumbs under his cotton vest, the engineer leaned back from the table, glancing around for agreement.

He received it from Neils Grurden. "That's correct. We got water, not too much at first, but we knew that if we kept drilling and digging we'd have more water than we could handle. Remember that, Abe?"

"That was why I was hired. On the other side was fast-moving water," the hydraulic engineer said, his head bobbing in affirmation.

"So you sealed it up," Getts pressed Grurden.

"Well, we didn't plug it, if that's what you mean. We just left it and built our drifts away from the west. The show wasn't all that good, anyway. We only stayed maybe three more years before the mine just played out," the engineer said.

"So," said Getts, "where did the water come from?"

"The water table," Abraham Penay replied in a surprised tone, as though it was obvious.

"Neils here said they thought the water was moving fast," Getts said, leaning forward. "That would mean there's a source nearby."

"Yes. No doubt. And it was fresh," Penay answered.

"So where did it come from?" Getts wanted to know.

"Oh, I see what you mean," Penay said and moved his pencil pointer to a spot almost two miles away. "Right here it is. Lake Simms. Natural reservoir for communities around here."

"There isn't a lot of rain here," Getts said, framing his next question. "We're not high enough for snow. What fills up the lake?"

Penay shrugged again. "We're not sure. Lake Simms is part of an inactive volcano and it's very, very deep. Thousands of feet."

"So if the water near the Salisbury mine comes from Lake Simms, there has to be a channel or a river system of some kind to make it flow. Isn't that right?" Getts wanted to know. Pete Dekins was watching Getts intently. Getts, very focused himself, made no eye contact with him. It was almost as though Getts did not want to be interrupted. Or stopped.

"Ah, that's what one would surmise, but in this case I'm sorry, but you're probably in error. What you are talking about is an aquifer system, the kind that runs through limestone or dolostone. Such as you have in the United States. Florida, is a good example. Places in Mexico and Central America have large rivers that run for hundreds of miles underground." Penay shook his head. "But gold is found in quartz. Alluvial placer rock."

Slowly shaking his head, unwilling to believe he may have been close to a possible solution, Getts at last looked up at Dekins. The general was sensitive to the

SEAL's frustration. "I understand where you were going, Bobby," he said. "Ever done any cave diving?"

"Once," Getts said, dejectedly. "One summer when I was at Stanford."

"Only one dive?" Dekins probed.

Getts nodded his head. "I was so scared I didn't want to go back inside."

"Then you're a lucky man, Captain," Abraham Penay said. "You have respect for your life."

The death of Psycho Cheetam struck Getts again, suddenly. He had been the team's best diver and his experience in caves, and his cool courage in deep water, was even now greatly missed.

"Wait a minute. If the mine water comes from Lake Simms, it has to get there through some kind of channel. Where does it come out?"

"Some of it keeps these wetlands aquified." Penay pointed to a flatland approximately three miles from Lake Simms and one mile from the Salisbury mine. "Most of it enters the area's water supply system, there." He pointed again at villages scattered about the map. "We lose a good deal through evaporation in the wetlands, of course."

"Then there has to be an entrance into the flow there," Getts said, looking around the room for confirmation. There was no argument, but then there was no enthused agreement, either. "Now, Neils, back to this Tauber shaft. Is the lower part still usable?"

"Huh?"

"You sealed the top. How about the rest of it?" Getts pressed.

"Well, I don't know. I don't know how much rock would have fallen to the bottom. Maybe a lot, maybe very little. There is no way to know," the engineer said, his fingers rubbing an imaginary itch at his temple.

"Well, there's only one way to find out," Getts said.

"You know your business better than I do," Dekins said, "but we don't have time for your people to explore underground rivers."

"I don't plan on doing it the right way, Pete, just the fastest. I'll do a bounce dive, map the route, and if it goes where we think it will, we'll go back in force."

Dekins shook his head. "I'll need approval from Washington."

"No you don't. You've got approval on your collar," Getts said, referring to Dekins's rank of brigadier general. And Getts knew Dekins was stalling, not wanting Getts to take the risk that he was planning to take.

"Bobby—"

"Pete, you're doing the negotiating, I'm in charge of the assault. You're not going to start changing hats on me now, are you?" Getts said.

Getts sent for the rest of the Green Solitaire team. He would have Steve Haskins, Dean Banks, Rick Heggstad, Snake Chandel, and Waco Miller for the assault team, assuming he could find drift five in the dark, far underwater, and deep underground. Peach and Eddie Knowles wouldn't be back from Botswana in time. He couldn't afford to wait. At most he would have five men—including himself—to make the swim while one man stayed on the surface and supported the men underwater. For the next three hours, Getts, his swim team, the engineers, and Dekins studied every nuance of the maps of the Salisbury mine, and the surrounding mines they could get their hands on. There were some mines on the Main Reef that were over two miles deep. The entire complex, covering hundreds of square miles, was a lattice-work maze of thousands of shafts, drifts, and adits that went everywhere and nowhere.

It was understood that the only way drift five in the

Salisbury mine could be located was by precise measurement and compass bearings.

"What we need, Bobby, is an uplink to an IO bird," Haskins said, his eyes wandering over the engineering drawings.

"What for?" Getts asked.

"Image mapping. They could use doppler radar for IPPs," Dekins put in, immediately seeing where Haskins was going. Image Operations was the state of the art data gathered by imaging orbiters, satellites, and aircraft equipped with EHF radar. In this case, Haskins wanted their capabilities for IPP—impact point predictions. It was possible, at least on the drawing boards, to locate spots on the earth that have particular densities—or lack of densities, such as in the case of a shaft or a drift.

"Pete, you can call it in to the NRO but I don't think we have the time or the equipment at this end to pull it off," Getts said.

"We got radios. They can send the stuff here and we can relay it to you. You have clamshells."

Dekins was referring to the diving helmet that resembled a clamshell that was equipped with radio com to not only fellow divers underwater but to the surface, as well.

"I don't see another way in or out," Dean Banks said. Dean would be Getts's swim partner on both the bounce dive and the assault, assuming the attack could be mounted.

"Okay," Getts said to his team, "let's load up the dive gear. Put it under a tent in the wetlands. We'll stage everything out of there." If they could not find the source of water that led to drift five from the wetlands, there would not be time for another search.

The four bodies of Boris's guards were stacked into their rented Nissan sedan, the doors locked, and the car left inside the garage. There was no way they could be buried without drawing attention. It would not be a fragrant odor that would greet whoever opened the car door. Nor was there anything that could be done about the fifth man whom Knowles gunned down in the streets of Gabarone. Still, there were likely no overt clues that would immediately lead police investigators to the house on Safari Street. Boris, once the suave man of the world, now sat, wringing hands, his body shaking despite the balmy air of southern Africa.

"Here, Boris," Peach said as he offered the Russian a glass of Pepsi stiffened with a generous shot of vodka. "You're going to feel wonderful after you drink this. Calm down. We're not going to hurt you."

"You killed them," Boris said, pointing a finger at the SEAL.

"Yes, that's true, Boris," Peach soothed, "but they were bad people. Terrorists. You're not a bad person, are you? Of course not. Hey, when you leave this house in a day or two, you're going to go straight to Hollywood, California, to sell your story. I know you can get behind that! Right, Eddie?"

Eddie Knowles stretched his lips wide apart, looking like a great white shark on the trail of a dinner-size mackerel. The effect was not exactly what Peach was looking for to reassure the shivering Russkie. Boris looked hopefully toward Melissa.

"Well, you can't have Melissa either, Boris. She's my girlfriend," Peach said, winking at HRH. Melissa fluttered her eyes in response. "But there will be others. Lots of others. You see, Boris, if you work with us my government is prepared to pay you a reasonable amount of money. Reasonable? Hell, a small fortune, plus a nice house and a car to drive."

"What kind of car?" Boris asked.

"Well, ah, I don't know. What kind do you think, Eddie?" Peach asked Knowles.

"The Ford line is good. Chrysler puts out a fine car, too, especially in vans and wagons," Eddie responded seriously.

"Boris doesn't look like a van guy to me," Peach said.

"Boris is going to have a luxury car. Aren't you, Boris?" Melissa purred.

"But you see . . ." Boris gulped, looking from Eddie to Peach to Arthur and Maury, his eyes shifting fast enough to follow a Chinese Ping-Pong match. "I must refuse. I do not want to say no but I must."

"We thought you might. But there's another way," Peach said, sitting down next to the Russian.

"Yes?" Boris said, his eyes opening wide with hope.

"We kill you," the SEAL said, simply.

"But no!" Boris said.

"But yes," Peach responded. "Other lives are at stake, Boris baby. Your choice is that you come over to our side and collect a nice pension and live in a nice house and drive a sexy car in Hollywood—"

"With movie stars running all over the place," Eddie interjected.

"—or we pump a bullet into your brain and dump you into the car in the garage," Peach finished.

"They will kill me, too," Boris almost cried.

"No, sir, by golly, Boris. Not while your friends—that's us—are here to protect you. And not while you're going out on the town with movie stars, either, because we'll have somebody protecting you there, too."

"Hey, Peach, how 'bout plastic surgery?" Eddie suggested.

Peach shook his head. "Look at the man. See that nose and chin? Who is he? I'll tell you who he is: Henry Fonda."

Eddie looked at Boris again but said nothing.

Peach turned to Melissa. "Is he Henry Fonda or what?"

Melissa only vaguely remembered what Henry Fonda looked like. She bit her lip, walked around to the side of Boris and looked again. "Ah, yes. The profile. It's—"

"Henry Fonda," Peach urged.

"Henry Fonda," she agreed.

"So no surgery or anything like that for Boris, here. Now look, Boris, we're running out of time. The encrypted software is on the Net again by now. I want you to pick it up just like you always do, and run it on your computer—by the way, what are you using to crunch the numbers?"

Boris's face brightened. "Parallel processors. The Cray Y-MP," he beamed, looking around for recognition.

"That's an American machine, isn't it?" Peach asked.

"Oh, yes. It is using vector arithmetic in Cobol. Four GL, it is called," the Russian said.

Peach and the others glanced around. Though they had searched the house and found two desk-size computers with two large screens, there had been nothing to resemble one of the giant Cray computers, which need special containment rooms with hermetically controlled climates. Boris could read their confused faces and his smile grew larger and larger.

"Okay, Boris, lay it on us. How do you do it?" Peach asked.

"I am a certified technician on the Kepler Project, eh? You know of it. International Astrophysics Association. The antenna—" Boris jerked his thumb toward the roof of the house—"pick it up. Mainframe is in MIT. I send and receive right here." Boris giggled. Peach felt like giggling, too, but for an entirely different reason. Part of the big puzzle just dropped into place: Boris was turned.

"Okay, I don't give a shit how you do it, but when you get through running these numbers, you're going to make your call to Felinda and tell him the son of a bitch checks out five square. You got that?"

The Russian's face sobered. "Yes. I got it. But I don't call Felinda. He is not my contact."

Chapter Eight

Bradley Wallis had tried for more than two hours to reach the Green Solitaire command center. He had used the highest levels of clearance but the delay was not a case of low priority, it was simply that General Dekins's com and data lines had been overwhelmed. It was only due to the fact that the NRO (National Reconnaissance Office) had all but given up trying to jury-rig an impact map and, more importantly, a nav system for Getts and his SEALs to use to find their way through the flooded subterranean strata that would lead to drift five. When contact was finally made, it was Pete Dekins who answered.

"I do hope Bobby hasn't jumped off, yet," the aging spy said over the satellite hookup.

"Ah, I wouldn't like to discuss that, Bradley," Dekins said into the mouthpiece.

"We are secure, aren't we?" Wallis responded, slightly piqued.

"I damn sure hope so. But he isn't here. I'll relay a message, if you'd like," Dekins said. No reference to a special operation would pass his lips as the troops were jumping off or about to engage the enemy. If the walls had ears and the SEALs got killed, Dekins would want to jump into the pit of hell with them.

"Hmm. Well, I suppose you should be the first to know, in any case. You are the man in charge. We think we know who's behind all this. Are you interested?" Wallis asked.

"Very much," Dekins said, gripping the phone tighter.

"I won't tell you how it all came about, but if you know anything about ECHELON you can guess. We think we know where the money is coming from to finance this whole enterprise. And the deeper we dig, the bigger it gets," Wallis said.

"Understand. You found the bank account?" Dekins wanted to know.

"Yes. It's very interesting about how the money flows in, but even more interesting to you and Getts is who is taking it out. Am I right?"

"You know who it is?"

"Yes. And you won't like it at all, General."

The wetlands was little more than a scummy pond, Getts and his team saw as they finished placing their dive gear inside the tent nearby. Near the watering hole grew reeds and algae, while a soupy mixture of green slime floated in clumps on top of the water. The pool itself was little more than twenty-five feet in diameter and Getts, on his hands and knees looking downward as he held a light underwater, could see nothing but black. While the surface of the water was warm, he knew that farther down it would be cold. The time was now 0616 hours and the day was already becoming warm.

"Let's do it, Deano," Getts said to Dean Banks, his swim partner. The plan was for Getts to wear a single 72 cubic foot tank of 2,400 psi on the first dive. Double tanks would have been better for safety reasons but he feared the openings he was looking for might not be large enough to allow the two-tank system to pass through. Banks would wear a double set and tow along an additional tank in case Getts had to go deeper than one hundred feet for any appreciable amount of time, and needed to decompress on the way up. The tank would be left at the eighty-foot level for emergency purposes if anything went wrong with Getts's system.

Getts would carry a reel of line, tied off on a rock or perhaps a piton driven into the stone walls of the cave, so that he could find his way back. Each diver carried two lights attached to his helmet, body weights, a dive knife strapped to their legs, and an underwater writing tablet. Getts considered wearing an inflatable buoyancy vest but chose instead to dive slim.

The operation was planned to have Getts rapidly descend into the system, go as far and as fast as possible, laying line, making notes, doing a general recce, then return to the surface as quickly as he could. Depending upon what the first recce revealed, they would plan a larger penetration with the entire dive team. As Getts and Banks were inside the river system, Snake Chandel, Steve Haskins, Rick Heggstad, and Waco Miller would support the mission from above. Two men, Heggstad and Miller, would suit up and, with tanks within arm's reach, would sit in the shade of the tent ready to dive into the water and render assistance should an emergency arise. Haskins would monitor the radio.

As Getts plunged into the water he was immediately shrouded in deep black, the sides of the cave invisible except by touch. As he descended past the thirty-foot mark, however, the water began to clear somewhat and his helmet-mounted lights began to penetrate the murky gloom. The rock walls widened to approximately fifty feet with the floor dropping at a steep down-angle of about sixty degrees. Getts followed the slope, paying out line from his reel.

"Tied off?" Getts said through his radio to Banks, who followed forty feet behind.

"Roger, go," Banks returned.

As Getts passed through eighty feet, making notes of depth, direction and visibility, the rock cave narrowed to four feet in diameter. He could feel the flow of the current, which he estimated at two to three knots.

Within eleven minutes Getts arrived at three chambers—he did not know if they were mine drifts or aquatunnels. He was almost one hundred feet down and had about forty minutes of air left. He tried to determine which chamber flowed fastest but it was difficult to gauge without a flow meter. At last he chose the farthest on the right because it seemed to offer the largest opening of the three, though they were all snug. Getts got his shoulders through the opening, then it became tight. His tank hung up on the rocks above yet he managed to kick his way through. Arriving on the other side he realized that one of his two lights had been torn away from his helmet. He considered returning to the surface, or at least to the fifty-foot level where Dean Banks would be waiting. But there were other lives at stake.

The sides of the inner cave were hard rock and very black, reflecting almost nothing from the light of Getts's remaining lamp. He swam horizontally for about five hundred feet until he came to the end of his safety line. He tied the second, and last, line to that and paused to make notes on his tablet. He noted his direction as indicated on his wrist compass: he was moving upstream, northwest. He knew that he had to turn back within the next few minutes, as his air at this depth was being used at a faster rate than originally planned. Up ahead he saw that the cave narrowed into what might be a mission-ending bottleneck. He had to find out if this was going to be their end.

The water here was flowing at a noticeably faster rate than at the last opening. Again he wedged his shoulders into the hole and kicked. Again his tanks and regulator scraped the top of the channel. Suddenly he could not move. He kicked harder but he could go no further, and when he tried to push his way back with his hands, he seemed only to lock himself in place.

Getts could feel the onset of panic attacking his brain. He stopped moving, laid still, and consciously fought to regain control of himself. He was gulping air in sharp intakes and he had to bring his breathing rate down or he would quickly deplete his remaining air.

"Deano, this is Getts. I've got a little problem here," he said into his lip mike.

There was no answer.

"Deano, Getts. Do you read?"

In the near total darkness and utter quiet around him save the gasping rattle of his own labored breathing, Getts knew that he had to get himself out, that there would be no one to save him.

He exhaled as completely as possible, reducing his chest size by centimeters, then kicked as hard as he could with his flippers. Suddenly he was through the opening and into yet another, larger chamber. He could not feel a current of any consequence. Once free of the claustrophobia-inducing vise that had nearly drowned him, Getts saw that he had just enough air in his tank to return to the eighty foot level and the emergency tank. He was already experiencing the difficulty of thinking clearly, a result of the onset of nitrogen narcosis, of staying too deep too long. He reached for the safety line that would guide him up. It was gone, slipped from his hand.

Frantically Getts searched for the line but his single remaining light, just now beginning to weaken, could only penetrate a few feet in any direction. He had no idea how large the cave was, or where the hole was that he had swum through barely two minutes ago. He swam in the

direction he believed it to be but arrived at a dead end. He
turned and swam in a different direction feeling for a wall
of the cave, worried that he might be inside a vast chamber and swimming deeper into it, rather than out toward
the opening.

Again he fought against panic. He swam down. Or
was it up? He did not need to look again at his air gauge
to know that he would not last much longer. He desperately needed to know which way was up and, finding a
small loose rock from a ledge, allowed it to fall from his
hands. It went "up." So Getts turned and swam in the opposite direction, toward the true surface of the earth. For
an impossible period of time he swam toward what he
hoped was the hole in the cave wall whence he had come,
only to arrive at another wall. He turned his light so that
he could see his exhaust bubbles, hoping that he could
follow them up and out. But the bubbles merely rose out
of sight, to hang against the roof of the cavern.

His air supply was now so low that he had to suck hard
to get a breath. At yet another dead end Getts could feel
panic rising again, this time almost overwhelming him,
and he began to see himself in the throes of death, imag-
ining how it would feel to die down here in this black
water pit. He had known other divers who had lost their
minds completely and tried to scratch their way out, ripping their fingernails out of their hands against rocks one
hundred feet thick. It was a hard way to die and as Getts
sucked hard at his rapidly diminishing air, he considered
simply removing his mouthpiece. That was the easy way.
He wanted to die with dignity, like a man. He did not
want a SEAL team to bring him to the surface having torn
at his face in agony, frantically digging like a trapped animal against the sides of his watery black tomb.

A voice inside his head shouted at him as though
through a fog: *You aren't dead yet! Fight back!* He had

been slowly swimming from side to side of the cave, bumping into the wall before his light, growing still fainter, illuminated the dark rock. Then the light winked out. He shut it off in order to conserve what little power was left in the batteries. On what he thought would surely be the last few kicks of his flippers, he bumped into another wall, either ceiling or floor, his helmet taking the blow but still causing his neck to hurt. As he put out a hand to push himself away, his arm went through nothing but water. A hole! Hoping that it was the same one through which he had entered, Getts forced himself into the cramped space with leg kicks that took almost all of his remaining energy, to the other side. He snapped on his light, which, after winking on, immediately diminished to blackness. It was now completely dead. But in that moment of light Getts had spotted the yellow safety line. Or had he? Frantically he searched the mouth of the hole with his hands. Had he felt it? Yes! His fingers gripped the line and he began to pull himself blindly hand over hand, at first horizontally inside the cave chambers, then upward, his lungs heaving desperately for air.

After pulling himself through the last narrow opening, still below the eighty-foot level, Getts gave out. His last conscious thought was that he had almost made it.

Fifteen minutes later on the surface, Getts was revived on pure oxygen being pumped into his mouth, his fire team gathered anxiously around his prone body. He heard Deano talking into his ear, "I coulda pulled you out a lot sooner but I had a catfish cornered down there. Put yourself in my place, Skipper. Would you pull an officer out of the water or would you spear a trophy catfish?"

"I would have pulled the guy up," Miller said. "I don't think it matters if he's an officer."

"But, it wasn't just one catfish, was it, Deano? I mean,

it would take three or four of those babies to make a fine meal," Haskins said with a straight face.

"Yeah, well, I could just see Peach coming back to the team and asking where Bobby is, and me saying that I left him down in the hole because I was looking for a snack. That's why I went down after him," Dean said.

"I think you did the right thing," Miller said.

"It's a matter of taste," Heggstad said.

Getts was already starting to experience numbness and tingling in his fingers and toes, early signs of carbon monoxide toxicity. He would have to go back down, starting his decompression at about one hundred feet. Haskins and Miller would go down with him this time, just to make sure he didn't get lost, they said.

Heggstad and Snake Chandel made the second recce dive, working closely from Getts's drawing and compass fixes. They also tried to clear the narrow openings through the chambers that had almost trapped Getts, but they dared not use explosives lest they alert Felinda and the terrorists. They attempted to use manual tools—sharpened steel bars—but the rock was hard and their air supply limited their heavy efforts underwater. They would need to think of a different method of getting men and materials into position for the assault into drift five.

Three quarters of a mile into the system, Snake and Heggstad reached the first of the flooded drifts within the main reef near the Salisbury shaft. They carefully drafted and plotted the drifts that were closest to drift five, then narrowed their best estimate to one.

Preparations thus made, Getts hoped that Peach's success with the Russian in Botswana would fool Felinda, and that the terrorist would let the hostages go. If not, the SEALs were ready to go to work.

Back on the surface Getts made a hurried trip to the HQ for a badly needed meeting with Pete Dekins. The two men agreed upon what had to be done with all parties who were involved in the kidnapping and murders, and plotted the close time coordination and support of the assault that would take place within the next twelve hours if Felinda had not released the hostages.

Before Getts departed for his dive, Dekins informed him that Bradley Wallis at the H. P. Carlisle Foundation had discovered the person who had devised and supervised the entire terrorist operation. Dekins thought Getts would have been shocked, but the SEAL only nodded his head, as though he already knew.

"Has the president been informed?" he asked.

"Oh, sure. But in fact I think Bradley told us, first," Dekins said.

After the severed phone line was repaired, the atmosphere at the Safari Street house was almost festive as they waited for Boris to complete the connection to South Africa. The individual the Russian needed to report to was out but was expected to return within the hour. Meantime, Peach lingered on a patio in the rear of the house, in an atrium shrouded from outside eyes.

"Proud of yourself?" Melissa asked Peach, her eyes sparkling.

"I'm always proud of myself. I'm proud of you, too," he said.

"Just because I'm the most beautiful woman you've ever seen?"

"I hadn't noticed. I give off such dazzling light that everything around me just kind of fades into the background. Know what I mean?" Peach said, putting his arms around her waist.

"It wasn't long ago when I could have had your head chopped off for talking to a princess like that. I think I can still have you flogged."

"Would you like to do that?" he said. "Have me whipped?"

She put her lips to his chin, then slowly shook her head. "No. I wouldn't want to hurt you. I don't even like to think about that," she said. He bent to kiss her on the mouth. The strength in his arms lifted her onto her toes and she could feel the entire length of her body pressing wonderfully against his. They kissed long, passionately.

"Peach . . ." she began.

"Yeah?"

"You're very special to me," she said.

"I feel the same way about you," he said.

"You do?"

"Mm hm," he said, kissing her again, running his finger across her breasts.

"Then why don't you get out of the navy and live with me? We could get married," Melissa said, amazing herself to hear the words come from her lips.

He held her at arm's length and looked at her closely. "Are you serious?"

"Yes. I can't imagine spending the rest of my life without you. At least I don't think I would want to do that," she said.

"What would I be? A prince or something?" he asked, a huge smile on his face.

"Yes, but we would keep that side of our family obligations to a minimum. I have seven estates and twelve houses scattered around the world. I haven't even been to all of them, and I have more money than I could spend in two lifetimes. That's what the royal councillors tell me, anyway. We could do whatever we wanted, whenever we wanted, and wherever we wanted. Doesn't that sound wonderful? And I'm not a possessive woman. I'm not jealous of anything. At least I never have been before."

Melissa paused to regard Peach whose eyes focused intently on her.

"Could I have all the guns I wanted?"

Melissa nodded her head, vigorously.

"Could I have a submarine for myself?" he asked.

"I don't know. I think you would have to share."

"I'd want my buddies to hang around," he said.

"Of course, darling. We would entertain your SEAL friends lavishly," Melissa said.

They kissed again deeply. "I'd have to talk it over with my CO," Peach said, ingenuously.

Later, Peach listened on a telephone extension while Boris made his report back to South Africa. He said that he had run his tests and that the software was correct.

"You took less than half of the time to test the system this time. Why?" the voice from South Africa crackled with skepticism.

"Because much of the work had been done on the first transmission," the Russian said after a moment's hesitation. For a protracted period of time there was silence at the other end. Then the voice spoke again.

"Did you simulate a launch and SFTIP?" the voice demanded sharply.

"I, uh, no. It was not part of my requirements," the Russian said anxiously. He had not expected to be challenged in his work. Simulated Flight To Impact Point was SOP for verifying guidance system technology but Boris was frankly surprised that his contact knew about such sophistications in engineering procedures.

"You did it for the first transmission test. Why should this be different?" the voice demanded.

"Well, I, uh, found the mistake from the first encryption, and I thought time was of the essence, you see . . ." Boris's nervous voice trailed off.

There was no response from the other end of the line.

Boris looked at Peach, whose face was grim as he listened intently.

"Put Dtrakka on the telephone," the voice ordered.

Boris looked pleadingly at Peach. Peach did not meet his eyes. It would be no use.

"Ah, Dtrakka is in town," he croaked, knowing that his thin lie sounded precisely like what it was.

"One of the other men, then," the voice demanded.

"They—they are all with him. With Dtrakka," Boris said, wiping heavy sweat from his brow.

The line clicked and went dead. Boris slowly replaced the telephone in its receiver. "He knows." Boris licked at his lips. "I have done what you told me, and now I have to get out of the country immediately. You don't know these people!" The Russian fell silent as Peach ignored him, and turned to his TS-300 and punched in the identifier. After a moment Pete Dekins's voice responded.

"Dekins."

"Peach, here. They didn't buy it," Peach said. "We're on our way back."

"Stand by, Peach," Dekins said.

"Roger," Peach replied, and waited. He recognized the next voice immediately.

"Remove the pit viper," Peach heard Getts say into the TS-300.

"Aye, aye," Peach acknowledged. "Quietly? Or do we want to draw a crowd?"

"The world doesn't need to know," Getts said.

"Understand. Out," Peach said before replacing the hand piece.

Getts, Waco Miller, and the engineers had gone over the problem a dozen times. Waco was the best explosives man on the team. All the members were very well familiar, even had great expertise, with most conceivable flavors of explosives, but Waco brought something else to the table. He had a feel for just how little explosive was needed to accomplish a given job, and he knew it without making calculations, which, in the field, were wrong more times than they were right. Common thinking seemed to be that if sixteen ounces of Amatol would do the job, then two pounds would make damn sure. After all, they didn't want to make a lot of noise, then wind up on the outside of a door that should have blown in.

But Waco never missed. He thought it was the mark of an amateur to overcharge. And in the present case, where Getts and the fire teams had to use an explosive device and still be quiet in the process, the smallest explosion and the least amount of noise was essential. The underground river water touched the outermost arm of drift five at 2,410 feet from the Salisbury shaft. It was hoped that a hole small enough to serve as an entrance into the drift from the river could be blown with a precisely placed circular cutting charge and blown without being heard nearly a half mile away at the main shaft. But sound travels with clarity within a tunnel of hard rock.

So Getts and Pete Dekins had planned a deception. At an exact moment of time, Dekins would create an explosion on the surface of the Salisbury shaft by igniting the fuel tank of an army truck along with ten pounds of RDX, more than enough to be felt by Felinda and his Ts at the bottom of the shaft. Getts's cutting charge would go off simultaneously, hopefully masking the commandos' entrance into the drift.

An endless list of negative possibilities could occur. The underwater charge may be too little or too much. The debris of blown rock could fall back into the river cave and block the entrance to the drift. The charge could cause a collapse of the underwater drift in which the SEALs were located. Finally, there were not enough spare air tanks available for the SEAL team to use for decompression if they had to retreat after the explosion. Obtaining more air tanks was possible, of course, but Getts considered that security would be compromised—at grave risk to the hostages—and that there was not enough time in any case since Felinda might be killing hostages even now.

It had to be a one-way trip, one Getts had a distinct uneasy feeling about.

This had been a dirty fight from the opening shot, and it had only gotten worse. Whenever he nodded off for a few minutes during the past seventy-two hours, Getts had nightmares. Always in the end of his face-off with death, he would die. He was in a dark, wet tomb when he suffocated. In his fast-playing dreams, he tried to kill himself, tried to get his pistol out of its holster and put it into his mouth so that he could pull the trigger and escape the torture. But he could never, ever, quite get the job done. So he died in agony.

But that was in his dreams. Now he was already eighty feet deep, five hundred fifty feet horizontally along the river system leading from the wetlands pool, following the previously laid safety line toward the bottom. Behind him he towed a water-tight bag containing a 9mm MP-5N submachine gun with one hundred and eighty rounds of ammunition in four custom clips, two flash-bang grenades, two pounds of plastique explosive, a pair of slip-over shoes, rope gloves, and one hundred fifty feet of light climbing rope. A knife was strapped to his leg, a pair of 2,600 psi tanks on his back. Each SEAL towed a similar load of lethal tools as he followed the man in front of him through the blackness of the frigid water.

The plan was for each SEAL to remove his tanks two times, at each of the bottlenecks that Getts had charted on his first bounce dive. They would then push the tanks through the narrow opening ahead of them, wriggle through, and replace their tanks and mouthpieces until they reached the next narrow door through the underwater cave. The maneuvers would be risky but less dangerous than trying to get through the openings with the bulky tanks still attached to the swimmers' bodies.

Getts passed through the narrow entrance to the second cave, pushing his double tanks ahead of him, replacing his mouthpiece, shrugging into his tank harness once more, then pulling his weapon bag tow line through. The procedure was troublesome and time consuming, but it was safer. When Waco appeared at the narrow, Getts helped to pull his tanks through to the other side, then yanked Waco forward through the hole in the rock walls. He helped Waco back into his harness, then swam off, leaving Waco to assist the man behind him—Dean Banks—in the same way. Behind Banks was Snake Chandel, then Steve Haskins, with Rick Heggstad at trail.

Getts had made a decision only two hours before that he hoped he would not come to regret. Normally on any diving mission, there would be SEALs above who would remain throughout the dive to give whatever support might become necessary. In this case, in order to kill terrorists, Getts needed every team member to join the assault into the Salisbury shaft. If the mission went as planned, the team would exit—with the hostages—up the main elevator shaft of the mine. If things went wrong in the water, or inside the mine—well, they would all be dead anyway.

Strangely, it was Major An Louden who offered to put two of his trusted men, familiar with diving, at the wetlands water hole while the SEALs executed their assault. Because of mutually shared moral values, far different from those held by the murderous General Boord, Getts found that he trusted An Louden, and he had gladly accepted the deputy security chief's extended hand.

At ninety feet Getts could hear music. For an instant he was alarmed, believing that his brain was once again being poisoned by a faulty gas mixture, but he then recalled that air bubbles from his exhaust valve sometimes created the sound of wind chimes as they floated upward to the top of the cave.

At 110 feet, 1800 horizontal feet from the wetlands pool, Getts checked his air supply again. He was alarmed at how much air he had used to arrive at this point. The process of each diver removing his gear at the choke points had taken much more time than he had estimated. His pressure indicators told him that he had seventeen more minutes of air, including his reserve. It would be enough if nothing went wrong, but they could not afford to have a piece of equipment hang up on a rock, or experience a regulator malfunction, or have a diver begin to gulp air at a higher rate than normal.

Getts arrived at the end of the cave where he had turned back on his first dive. He was now navigating according to the drawings sketched by Snake and Heggstad. The final entrance from the river into a mining drift loomed in front of him and Getts swam through, his light barely reaching two feet into the faster flowing water, now stirring up fine specs of silt. A diver's flipper, if he was not careful, could raise enough sediment to black out the entire cave and leave the divers entirely blind for hours, even with a light in hand. On the other side of the entrance to the drift, Getts faced a choice. A clearly discernable drift—from a mine other than the Salisbury—lay straight ahead, to the northwest on Getts's compass. Another drift, angling to the right in a more northerly direction, was nearby. The drawings in his hand indicated three entrances. Was he in the wrong place? Was he merely reading the handdrawn charts incorrectly?

"Snake," he spoke into his lip mike, "I'm at the first drift. I see two. You say three. Which is it?"

The response from Snake was weak, the underwater radios not operating at top performance level inside these narrow rock walls: "First right."

"Understand first right," Getts said, already turning in that direction. Snake made no correction so Getts continued on. He continued swimming into the current. The force of the water was much stronger now, and it was with great effort that Getts maintained an even breathing rate. Even under normal conditions, air was used up exponentially faster at this depth than near the surface of the water. After entering yet another drift by following Snake's chart, he searched for the location they had agreed was most likely to run directly under the Salisbury drift five.

Most likely being the key words. Now that he was once again underwater with not enough air to retrace his route to the surface, Getts felt a stab of panic at the thought that it was only calculations and estimations that separated him—and his men—from life or an agonizing death.

Maneuvering by the touch of his hands and peering intently through the murk lighted only weakly by the glow of his flashlight, Getts chose a spot above that he fervently hoped was underneath the drift. His air supply indicated four minutes. He turned and was relieved to find Waco Miller immediately behind him, already opening his bag of pre-shaped plastique. Waco, Getts knew, had been watching his own air gauges and realized that the entire team was just about out. Like Getts, they had switched onto their emergency supply more than ten minutes ago.

As Getts watched Waco place his cutting charges into a roughly round pattern in the ceiling of their drift, he noticed that air was no longer flowing easily into his mouth: he was sucking it out. He turned his head to see his teammates packed close together, waiting calmly for their comrade to finish his work. Though they were minutes from death in a wet hole, not one of them panicked.

Waco indicated that he was ready to blow the hole. Getts knew that his radio communication with the surface—and thus to Pete Dekins who would set off the diversionary explosion—would not function, but he gave the signal anyway. "Wetlands, fifteen seconds to blow. Count now, thirteen, twelve, eleven . . ." Longing for a breath of fresh air, Getts did not allow himself to consider what would happen if the cutting charges failed to open a hole.

He gave hand signals to his men who, in turn, passed on the signal to the man behind him. The team flattened itself against the rock walls. There would be a concussive blast from the charge. They expected it might even be painful but if Waco had done his job correctly, the force of the blast would be directed upward.

". . . five, four, three . . ."

The truck, already set afire and packed with RDX, exploded with a tremendous roar, sending wheels, tires, and whirring pieces of metal into the air, then showering it all down around the entire platform. The detritus rained upon the heads of South African military personnel, swarms of international media, and civilian gawkers who had accumulated at the edges of the fences surrounding the Salisbury mine complex.

Dekins at once began shouting into the telephone that connected him to Felinda and the hostages. "Hey! Felinda! Goddamn you, Felinda! What the hell is going on around here? You double-crossed me, you bastard!"

The terrorist's voice was equally loud and excited as he screamed back at Dekins. "You! Who do you think—what is happening?! Answer me or I will kill your filthy—"

"You double-crossed me, you son of a bitch!" Dekins shouted back in pretend anger. "We gave you the software just like we said we would and you went back on your word! You lied! You lied!"

Felinda, for a prolonged moment, was shocked into a confused silence. When he spoke again his was the voice of question. "What happened? We felt a shock down here. An explosion! If you are trying—"

"Trying, my ass. You blew up my supply truck, killed three of my people plus I don't know how many South African soldiers. What kind of shit are you trying to pull?" Dekins said accusingly.

"It is *you* who lie! Do you hear? I—we—have done nothing. But I am about to carry out what I said I would do! The guidance code was again corrupted!"

"Don't tell me you weren't behind this bombing. Nothing happens around here unless you want it to happen. If we have learned anything in the last four days it is that you call the shots around here. Your people planted the bomb. Who else could it be?"

Again there was no response from two thousand feet under the earth. It was imperative that Dekins keep Felinda talking while Getts—if he and any of his men were still alive—could get into position.

Getts and his team were completely blinded by the instant mixture of water, silt, and pulverized rock as the explosion sent a shock wave smashing against their bodies. Still, it was not more than they expected, certainly not

more than an NFL quarterback takes when he's blind-
sided. Getts immediately turned toward where the hole
leading into drift five should be, helping Waco claw at the
small rocks above and to the side of the chamber.

Getts was sucking hard on his air hose and getting
nothing. Just at the moment when death was at his shoulder and the thought raced through his head that he had
killed his men, his hand struck through the surface. He
quickly braced one foot against one side of the rock wall
and, while kicking with his fin on the other leg, wiggled
his shoulders upward and through the newly made hole
above. Rolling immediately onto his side—and onto firm
ground—Getts stabbed his flashlight back down the hole
to give guidance to the next man coming up.

Waco popped through next, rolling onto his side and
tearing off his mask, gasping for air. Then came Snake,
Dean Banks, Steve Haskins, and Rick Heggstad, each
one helping the next up through the hole. For several seconds the SEALs sat on the floor of the drift, the water beginning to rise slowly around them—and gulped fresh air
into their lungs, battling back from the verge of hypoxia.
Within thirty seconds they had recovered and wordlessly
stripped off their tanks, flippers, and other diving equipment and silently retrieved weapons, grenades, and small
com radios from their underwater weapons bags. They
slipped the headsets of their radios onto their ears under
the hood of their wetsuits, which had the effect of making
them look eerily like Batman—only much deadlier.

While Getts considered using night-vision glasses for
this assault, he rejected the idea because the killing zone
would be bathed in light and the period of time it took for
their eyes to adjust from the glasses to real light was several minutes. They simply did not have the time to wait
for that accommodation. Guns loaded and safeties off,
they began to move down drift five at a rapid pace.

The SEALs still had a formidable task before them. The hostages were still about seven hundred feet below them. Access to their level was through one of three adits into the mine. The first and main adit was, of course, the Salisbury shaft, but their first objective was to locate the second adit, the Tauber shaft. The SEALs were performing a slow jog, running along the abandoned drift around chunks of fallen rock, pieces of reinforcement timbers, and a light rail line that once supported ore trolleys. The air was dank and warm, but it was immeasurably better than what now remained in their discarded SCUBA tanks.

Getts knew that the Tauber shaft was less than two hundred yards directly ahead, and he prayed that they would not find it covered with rocks or filled in with earth. His body was perspiring freely inside his wet suit but he was driven by adrenaline coursing through his system. His mind was sharpened with the almost certainty of combat that was, he hoped, only minutes away.

At the bottom of the mine, Dorothy could see that the girls were in various states of fear, anger and hysteria. All had been raped repeatedly. And they had been beaten, as had the boys and the men. Amazingly, only Bishop Kimo Jimini appeared unscathed except for the gash on his arm, a fact that Dorothy had thought was odd since the bishop did not spare any of the terrorists a tongue-lashing, including Walter Felinda. The Anglican showed no fear of their tormentors despite their horrible brutality and their shouted threats.

Dorothy's deepest dread, she was surprised to realize, was not for herself but for her husband, Ronald. She had always known that she had loved him desperately, but she never imagined that she adored him more than her own life. In a cataract of emotions, Dorothy remembered the

endearments and tenderness in which Ronald had
wrapped her for their entire existence together. He was
more than devoted and it hurt her to know that he would
never leave her to save himself. If she had anything with
which to bargain with their torturers, she would have
done it. But she had nothing to give, and that made her
sad.

She watched him now, trying to reason with the raving
madman that was Felinda. She could not hear what was
being said but she could see them standing in an alcove of
rock, Ronald appearing quite calm, the Zulu general waving his arms wildly, eyes bulging, his very countenance
frightening to Dorothy. She felt that soon the terrorists
would resume their butchering, this time of all of the
hostages. The insane general's men were agitated, threat-
ening with their guns and their long knives, while at the
same time confused and without clear orders. The decision had not yet been made, Dorothy could clearly tell by
their milling motions, but she also felt that it would not
be very long now, perhaps only minutes away.

"Darling—" Ronald began as he slowly returned to
her side.

"I know," she said, touching his unshaven face. "Stay
with me for a minute. Just hold me."

"Don't worry," he said softly into her ear. "Nothing is
going to happen to you. I promise. I'll make sure of it."

She smiled up at him, nodding her head so that she
conveyed to him that she had been successfully reas-
sured. She knew better, of course.

Getts was now second man with Heggstad at point.
Heggstad halted, and flashed a hand signal to use caution.
Getts could now see the Tauber shaft ahead. The team approached the shaft entrance, which was nothing more
than a square box of heavy four-by-eight-inch timbers

NAVY SEALS: GREEN SOLITAIRE   213

surrounding a hole in the ground. A padlock held fast a
latticed metal door. At Getts's nod, Heggstad squeezed
off a three round burst form his suppressed MP-5 into the
lock, popping the hasp open.

Getts looked upward inside the shaft, his flashlight attached to his head lighting the way. The power of his
flashlight was insufficient to pierce several hundred feet
of blackness above. As he pointed the beam down, the result was the same. He could see, however, that there was
no obstruction in the shaft for a considerable distance.
With each man carrying 150 feet of rope, they could descend a total of 900 feet. According to the engineering
schematics of the mine, they would by then be at the bottom of the mine, inside drift nine, at 700 below drift five.
They could be confident that they had more than enough
rope.

Attaching their war bags to their harnesses and sling-
ing their MP-5s to their backs, the SEALs signaled to
Getts one by one that they were ready. The first line was
attached by Heggstad to a solid wood timber that com-
prised part of the elevator box. The second man down,
Getts, checked the knot, as did the third man in line,
Snake Chandel. Wordlessly, the SEALs swung over the
side of the black pit and began rappelling down the shaft.
Twenty-five feet from the end of the rope Heggstad
reached the first warning knot in the rope, telling him that
the end was near. He chose to pass two more knots before
tying off a second rope to the first. As before, Getts
checked the knot before following his point man on the
second leg.

Despite the special material of his climbing gloves,
Getts's hands were almost hot as he rapidly rappelled.
His shoulders and arms ached from the unrelieved strain
put upon them not only by his body weight but by that of
his equipment. While the discomfort was mild at this

point, he knew it would only get worse before they reached the bottom. At what Getts estimated was the 550 foot level, the SEALs found the shaft blocked. They did not expect to confront an elevator, but there it was stuck on its rails, suspended below them while they hung above the stuck car another 150 feet above drift nine. Signaling up the line to halt, Getts quickly discussed their options with Heggstad.

"We gotta go through it," Heggstad whispered over his lip mike. The other SEALs, dangling motionless on the line above them, could overhear on their radios.

"Agreed. No way around," Getts said, tersely.

"I'm going to tie myself off and go in," Heggstad said.

"Roger," Getts replied, taking Heggstad's MP-5 and war bag into his own hands and attaching them to the rope. Getts, like the SEALs above him, clamped his ascender/descender closed, the strain of the rope now around his waist. He was unable to loop the rope at foot level to take some of the weight off, and as the bite of the line cut into his guts and ribs, there was no choice.

Heggstad detached himself from the rope holding his comrades so that if the elevator fell, it would not drag all of the others along with it. The risk was that in putting weight on the stuck elevator, it might dislodge and go crashing 150 feet to the bottom. The SEALs had room in their packs for nothing more than a flat, high-tensile steel tool for dislodging rocks and obstructions in the waterway. Heggstad now used the tool to pry his way through the rusted metal screening of the top of the elevator car. Once he had fashioned an opening large enough to accept his body, he lowered himself gingerly onto the floor of the car. As he took a single step toward the front where two narrow gates served as a door, the weight of the car shifted and the car groaned against the rails. Heggstad hesitated. He could feel himself begin to sweat. He looked over the edge of the doors, down into the elevator shaft. He could not see the bottom, nor was there room for a man to slip between the elevator car and the wall of the shaft.

"Bobby," he said into his lip mike, "we can't go around the car. We gotta go through the floor."

"Understand," snapped Getts.

"Need you to tie off the car from the top," Heggstad said.

"Roger, will do," Getts said.

Getts motioned to the man hanging above him that more rope was needed. The entire team had heard the conversation between Getts and Heggstad and understood the situation. The last man in line was Steve Haskins who, even before he received the order, was lowering his length of rope. It was the last that the unit had. Getts measured off as much as he dared—fifteen feet—and cut it cleanly with his fighting knife. Releasing line through his ascender/descender, Getts put himself in a position to reach below him and put one end of the rope length through the eye of the lowering block on the elevator. Laboriously, he reached toward one of the rails that guided the car upward and downward. Unable to reach the rail, he leaned his body into a horizontal position and placed his foot against one side of the wall and kicked out. The weight of the SEALs tied above him dampened the movement of the line but after a second kick Getts was able to grasp a handhold onto the rail. He was now able to run the other end of the fifteen foot line through the rail, then had to repeat the process two more times until he had enough loops to hold the weight of the heavy elevator car. He used a clove hitch to secure the open end of the line to the rail.

Below, Heggstad was prying a second, then a third piece of flooring from the bottom of the car, his body

bathed in sweat, his wetsuit raising his core temperature
to an uncomfortably high level. As he worked on the
fourth piece of decking he strained with all of his might,
but it would not break away from the steel frame to which
it was bolted. Then, at his side, he felt the presence of
Getts. Together they slipped the steel pry bar under the
heavy wooden deck and pulled mightily, one on each
side. Suddenly there was a loud pop as the wooden member broke into splinters at the point it was bolted. They
waited silently, listening for a reaction—any foreign
sound—that would indicate they had been heard down
the shaft and through the length of drift nine. After several minutes they began to move again, each SEAL
hooked back on their lines and dropping into the elevator
car and then out the bottom, continuing their descent into
the black hole below.

They had now been in continuous action for three
hours and twelve minutes. Every muscle in their bodies
was crying out for relief when, looking down once more,
Heggstad finally spied the bottom of the elevator shaft.
Their rope hung just eight feet above its floor.

Dropping silently onto the rocky surface of the shaft,
the team took no more than four minutes to empty their
war bags of ammunition and grenades. The six men
formed two fire teams, each team responsible for one side
of the drift, including any rooms that might be found
along its sides. Getts took the lead of fire team Alpha
while Heggstad led Bravo. They expected to travel no
more than two hundred and fifty feet before arriving at
the main room serviced by the Salisbury elevator shaft.
The SEALs' eyes were trained to operate in the faintest
kind of light and they felt entirely capable of moving
silently and swiftly down drift nine with only one
shrouded flashlight illuminating the way.

*   *   *

Felinda heard the screams of the girls from the Netherlands. They and the Americans had to be punished. He
had ordered the girls to be brought before him, to the big
room, and he would open the telephone to the line above
so that General Dekins could hear what they had forced
him to do.

He had to kill the Dutch woman who was in charge of
the smaller ones—she had become insane, clawing, raving, and screaming. He had enjoyed doing the killing
himself and did not in the least mind the gouges of flesh
she had taken out of his forearms as he strangled the life
out of her. It had, in some way, felt more like a real kill,
one that he might have done in the bush as a very young
man. He had finished her off by cutting her head from her
shoulders, an end she richly deserved, in his estimation.

But he had not sent her remains up the elevator. For
reasons he could not fully fathom himself, Felinda was
just a bit confused about what he would do next. After all,
he and his men were in a deep hole in the ground, and
without the hostages, what would they barter for their
own safe way back to the surface?

He would certainly have to kill them. Or most of them,
because the Americans had tricked him and his colleagues. They had refused to comply with his orders. And
he would have to do as he promised. Still, until he was
certain of how he would proceed . . .

The screaming suddenly stopped. Had his men finished off the European scouts? A sudden rage swept over
him. He had not yet given the order! He turned to a
sergeant near his elbow and commanded him to look into
the west rooms and report back immediately.

General Johannes Boord had never before been
awarded a medal from a foreign country, least of all a nation of huge international importance such as the British

Empire. He was uncertain of exactly which honor would be bestowed. His secretary had made a mild attempt to find out but she remained unclear herself, even after calling back the British embassy to reconfirm the time he was asked to appear. Well, no matter, he thought as he turned again in front of the full-length mirror mounted on the door of his office bathroom. He at first had worn his black tunic with black uniform trousers, with the red striping down the sides, but somehow it seemed too formal for a daytime occasion. He then changed to a white coat that was faintly reminiscent of colonialism, the notion making him smile at the irony. And he rather preferred the contrast of the brightly colored ribbons that already festooned his breast upon the white jacket as opposed to the black dress. He even considered wearing khaki, projecting the aura of a rugged, highly challenged African official deeply committed to his sworn duty. He imagined himself after receiving the Royal Cross of the Something-or-Other Order, self-effacingly declining the offer of food and drink in the company of a grateful embassy staff, bowing slightly at the waist, then pirouetting grandly to return to his important ongoing business.

The award, he understood, would be given in a ceremony presided over by no less than Her Royal Highness, Princess Melissa Radford-Gayles Witherspoon, Duchess of Kent, Countess of Beaumont. Of course, he knew that her jet aircraft had brought her to South Africa a week ago, apparently so that she could convey the deepest concerns for the hostages' well-being on behalf of the British royal family. Well, it was good public relations, he thought, and whatever else the Windsor ladies were good for they were at least harmless. As General Boord stepped through the door of his private office into the larger room containing the desks of his minions, heads turned, no doubt impressed with the resplendence of their chief. Out of the corner of his eye he could see his secretary smile and nod her head approvingly as he strode past her anteroom. He was certain that they all knew he was on his way, in the company of his bodyguards, to the British State House. He was early, but he did not wish to offend his newly subscribed benefactors by arriving late. His driver was subjected to only a cursory check at the state house compound front gate, then given directions to what was referred to as the south entrance. The smartly uniformed marine then saluted him as they entered the grounds. He was well up the curving driveway before he realized that the trailing car, containing his personal bodyguards, had not been admitted. As he turned in his seat to look out the rear window, he could see that a heated argument had begun between his men and the gate guard.

"Felix," Boord said to the driver, "tell Arnaud that he can wait outside the walls. I am perfectly safe here."

"Yes, General," the driver said while reaching for his cell phone to relay the order.

At the south entrance to the building a royal blue awning stretched twenty-five feet to the edge of the driveway in order to protect visitors from the harsh African sun. General Boord's door was opened by a well-disciplined, militarily correct Royal Marine sergeant who snapped a wonderful salute as only the British can execute. The general had only begun walking up a crimson carpet when another man dressed in civilian clothes moved briskly to meet him, his hand extended.

"General Boord, welcome to State House, sir. My name is Arthur Carlin. Her Royal Highness has asked me to escort you to the chambers where the ceremony will take place."

"Thank you," Boord said, unsure whether or not the man was beneath him in comparative rank but taking his hand nevertheless. He was in an expansive mood and could afford to err on the side of tolerance. "Tell me, am I to be the only one to receive the, ah, medal, or will there be other awards bestowed?"

"You are the only recipient, General, and I must say that we are all looking forward to the event," Arthur said as he led the general down a long corridor, taking two turns before they arrived at a plain door. General Boord was impressed by the fact that the Royal Marine at the door had fallen into step behind them.

"If you don't mind, sir, we would like you to wait in this room. You are just a bit early and there are still some details to be finished before we begin."

"Of course," General Boord said, waving his hand in the air.

The general was surprised—and a little disappointed—that the room in which he was asked to cool his heels appeared to be little more than a storeroom for miscellaneous goods and supplies needed to run an embassy. Flags of many nations were rolled up and protected by dust covers, alongside portable tables with folded legs, numbers of chairs stacked in twos, a kitchen service center with two large coffee urns, and a sofa pushed up against one wall, while a rolled carpet occupied the center of the room. The general was not surprised by the presence of others in the room, since a significant rite was about to be staged and help would be needed. There were two men in addition to Arthur Carlin and the Royal Marine, wearing civilian khaki clothing. They did not seem properly dressed for the lofty ceremony that lay ahead, but it could also mean that their work would be offstage.

"How do you do, General Boord?" the largest of the men said as he stepped forward. "Remember me? My name is Peach and this is Eddie Knowles."

When the general extended his hand, Peach buried his fist deeply into the general's stomach. As the general fell to his knees, his last conscious thought registered the unmistakable odor of chloroform.

Lighting in the drift rooms was dim, but being experts in night operations, Getts and his team was able to move swiftly ahead. There were two rooms within drift nine east. The SEALs could see that in the room on their left was a woman who appeared, from the photographs the SEALs had been shown, to be Dorothy Mauser, wife of Ronald Mauser of the CIA. Ron Mauser, visible to Getts only in profile, kneeled near his wife, enclosing her in his arms. There were two Ts watching over the Mausers and the African-Americans teens and adults. One of the Ts, a small but muscular man, harangued the hostages in a shrill, uninterrupted voice as he gesticulated, waving his arms and drawing back his fists as though prepared to strike. The hostages were quiet for the most part, but their fear was stark upon their faces. From his position, Getts could not see the room on the opposite side of the drift. The Ts were not looking in his direction. Getts cautiously moved from the deepest shadows into a lighter part of the drift where he would be exposed enough to be recognized. His movement caught the eye of Ron Mauser. For a long moment the two men's eyes locked. Getts made a hand signal to Mauser, querying him about the room across the drift. Mauser turned his head away from Getts but slid his right hand down his leg and held up two fingers.

Getts pulled back into the shadows and hand-signaled Heggstad that there were two Ts in each room and that his own team would take the Ts on the left. Heggstad and Bravo would take those on the right. Getts withdrew his knife from its scabbard on his leg. This was to indicate

how the first Ts should be taken out if possible. A round
fired from a silenced MP-5 was quiet enough, but the
clack of the receiver's mechanism could alert Ts farther
up the drift in the main room of the Salisbury shaft. Getts
pointed his knife at Snake Chandel, meaning that Snake
would take the second of the two Ts on the left while
Waco Miller would back them up with his submachine
gun. Silently, each team crept into position, as close to
the rooms as they dared get, using the shadow of rock
walls to mask their approach.

Snake took the nearest T, as Getts moved on the next
man three steps over. Snake, his free hand clamping over
the T's mouth, drove his combat knife deeply into the T's
back and twisted hard. The man fell dead in his arm without a sound, his vertebrae severed. Getts grasped his target around the chin but the man had become alert because
of the nearby motion. When Getts hit him with all of his
strength with his knife, the blade penetrated the man's rib
cage. But because of his wiry, twisting body, the T slid
down and away from Getts's grip. The man opened his
mouth to yell even as Getts fell upon him and stuck the
knife directly into his throat.

The man's shout had died in his bubbling neck wound.

Ron Mauser had tried to cover the sound by raising his
own voice in pretended protest against a guard, but the
captors in the main room could already be seen looking
down drift nine east.

"It's torn," Getts said into his lip mike to the other
SEALs. "Go! Go! Go!" he commanded.

Following a well-rehearsed drill, the SEALs of both
fire teams tossed flash-bang grenades in front of them
while rushing into the main room, snapping off three-shot
bursts into anyone who had a weapon in his hand. The Ts,
who once appeared to be an organized military unit, were
suddenly disordered and confused. They realized fear

when they turned and saw large men in black rubber suits, their faces painted, strong and determined, firing rounds from guns that never seemed to miss a target.

Getts immediately was grateful that in their abject fright at their imminent death, the Ts' attention was not directed at the hostages. Instead they looked for ways out. And there were none.

After finishing the Ts in the second room of drift nine, Heggstad, along with Steve Haskins and Dean Banks, made a right turn at the next drift—drift ten—where there was one additional room. This room was covered with blood, having been used as the charnel house by the Ts for rape and execution. The SEALs came face-to-face with five Ts, who were among Alise Willicaze, the second Dutch lady, and four of the surviving scouts. Haskins and Heggstad easily outgunned the Ts except for one who used one of the Girl Scouts as a shield. Dean Banks, arguably the most accomplished shooter on either SEAL team, unhesitatingly aimed at a corner of the T's exposed head and pulled the trigger. The back of the man's head disappeared while the T, eerily, seemed for an instant not to know that he was dead and he turned to look directly at Dean. Then his arm sagged to the ground and his knees buckled.

"Heggstad, nine west," Getts said over his radio.

"Aye, aye," Heggstad responded, motioning Haskins and Banks to follow as he raced across the intersection of the main room and into drift nine west. According to the photos and intelligence reports they had been able to assemble, there were still hostages in the mine, namely Bishop Kimo Jimini, Robert and Carol Herlift, American honeymooners, aged sixty and thirty-nine, Ben Levy and his wife, and the Reverend Dennis Johnson, on sabbatical from Boston College faculty.

They were all found in drift nine west, their throats

cut. Heggstad, Banks, and Haskins killed three Ts, the last of the living.

The assault had been underway for two minutes and thirty-eight seconds when Getts and his team, securing the main room, began their search for Walter Felinda. Among the conveniences found in the main room were cots upon which the terrorists slept when not tormenting their hostages, a tent containing a single cot and a telephone to the surface, and a chemical toilet located behind the tent, testimony to how well planned the kidnapping had been.

Waco Miller flung open the door of the chemical toilet to find no one inside, but he was suddenly hit in the chest with a burst of automatic gunfire. Hiding behind the toilet, Felinda fired through ventilation mesh. While Getts returned fire through the fiberglass structure, Dean Banks quickly went to Miller's side, dragging him away from the line of fire. Getts rolled to his right for a better angle on the chem toilet only to find that the small edifice blocked a drift leading off from the main room. Without looking, Getts knew that the drift was not marked on any map. Slapping a recharged magazine into his assault rifle, he dove into the darkness of the drift. He felt the rounds whistling by his eyes and ears before the sensation of hearing them registered in his brain. Getts realized that Felinda could see very well in the dark.

In a crouch, with his back pressed tightly against the wall of the drift, Getts held his flashlight at arm's length and snapped on the switch. In the next instant there was another burst of automatic gunfire, the loud reports echoing off the sides of the gold mine. Getts switched off the light and advanced quickly, diving for the floor of the drift as still another burst of gunfire sang over his head.

Lying quietly on the floor, he waited. He heard footsteps receding. Getts got to his feet and ran, dodging from one side of the drift to another. Coming to the first room to the side of the drift, he dove inside just as another long burst of gunfire ripped by, this one tearing at his pants, another round cutting across a muscle in his thigh. The sensation of burning was intense but Getts willed himself to ignore it and returned fire. Again he pressed himself against the wall of the shallow room as Felinda tore off another long burst. He was becoming anxious, his shooting technique betraying a lack of discipline, Getts realized. The SEAL stepped out of the room, ran ten steps up the black passage of the drift, then dropped on his belly. There was no answering fire.

Getts held his flashlight at arm's length and turned the switch on. Light once again stabbed down the drift, but this time no gunfire followed. Getts rose into a crouch and began to move cautiously down the drift. There was no light at all deep inside the drift and Getts did not want to reveal his own position with his flashlight. He also knew that when he met Felinda, it would be up close. Very close. Silently, Getts removed the magazine from his gun and placed it quietly on the floor of the drift. He then took his assault knife from the sheath on his leg and stayed absolutely still.

At first he heard nothing. Then came the sound of a small rock scraping against another. Getts tried to estimate the distance of the sound from his position. Twenty feet? Less? He remained motionless, straining to hear. Another sound came, caused by a footfall, fainter this time. Getts moved ahead with several rapid strides, then stopped and waited.

He listened. Then he heard the chilling noise of another human breathing. Now in a combat attack position, his knife held waist high, Getts felt the adrenaline pumping in his veins, anxious to lay his hands on the killer of women and children. Making sure his own breathing did not give him away, Getts controlled the expansion and contraction of his chest, breathing through his nose slowly, deeply. He sensed the movement of air close by. Then the blink of an eye revealing white orbs.

Putting up a blocking hand, then wheeling on bent knees and driving his shoulder and extended arm forward in a full thrust, Getts felt the knife penetrate Felinda's torso. Felinda gasped, a scream tearing out of his throat. Getts turned the knife viciously, pulled it out, then locked his left arm around Felinda's neck as he slammed the heavy blade deeply into the man's chest again, then again. The SEAL was surprised at the satisfaction he felt as the self-proclaimed general of terrorists fell to his knees, then pitched forward, his face striking the hard rock of the drift. Getts cleaned his bloody blade on the prostrate body of his enemy, then turned and felt his way back toward the main room.

When Getts returned to the center of the mine he was not surprised to see Ron Mauser holding a smoking MP-5. His jaw muscles pulsating after finishing off the last of the Ts, Mauser handed the gun back to Snake Chandel.

"Sorry if I took away some of your fun," Mauser said, "but that son of a bitch was mine."

"Don't give it a thought. Where's your wife?" Getts asked, his eyes narrowing.

"She's back in that room, taking care of the others. That's how she is," Mauser said.

"Good," Getts responded, then grabbed Mauser by his lapels and slammed him roughly against the side of the mine shaft. "Get your hands against the wall—spread your feet!"

"What are you doing? Is this a joke?" Mauser said over his shoulder.

Getts, in no mood for discussion, patted down the CIA man. Not to the SEAL's surprise, Getts came up with a compact Walther 9mm pistol holstered inside of Mauser's trouser leg.

"What was this for, suicide?" Getts held the gun up to Mauser's eyeballs.

Mauser shrugged. "I figured to shoot it out at the end. And save the last two for Dorothy, then me."

"You're a good liar, Mauser, but you better keep your mouth shut from now on. You're going back to the U.S. to stand trial for the whole mess, murders and all."

"Who the hell are you—?"

Getts slammed his fist into Mauser's kidneys. Mauser grunted in pain.

"I don't want to hear your bullshit. It'll be a long time between now and your trial, appeals, and all the legal delays before they pump the chemicals into your arm, asshole. But if you keep running your mouth, so help me god I'll gun you. Dig it?"

Mauser started to move his mouth and shake his head, then stopped. "Okay," he said meekly. "How did you know?"

"You people were moving a lot of cash and diamonds. I understand the NSA unscrambled your bank account and found out who it was connected to. It was connected to you. Is that what you did it for, Mauser? Money?"

Mauser nodded his head. "Isn't it always?" He averted his eyes for a long moment, then said, "Felinda. I didn't know the man was an animal. I didn't expect that. I figured I could keep it all . . ."

"All what?"

"Under control. I thought I could handle him. Like the others, you know?" Mauser said. "I—I got blind by it all. The money, the excitement of pulling it off."

"And Boord?" Getts demanded.

Mauser shrugged. "A cash-and-carry partner. You

can't pull off something this big without that kind of support. Hey, everybody's for sale."

"Not everybody. What's the price tag for selling out your country?" Getts asked.

"I didn't figure it that way," Mauser said defensively, but was still unable to meet Getts's eyes.

"You didn't, huh? You just wanted all the terrorist countries in the world to have new and improved cruise missiles in the name of fair play. Is that it? Do you know what I think, Mauser? I think they ought to hold your execution in Yankee Stadium. They'd sell it out."

Within minutes the elevator car at the Salisbury shaft was filled with the survivors. It was agreed that bodies would follow on the second lift, though Getts saw to it that Dorothy Mauser left on the first elevator. She would be escorted to her hotel and told that her husband was returning to the USA under arrest. Getts hated the thought of the woman's anguish.

All of this was done in a tidy fashion, with the exception of the corpses of the Ts which were left where they fell. It had been decided that the mine would be closed, sealed for all of eternity.

While Pete Dekins remained with the survivors, the third elevator operation brought down the long-separated comrades of Peach and Eddie Knowles. There were handshakes and bear hugs all around, every man glad to see that the SEAL team emerged from the assault alive and with only a few scrapes and minor flesh wounds for the experience.

"Did you get him?" Getts asked Peach.

"Did you expect the smartest, most handsome, strongest fucking warrior in all of America's armed forces to fail in his assignment? Is that what you are asking, Bobby?" Peach said.

"Yes, and unless I'm right there to make sure you put

your boots on the right feet, I worry about you. Call me old-fashioned," Getts said as he followed Peach and Eddie back to the elevator.

There, on the floor of the car, was a rolled carpet, tied firmly in several places. When the bindings were removed and the carpet spread out, General Johannes Boord lay bound and gagged in the middle.

Getts approached the general and squatted by his side.

"Well," he said, glancing around at the cavernous walls of the mine, "this is it for you, Johnny. When we go up that elevator for the last time we're going to blow the shaft behind us. You'll still be here. Plenty of air for you, lots of water as soon as the river fills in here. You won't have much to eat but, hell, you've destroyed enough human flesh just for entertainment, so eating a few of the cadavers might just tickle your fancy."

Boord's body twitched, his eyes bulged. He tried to shriek but the heavy tape over his lips kept the sounds inside.

"You'll get out of those ropes sooner or later, John. Then you can make yourself a lot more comfortable," Getts said, rising.

"I got him some candles, Bobby," Eddie Knowles said, laying a box on the carpet near the general. "Matches, too."

"Why, hell, Johnny," Getts said, "I'll bet you'll remember Eddie's kindness for the rest of your life. Now, am I right about that?"

Getts gave the bound general a jaunty wave as he and his SEALs walked toward the elevator.

Epilogue

Peach spent five more months in SEALs before resigning his warrant and traveling to Bermuda to join Melissa in one of her stately homes. They were married in January of the following year in a small, intimate ceremony of 850 guests.

Eddie Knowles continues to serve in the SEALs, as do Snake Chandel and Waco Miller. Dean Banks left the navy when his hitch was up and married a teenaged girl. He works as a debt collector for a small finance company. He complains to his old swim buddies that he hates his job.

Steve Haskins also left the navy when his hitch was up and finished college. He is now a high school football coach in California.

Rick Heggstad finished his tour in the navy and settled in Texas. He was arrested for illegally selling arms and explosives to foreign nationals and at this writing is out on bail awaiting trial on federal charges.

Five months after the Green Solitaire operation, Getts traveled to California's central coast to locate Psycho Cheetam's widow. She no longer lived in a modest house but in nearby affluent Santa Barbara. Getts reached the main house through a high, wrought-iron gate and a quarter mile driveway. Arlene had remarried, telling Getts that her life was interesting for the first time in her life now that she associated with a "better class" of people. Her current husband, a natural gas company investor, did not drink—in contrast to Psycho. She never understood why he was called that, anyway.

Ronald Mauser was indicted on an array of charges that included conspiracy to commit international terrorism, murder, and several other related charges. After more than a year of exhaustive debriefings, his trial date has been set.

Captain Robert Getts is still on active duty with the U.S. Navy but has applied for a medical disability separation.